Spotlight
Emma Ellis

This book is written in British English.

Cover by Miblart

TRIGGER WARNINGS.

Please note, this book mentions domestic violence, child abuse, substance abuse, miscarriage, and infant death.

Chapter 1

'Once upon a time, there was a little boy—'

Harriet Chapel's class of ten-year-olds, sitting cross-legged on the floor, all stare at her. Elbows on knees, chins in hands, leaning forwards, wide-eyed and silent. Story time is their favourite when it's Ms Chapel telling the story, so the other teachers say. The children rave about it all day. She does all the voices, making them laugh with the mean gruff ones for the villains and the high-pitched squeaky ones for the heroes. She could listen to their laughs all day. It's the best applause.

'—and the little boy took out his sword—' She stands, holding an imaginary sword in her hand. The class all have their hands pressed into their cheeks, jaws agape, as still as they've ever been. '—the dragon spoke to the boy and said—' the thirty ten-year-olds inhale sharply and grin as they wait to hear the dragon's voice for the first time.

At the back of the class, leaning against the door frame, arms folded and wearing an amused half smile, is Theo. Her old childhood friend who saved her when she was at her lowest moment, the man who gave her a home. She has so much to thank him for. He works part-time in the workshop and is a firm favourite with the children. Perhaps it's the way he can make a broken old fan work again. Or perhaps it's because he enjoys what he does so much it shines through.

'Mr Lawrence,' Harriet says before she says the dragon's line. 'Why don't you come and play the part of the little boy, so I can put all my efforts into being the dragon.'

The class cheers and claps. He gives Harriet a narrow-eyed look that says *I'll get you back for this,* and walks over. The class all giggle as he pretends to sulk and drag his feet over in such theatrical fashion, Harriet thinks he should be the one teaching drama.

He takes a copy of the script, then clears his throat.

'No little boy shall best me!' The dragon roars and fire shoots out of its mouth in the form of rustling paper and wiggling fingers.

The voice for the little boy is animated and laced with all the enthusiasm the class is showing. He walks around as if he is a puppet on strings, holding the imaginary sword as if it weighs a ton.

'I slay thee, evil dragon,' the little boy says with a whimper and a grunt as the sword is too heavy to lift.

Despite its weight, he plunges the sword into the dragon's heart. The beast spirals from the sky, its wings flailing and weak. The dragon lands, impaled on the castle wall, and with its dying breath, says, 'In the name of Dragonsville, I swear, we shall seek revenge.'

Cheers erupt from the ten-year-olds, and the two teachers take a bow.

Harriet sits back in her chair, Theo pulling out one for himself, and they wait for the class to calm.

'Now you know the story,' Harriet says. 'But the question is—what happens next? I want you all to come up with your own play, in groups of three or four, about the little boy and the dragon's revenge.'

'But, Miss!' Ashleigh never puts her hand up to ask a question.

Harriet doesn't care. Eagerness should come before such formalities, but if the senior staff catch her letting Ashleigh get away with it, they'll only moan. Again.

'Remember to raise your hand, Ashleigh.'

There's a huff and eye roll that tells Harriet the young girl would do brilliantly on stage. 'But, Miss. The dragon is dead!'

'Well, maybe there are more dragons or maybe he isn't dead. Maybe there are people who loved the dragons and want revenge. Use your imagination.'

Ashleigh's eyes widen with every idea and, along with the other children, she jumps to her feet. A few of the children are upset over who gets to work with whom, the usual ones being left out, and Harriet intervenes to rearrange the groups. Then she has a few moments to sit back at her desk and observe. She loves inspiring children's imaginations more than anything. As they get to work pretending to be dragons and brave slayers, in all their faces and giggles and actions, she sees the boy she misses so much. They all remind her of Oliver.

It's been three years since she said goodbye to Oliver at the warehouse and still not an hour goes by that her heart doesn't ache for him, doesn't wonder what he's doing right now, hoping beyond anything that he's happy. The children she teaches bring her so much joy, but there isn't a joy that compares to what a child offers their parent.

'Thanks for your help,' she says to Theo. He's in his tech coat, dusty and covered in paint, glue, and God-knows what else. Hardly the attire for a dragon-slayer. 'Oscar-winning performance.' She smirks.

He laughs. 'Well, the kids seem to think so. Any protégés?'

'They're ten-years-old. I just hope it helps the shy ones come out of their shells a bit.' She watches them reenact the boy slaying the dragon, the dragon's flight, even the most reserved of the children getting involved.

There are five MechaniKids in this class, all much smaller than the other children since they have the bodies of six-year-olds, though their minds are progressing rapidly. They learn like they're made of sponge, sucking up information. MechaniKids are common now since the incentives to adopt them were increased to benefit the parents' human children. There's less taboo with having them in classrooms and publicly known to be bots. The company who makes them, Truly Realistic Intelligence, pay their electricity bills, guarantee wattage supply, and put money in trust for university fees for the families' human children.

'Not much work going on in salvage studies?' she asks Theo.

'Waiting for some supplies to be dropped off. I just got a call to say a huge haul is coming up, so that should keep us busy.'

Some scuffles break out, the human children telling the MechaniKids they're not welcome in their group, their small size making the MechaniKids a prime target. Harriet gets up to intervene. Someone has to look out for all the children, to teach them that different doesn't mean bad, that all the children should be included.

Harriet untangles blonde curls out of the clenched fist of another child. 'Polly, do not pull hair. I've already said Lexi can be in your group.'

'Her kind can't do drama,' Polly says, stretching out the As in drama and spitting out her tongue at the end. She has a hard face for a ten-year-old, a natural tightness to any smile. 'My daddy says so, anyway.'

'That's enough,' Harriet snaps. 'Be nice.'

'I'm not being nice to *that.*' Polly narrows her eyes and glares at Lexi.

'Okay, Polly. If you don't want to work with Lexi, then you won't work with anyone. Off you go to the corner.'

Polly folds her arms and stomps off, kicking over a chair on the way.

Harriet takes a breath as the class gets back to work, then sits at her desk with Theo. She finds being cross with any of the children tricky to maintain. Their tantrums are adorable and only demonstrate their need for mentorship. She watches Polly sulk in the corner and wishes she could give her a cuddle, explaining it's normal to get upset sometimes and it's part of being a child. Harriet's not a natural disciplinarian at all. When she first took Oliver home, she was told he was a clean slate and needed to learn everything, but isn't that all children, not just MechaniKids? These children don't know how they're going to colour the world yet. They're flowers not yet in bloom.

'You're lucky it's just drama,' Theo says. 'I had a child in my class stab a MechaniKid with a screwdriver the other day.'

'It's those damned union protests outside. They're stirring up so much nonsense, it's getting to the parents.'

Every evening after work, Harriet and the rest of the faculty have to push past the protests that are calling to stop the integration of bots. The poor MechaniKids at the school are also subjected to the chants and abuse, the protestors not caring at all who they upset or the knock-on effect with these kids' family lives. It's only small protests right now, but there seems to be little action taken against them. Oliver is at the MechaniTeen Institute and Harriet only hopes tolerance has improved by the time he gets out and he's currently oblivious to the animosity. Though his release date could be today or in two years. How would she know? TRI took him away, and she's heard nothing since. She's not a parent to them. She is—was—nothing more than a temporary owner of a bit of tech.

She's been posting about the protests and her concerns on the social media, *Get Level*. She has an anonymous account for the purposes of the group. *Shamed Parents,* they call themselves—the parents whose children were taken away by TRI. There's so much hurt in that group. So many empty arms where their children should be.

'One bit of tech advancement has brought out all the crazies,' Theo says with a tut. 'How are you holding up, anyway? That's why I came here, by the way, not to be in a play.'

She laughs. 'Well, so far today I arrived two hours early and spent that time drinking three cups of coffee, rearranging the furniture, looking through workbooks and fiddling with displays before these toerags arrived.'

'Dexter not hinted at anything?'

Harriet bristles at the mention of the headteacher. Dexter Eamon is the sort of head teacher Harriet would have had nightmares about as a child. Six foot five, a face redder than a beetroot, and a booming voice that makes the littlest children cry just when he says good morning. When Harriet first met him, she assumed under the strict, whip-cracking exterior he shows the children, there would be a kitten underneath, a friendly face up for a chat, one she could confide in during break times. She was wrong. If anything, he tones down his bullish personality for the children. He lives on level 90, so the gossipers say, and clearly thinks his shit doesn't stink.

'I don't want to ask,' Harriet says. 'I don't want to sound too keen. Knowing Dexter, he'll probably deny me a MechaniTeen assistant out of spite if I show how much I want one.'

Theo nods and gives a sympathetic smile, as he knows it's not just any MechaniTeen assistant Harriet is hoping for. She's hoping for Oliver.

It's ridiculous to think that out of all the MechaniTeens joining them for their work experience placement, it could be Oliver assigned to the school. But she's too high on caffeine to keep her mind still and rational. Luckily, the children match her energy levels, and they don't notice how twitchy and restless she's been all morning.

Dexter Eamon's voice bellows through the corridor. She bolts upright, her eyes locking with Theo, and she bites her lip.

'Good luck!' he says, and leaves the classroom, leaving the door open.

Harriet peeks down the corridor. Dexter hasn't rounded the corner yet. She shuts the door, resisting the urge to press her ear to the glass window and listen.

'What's going on Miss—'

'Shh!' she hushes one of the children. 'Everyone, see how still and quiet you can be for a minute. Do your best impression of a statue.'

'But there aren't any statues in Dragonsville!' Ashleigh says.

'Some dragons have the power to turn you to stone!' She hisses like a snake and the class all gasp.

They all stand to pose, some on one leg, some pretending to hold books and staffs, and for a glorious minute, they are perfectly still and quiet.

Harriet inches closer to the door, fingers crossed, holding her breath as she waits for Dexter and the work experience teens to arrive.

'We obviously don't want the teens interfering with any important lessons,' Dexter's voice is now clearly audible, and he sounds as disgruntled as ever. 'But there's plenty of cleaning to keep on top of and making sure the children don't cause trouble.'

Footsteps approach and Harriet stands a little way back from the door. A swell of pride fills her when Dexter walks in and the class is still silent. Perfect statues.

'Relax now, children,' she says. 'Sit back on the carpet. What excellent statues you all make! Say good afternoon to Mr Eamon.'

They giggle, sit, and say their good afternoon in a slow droll.

Harriet smiles, but has to stop it from faltering when she sees Dexter with his bright red and smarmy face. He looks like he enjoys dishing out disappointment. Behind him the teens are standing, and they all step out, one by one, and Harriet's morning energy drains to nothing.

Three MechaniTeens. They're all perfectly lovely and polite. But they're all girls. None are Oliver.

Chapter 2

Oliver

I think, therefore I am.
   Rene Descartes

***

Bots aren't meant to dream. That's what the manual says. There's an FAQ section on the website that Oliver sneaked a peek at once. It says that bots don't have minds that need to process thoughts, and going on standby is the system reboot they need.

Yet Oliver dreams. Every time he is on standby, he dreams of his mother.

He dreams of the days when he was a little boy, scaling the climbing frame, begging her to watch just once more. He dreams of her voice and her hugs, her encouragement and love. Though, more often, he has bad dreams, ones in which she's not okay.

When he's on standby and one of those dreams plays on a loop, he can't wake up. He can't move. Paralysed, he has to watch again and again as Anthony hurts his mother. Only in his dreams, he's a spectator. Observing and unable to intervene.

In his good dreams, he remembers her promise. That she'll never go back to Anthony. Oliver told her he doesn't need her anymore, and he hopes she doesn't need him.

Bots don't have hopes or aspirations. That's also what the handbook says.

His MechaniKid days were meant to teach him about the world, yet he never learned about loneliness. He never learned what it would be like not to have a mother. He recalls when he was a little boy, looking out of a vast window, at gleaming buildings and endless sky. From there, when he was younger, he really believed the world was something beautiful.

Time passes twice as quickly for him as it does for human children. He learned that in class at the MechaniTeen Institute, where he's lived for the past three years. They told him this so he can understand humans better, rather than help him understand himself. He rarely understands his own mind, or mechanics, or programming, or whatever it is. The world he lives in now is too confusing, too conflicted. He was never going to fit in anyway. Outside of the Institute, he always knew he was different, but somehow, here, among his own kind, the world is even more of a square peg and he is even more round.

His roommates are all asleep, or on standby, to use the correct term. They're supposed to be on standby while they charge as it helps them charge more efficiently, but Oliver always asks the woman who does that to leave him on. She's nice and she smiles at him and always says okay. She doesn't ask questions.

That's Thomas's mum, Josie. She's extra nice to Oliver. He thinks that's probably because she tricked his mum into handing Oliver over to the Institute and feels bad about that. But Oliver's pleased things worked out that way. If she didn't, he'd be even more alone.

He didn't want to tell her about his bad dreams. Josie might think he's not so grown up or being silly, or that he's still a kid. Admitting he's sometimes afraid doesn't seem like a good idea here. Some of the other MechaniTeens would find it funny or hurt him. Of course, bots aren't meant to feel physical pain but it does hurt, somewhere deep inside, the same place where he felt love. He hasn't felt that love for a long time. There's an empty feeling, a longing to love. It's strange that an empty feeling is so heavy. Strange how such emptiness can crush.

Oliver fumbles against the wall to find the light switch. They told him a while ago they'd update his eye programming so he could see in the dark better. Half of his group were told that. The other half weren't, though they're not sure why. There's a lack of questions among some of his peers. They accept what they're told, like they were never taught to be curious. Oliver doesn't see the point in night vision. They always have lights in the Institute, not like in some places he remembers from before.

It makes him wonder, though, when he's fully grown, if they're going to send him somewhere to live in the dark. He's not afraid of the dark. He's only afraid of being alone, of never seeing his mum again, and there's no way she'd be happy living somewhere dark. If he could see in the dark and shut his eyes, would he see the inside of his own eyelids? Maybe. That'd be weird.

With the light on, he unplugs his charging cable and walks down the hallway. He doesn't need to get out of bed like he did when he was a kid, as they don't have beds anymore. Bots don't need to lie down, he was told by one of the staff when he asked. They can charge just as well standing up, and they take up less room. There's never much room in the communal area. It's windowless and boxy with no space for beds. There was always something cosy and comforting about lying down to charge. He felt safe.

Down the hallway there's a bathroom the humans use. MechaniTeens aren't meant to use it. They don't need to wash, but Oliver hates the feeling of grit and muck on his hands, and today really has been mucky. They spent all day lifting heavy bags of what felt like gravel and loads of dust poofed up. He only wants to rinse it off. He walks down the hallway, his feet making clanging sounds on the metal floor. There's no one around after standby time. The staff leave them all alone while they sleep, and so this is Oliver's time when he doesn't have to worry about what others think of him.

When he gets to the bathroom, he runs the tap and his hands go pale under the cool stream. The dust swirls down the sink and he's careful to rinse it away and not leave a trace. The rest of him is still grubby, but that's the best he can do for now.

He makes his way back to the communal area via the office so he can have a peek at the calendar. Another two days have passed since his last charge. At least time is going quickly.

In the communal area, he steps up to George, the biggest teen. And the meanest. He's fast asleep on standby. He doesn't seem so big when he's on standby. It shows how much of his size is posturing and volume. Oliver could cut his hair or his eyebrows, or maybe write something obscene on his forehead. He doesn't. If he did, someone might find out he's awake and they'd make sure he goes on standby. Josie might get in trouble. So he doesn't, but it's nice to imagine.

Bots don't have an imagination. It says that in the handbook too.

There's a tiny creature crawling across the ground. A beetle. Oliver crouches to watch its tiny legs scurry across the floor and he feels calmer as he does. The tiny creatures have always had that effect on him. He keeps watching until it finds a way into its hole, in the wall and out of sight. He used to love watching the birds and insects when he was a kid with his mum, especially spiders, but he so rarely sees anything besides bots and humans now. As soon as he gets out of here, he's going to find a spider and watch it make its web.

He plugs himself back in, turns the light off, then leans against the wall, looks into the darkness, and counts the days. Almost three years to the day since he became a teen. They say soon they're going to upgrade his hydraulics and biosheath to make him stronger. They do that to lots of the boys. He doesn't care about being stronger, but his body is sluggish after today, so it's probably sensible.

Three years down, two to go. Just two more years until he can get out of here, and hopefully be happy again.

Chapter 3

Harriet was silly to hope. The chance was so slim, yet she can't help the shrinking sensation in her chest and her shoulders rolling forward for the rest of the day. She has no teen with her yet. Today, they're only being introduced and having a tour of the school, but she wonders how long before she can ask the teens about Oliver. They might know him, or they can tell her about the Institute and she can picture him, his blue eyes, his messy hair, his cheek dimples, but grown up. A teen, yet still her kind and caring little boy.

That shrinking feeling gets worse when she realises she doesn't know what Oliver's teen body looks like. He could look totally different.

Harriet packs up the classroom, re-gluing the displays that have succumbed to gravity, and putting all the mismatched furniture back into place. Everything they have here is salvaged from the landfill. Harriet worked in a school on level 99 once, years ago, when she first met Anthony. Up there, all the furniture matches and is replaced every year. Harriet likes the higgledy-piggledy appearance of this furniture. It's less structured, more chaotic, as children should be. At least Theo and the rest of the workshop staff can fix up what's scavenged from the landfill. There's no way they'd throw things away so frequently here on level 5.

When she finishes for the day, she collects her bag and makes to leave, but a parent confronts her before she reaches the door. He's a large, brutish man with tattoos up his neck and gaps in his teeth. He looks like he could play the villain in action movies.

'Oi!' he says to Harriet, too loudly for how close he is. He's Polly's dad, and this is not the first time he's accosted Harriet in such a manner. 'I want a word with you.'

Harriet paints on her most professional smile. Her acting is clearly not done for the day. 'Mr Wilson. How can I help you?'

'You're favouring those bot kids over my Polly. Trying to force her to work with bloody robots.'

'I can assure you, that's not the case. Polly was being particularly unkind and violent towards a MechaniKid. I had no choice but to tell Polly to work alone.'

'They shouldn't even be in the class. It's not right. And my Polly should not be in trouble for being violent when it's just a machine.'

'Mr Wilson.' Harriet stands as tall as she can, which isn't very, focusing more authority into her tone. She's cowered to too many men in the past. She'll not pander to this bully. 'The school has an inclusivity policy. The MechaniKids need to learn human behaviour and they can hardly do that if they are being picked on.'

'You can't pick on a machine,' he shouts through his teeth. Some spittle ejects and lands somewhere on her blouse. 'You wait. Those bots are freaks, everyone thinks so. And we're going to make sure they fry like they're in Hell, where they belong.' He walks out, punching the wall on his way.

Harriet's breath stalls for a moment, her hand going to her stomach as her gut swirls. She exhales slowly, steadying herself. Polly's dad is angry. His threats are empty, and untrue. The bot haters are a small minority; almost everyone loves the bots. He's talking nonsense. She shakes her dread away, and makes her way out of her classroom.

It's easy to see where Polly gets her attitude. She's a sweet girl most of the time and very bright. It's hard for Harriet to undo the hate that's conditioned on her from home. Children don't understand time, how their decisions will stay with them, how misdeeds repeat in the mind like a grainy old movie. They're too young to know the mind doesn't have an off switch.

The parents should definitely have more compassion, though. Harriet wishes she could put the parents in detention, give them extra homework assignments to make amends for the attitudes they're instilling. No doubt Mr Wilson will go to Dexter, and she'll have a complaint to deal with.

Theo meets Harriet at the school gate, just inside so they can wade through the protest together. She sighs when she sees it and curses under her breath. As if she's not had enough of this shit already. Today is the biggest turnout yet. Signs wave around their head saying, *Humans first!* Harriet grimaces at their pathetic and overly simplistic platitudes as they carry on chanting, *Tech is trash!* And *Ban the bots!*

Each chant leaves a sour taste in her mouth and she dips her head. She can't help conjuring images of them saying the same thing to Oliver, insulting him, making him feel unwelcome. It's only words, she reminds herself. Sticks and stones.

Harriet and Theo keep their heads down and swerve their way through the gathering. From the lack of children with the protestors, it's clear they're not even parents. Just people who have taken it upon themselves to latch onto a cause that doesn't concern them at all. Luckily, most of the parents are ambivalent towards the MechaniKids, and plenty understand the benefits of having them in class. But it's always the hateful few who are the loudest.

'Flesh first!' one shouts right in her face, and she pushes him away. Not hard, but he's a scrawny waif of a man and her shove sends him hurtling into the protestor behind.

No way is Harriet going to apologise. She glares at him. 'Get out of the way!' she shouts and continues to push her way through. Ten hours she's been at work today, and this is the crap she has to put up with.

'Bot sympathiser! Human hater!'

'Oh, piss off!' Harriet shouts over her shoulder as she gets past the protest. She clamps her mouth shut afterwards, looking over at Theo to see he's biting back a laugh. She shouldn't swear so close to school, although she'd like to say much worse words.

Theo drapes his arm over her shoulders as they walk home. In the quieter streets away from the school, her disappointment sets in. She leans on Theo, letting him take some of the weight of her worries. She doesn't voice her disappointment. Theo will know by now none of the teens are Oliver. As much as Theo is a supportive friend, he can't comprehend how much she's hurting. A loss like Harriet's is something only a fellow parent could understand. She may have said goodbye to her boy, but she never stopped hoping and wishing. Never stopped imagining being part of his life again.

'Monty messaged,' Theo says. 'He's making fajitas tonight.'

Harriet smiles, as she always does to engage in conversation. It's camouflage for her pain. They walk home and she listens to Theo talk about his latest salvage project, some gizmo he's fixed, about what his partner, Monty, is putting in the fajitas, about a conversation he had with his parents. Harriet says nothing but nods at the right places as her mind travels elsewhere.

When they arrive at their building, Harriet does a double-take. There's an envelope sticking out of their post box. It's so rare to receive post these days. It's generally only used for eviction notices and lawsuits. Theo walks over to it.

'We're up-to-date on the rent, right?' she asks.

'Of course. And bills.' He looks over his shoulder to avoid prying eyes of neighbours, then takes out the envelope.

'It's for you.' He hands it to her. 'There's no postmark; it must have been hand-delivered. The new tenants must have brought it over.'

On the front, in spidery handwriting is Harriet's name, and the address of their old place. They moved almost two years ago when Monty and Theo needed more space for their furniture and electrical salvage projects. It's the first bit of forwarded mail they've received.

A frown creases Harriet's brow as she stares at it. She runs her thumb over the clumsy handwriting for a moment before opening it. When she sees the letter, her hand goes to her mouth and she blinks away tears.

'What?' Theo asks.

Her breath catches a moment before she utters her next words, as if her lungs are disbelieving. 'It's from Oliver.'

She can't walk up the stairs to their apartment right now. Her knees have turned to jelly. She sits instead on the step, clutching the letter and reading through her tear-misted vision.

> *Dear Mum.*
>
> *I hope you are having a nice life and not spending too much time worrying about me. You don't need to worry about me. I am much older now, and bigger. I am sure now I could reach the top of that climbing frame! Funny thing is, I don't really want to. I'll try to send another letter if I can at some point.*
>
> *We're so busy here. There is so much to learn.*
>
> *Thomas is my best friend. You remember Thomas? We do all our classes together. I also have some other friends, Evie and Mia, but I don't get to see them so much.*

> *We work a lot and are kept busy. I've heard sometime soon we'll be allowed out for a few weeks on work experience placements. I hope that when my time comes, I'll get to see you. But if not, it's only another two years and I'll be out of this place and be fully grown and in the workplace. That seems a little scary right now, but I am sure it'll be fun.*
>
> *In the meantime, I hope you're okay.*
>
> *I love you. Fly free.*
>
> *Oliver.*

Harriet presses the letter into her heart as she cries, then hands it to Theo to read.

'I wonder how long ago this was posted?' Theo says. 'They might not have re-delivered it straight away.'

'Why now?' She wipes her eye on her sleeve. 'He could have written ages ago, but now? The letter doesn't really say anything worrying but again—why now?' She begged TRI to let her have access, just a letter or occasional visit, but they flatly refused.

'You think maybe they're sending them to all parents now? Maybe the Institute has had concerns about parents, what with some teens coming out.'

'Maybe. But I know he wrote it. Fly free. That's our saying.'

'I'll bet there are parents everywhere missing them.' He sits next to her on the step and puts his arm around her. 'Those stupid protests are not representative. Those that love and loved their kids are just too scared to speak out because they'll get branded as crazy by the haters.'

'I bet you're right.' She doesn't mention her time chatting online to *Shamed Parents*. From Theo's perspective, she appears mostly like she's drawn a line under her time with Oliver. She is an actor, after all.

'And like he says,' Theo continues, 'he's reassuring you that he's fine. And you're more than halfway through his teen years. The next two years will pass in no time. Then you might be able to see him again.'

Theo's right. Time passes quickly. The last three have been the blink of an eye. Moving house, starting her job, and teaching is such a busy profession, time has whizzed by. But two more years without Oliver still feels like a life sentence. With the protests getting louder, she reconciles that Oliver being at the Institute isn't the worst thing. As much as she misses him, at least he's safe.

She walks up the stairs as Theo's phone buzzes. He stops walking to check it. When she's ascended a few steps and he still hasn't moved, she turns around.

Theo is staring at his phone, his face pale.

'What?' she asks.

'It's those Ban the Bot protestors.'

She sighs. 'For God's sake, what now?'

He lifts his head, his gaze meeting hers. 'They've blown up a tunnel. Says they're trying to blow up the Teen Institute.'

Chapter 4

Harriet watches the news with bated breath, biting her nails, and barely taking time to blink. Monty's fajitas sit on the table uneaten. None of them have an appetite. She's on *Get Level*, reading the panicked posts from other parents. You'd think TRI would give them some reassurance or updates. You'd think they wouldn't have to hear about their children from the bloody evening news. She tries calling them, but there's no option on the automated phone line for this. She needs to see her son. She needs to know he's okay.

'They caught the people that did it,' Monty says as he finds another news site on his phone while pacing the living room for the hundredth time. 'They're some bot-hating nutters.' His footsteps are soft on the white faux fur rug.

Everything in the living room is pale coloured or shiny, supposed to make the place feel less dim since the lighting is so bad down on 5. It's supposed to feel more spacious, Monty said when he decorated. A glitter ball hangs from the ceiling, as well as various other gaudy and kitsch ornaments he's found at scavenger markets. To add some cheer, he said, though it's going to take a hell of a lot more than sparkles and colours to lift

Harriet's mood right now. Whatever decor used to be effective fails to incite any positive emotion as she watches the news. The walls are closing in; the place darker than ever.

Harriet rubs her temples, unable to pull her eyes away from screens. TV to phone, TV to phone, is all she's been looking at, and her dry eyes burn. 'This is just crazy.'

'At least they got it wrong.' Theo says. 'It was just an old empty warehouse.'

'How many times are they going to get it wrong, though?' Harriet throws her arms into the air. 'How long before they get the right location? They need to move the teens.'

'But they're safe where they are,' Theo says. 'These bot-haters haven't found them yet.'

'Exactly. *Yet.*'

The *Shamed Parents* take little comfort in the update, some wondering if the news is even telling the truth. Would TRI admit it if the explosions were on target and destroyed their stock? They wouldn't risk the damage to their share price.

Harriet asks if any of the parents have had a letter. None have, not that they're admitting. It makes Oliver's letter all the more peculiar and worrying. Perhaps he had a hunch their time was coming to an end, that he was being held hostage, or . . .

Harriet thumps the side of her head with her fist. She can't think like that. She can't allow herself to imagine her son being harmed.

Monty sits again. The three of them huddle up on the sofa. Monty fixed up the sofa when they first moved in, improving the stuffing and reupholstering it in a neutral yellow, easy-to-clean material. In case of spillages, he said. They've never spilled anything on the sofa. A child might, though. Oliver knocked over paint pots at the refuge on more than one occasion. Monty made their home child-proof, just in case.

Monty turns up the volume on the TV. Harriet is wedged between her two friends who have been with her through all of her moods the last few years, who moved house to make sure they had room for her, who loved Oliver too. She doesn't tell them enough how much they mean to her. Right now, squished together on a sofa only big enough for two people, she lets their torsos hold her up so she doesn't crumple. Monty takes up as much room as Theo and Harriet combined. For someone born below ground, he's always been broad and sturdy. They joke his shoulders are wider than the doorframes. He moves around to sit at an angle and puts his arm around Harriet.

The presenter is Shelly Anderson, the usual evening reporter. Harriet met her briefly years ago when she interviewed the cast of a movie she was in. In her younger days, Shelly was more confrontational, trying to make a name for herself by being controversial. Now, she targets her questions more to please the viewers on the top levels, since they're the only ones guaranteed electricity in the evenings. The bias in reporting is the thing a patchy grid affects more than anything else. Why cater for an audience that may not be watching?

Shelly's face is deadpan. Her mousy, slicked back hair hangs to her shoulders, oversized spectacles sit slightly askew. 'Like it or not, bots will play a significant role in the workforce in years to come. So why all the upset? With us now, we have the head of TRI, along with a member of the anti-bot movement, calling themselves the Flesh Fraternity.'

The Flesh Fraternity. Harriet sneers at the screen, turning her head away for a second, contempt burning her insides.

The camera pans out to take in the seating area opposite her. Two men, sitting as far apart as they can on the sofa, stare at the camera. One with eyes like ice. The other with the kind of entitled smile and cut to his suit that tells the world he's never had to skip a meal or worry he won't make rent.

'Mr Chambers,' Shelly says, 'is TRI worried about the rise in public hysteria over bots?'

That entitled smile stretches thinner. 'Not at all, Shelly.' He has an open posture, man-spreading his way across the sofa to take up the entire camera view. This man is the head of the company that made Oliver. Harriet should feel some sense of appreciation towards him. But he oozes the kind of self-serving confidence that makes every one of her hairs stand on end. He reminds her too much of her ex-husband, Anthony. 'Hysteria sums it up well. This kind of reaction is completely irrational. Bots are harmless and will be doing the population a great service. Demand for bots, once the first generation is available, is already outstripping supply in some markets, so this really is a minority who have unwarranted concerns.'

Shelly nods, then turns her attention to the other man on the sofa. 'Mr Hill. As a member of the Flesh Fraternity, what do you have to say about tonight's events?'

The second man is less sharply dressed, and it doesn't take a genius to tell he's from the lower levels. His simple smock is brown and stained, his thinning hair spreads from his sideburns down to his chin in tufts that surround old scars. The makeup artists must have had their work cut out for them.

'Well, Shelly. Such acts are not what the Flesh Fraternity is about.' His voice is breathy, every syllable sounding like an effort. 'We believe these actions to be the work of another group, called the Human Front. But to say we are a small minority is wrong, as this proves. All employee unions are now backing the Flesh Fraternity and our message is clear. Machines masquerading as humans are the Devil's work, not to mention the damage they do to the electricity supplies on the lower levels.'

The Devil's work. Harriet snorts a laugh at that.

'That is simply not true.' Mr Chambers' tone is jovial, as if the other guy is making a joke. Perhaps the Devil reference really was meant in jest. Surely, no one could mean such a thing in earnest. 'Every household and workplace that has a MechaniKid or MechaniTeen has its electricity supply checked and guaranteed by TRI and paid for. If any household or workplace is concerned about their access to electricity, the solution is simple. Sign up for a bot.'

The lights in their apartment flicker, and the TV turns to static for a second.

'But there is no extra supply,' Mr Hill says, the sound and picture quality still grainy and muffled. 'For every household that has a boosted electricity supply due to having a bot, there are ten households that have their supply stripped to cope. TRI is stealing from the needy to provide these products. As I said, the Devil's work.'

Harriet rubs her forehead. The sheer lunacy bringing on a migraine.

Mr Chambers holds up his hands and cocks his head, his smile relentless. 'The attitude of the few who are bot-sceptic seems to be the attitude of people who are traditional and resistant to change. As such, at TRI, we are training the teens to take on traditional roles in society based on their gender. The male bots—'

Mr Hill scoffs. 'The fact you're even referring to them as if they have a gender is obscene.'

'We did consider non-binary bots, but from the traditionalists this was regarded as a bad idea. So, the bots have clear genders and their roles in the workplace will reflect such traditional values. Female bots are learning to look after children and domestic duties; male bots will be doing more manual labour.'

Harriet gasps, her mouth hangs open, and Monty mutes the TV.

'The world's gone mad,' Theo says.

'Gender roles?' Harriet says, her voice breaking into a squeak. 'What sort of work are they going to have Oliver do? That's nonsense. Oliver would like a role working with children, a nanny or teaching. Are they saying those sorts of roles are only for girls?' Job roles haven't been gender specific in over a century. Imposing ancient ideas on the most modern technology seems like an oxymoron.

Theo rubs her arm. 'Truth is, Harriet, he's a teenager now. You really don't know what he'd like.'

Her heart sinks a little as she realises the truth in this.

Theo runs his hand over his head. His hair is thinning a lot these days, a bald spot on the back. Monty lost all of his years ago, thinning hair being a trait of pretty much all below grounders. Theo's follicles hanging on is something of a miracle. His dad still has some hair, though. Good genes, he claims, though whenever he has any stress he says the rest will fall out soon. If stress caused hair loss, Harriet would be bald herself. Instead, hers takes less time to brush these days and shampoo lasts a lot longer. She's not in the movies anymore. Her need for good hair days are long behind her.

Theo gets up to make tea just as the electric dies.

'Fuck's sake,' Monty says.

'Electricity is power,' Theo says with a frustrated sigh. The mantra of the lower levels bites.

Harriet sits, rigid, every muscle tense, barely noticing the blackout. Two people were on TV arguing over whether or not her son should exist, and she hates them both. Oliver should have the right to choose what he does with his life. Choice is a human right.

But Oliver isn't human.

She sits back on the sofa, folds her arms, and shuts her eyes. If they're the two opposing sides, it's lose-lose either way. It's a dangerous world, she knows that. But it shouldn't be, not for her son.

Theo gives her a hug, the kind of hug that lets Harriet know he's there for her, that he's up for a talk when she's ready. He knows her too well, and knows that talking about feelings is too alien for her. He makes a joke, something light-hearted that she doesn't hear, but laughs at anyway. A tired, unenthusiastic laugh. Not a hearty, belly-cramping laugh. She hasn't laughed like that in years.

Theo tries to light her spark, like he often does, but she walks in the shadow of who she once was. She thought of herself often as a failed actor, a drop-out. But instead of playing her parts on the big screen she's in costume every day. She's a performer, a master of disguise. And right now, with the madness of everything, she feels as if her entire existence has been a show and she's playing the role of her life.

She goes to bed, and the food Monty prepared is left uneaten. It's a mother's job to worry. That's how Harriet consoles herself every time she frets and loses sleep. The feeling of dread and helplessness that claws at her at least makes her feel like a real mother with a real son. The world has gone mad, like Theo said, and she feels more than ever right now, like she's stuck in some shitty soap opera that gets its viewer numbers by throwing tragedy after tragedy at her. She's playing the part of the constantly wronged woman, the one whose storyline is always a tearjerker.

She deserves her pain. She's made so many mistakes. She never told her ex-husband she was born below ground, and being born and bred below made it likely any children she would have would be sick. Her baby Freddie lived only minutes. She misled Anthony, trapped him with his love for her. She's poison. Her body killed their baby. She wraps her arms around her stomach, feeling nothing but loss. Her misery is her karma.

Perhaps her life is a book, and somewhere there's an old paperback with yellowing brittle pages, that musty old book smell, one page dogeared where she left off, where she left Oliver, her newborn Freddie, her brother Tipher. Her boys, each given just one measly page, whereas they all should have had an entire volume.

That's all it is, she tells herself, when she tosses and turns until she is flushed with heat and knotted in sheets. That book is shut, but one day she'll be able to pick it up again, find them and they're all still there, still alive.

Chapter 5

When he first arrived at the TRI MechaniTeen Institute, Oliver and the others were told their teen days would prepare them for work one day. They had to get to know one another and learn some skills for the world of work. Oliver imagined it like the playground or refuge, where he could read to one of the other teens or get a toy to share with them. But there are no toys or books at the Institute. Not nice books anyway. There are textbooks to learn how to wire a plug or cut hair. Nothing like the books he used to read, as if they don't want them to learn about anything fun.

He likes the idea of being a teacher, like his mum. He'd love to look after children. Maybe a PE teacher, as he remembers teaching little Delilah to climb. But he's only had manual labour work experience so far.

His teen body was instantly strange. It didn't fit like he was used to and, as he was learning to navigate it, he was sure everyone was watching and laughing. Human children change gradually, so Oliver assumes they cope better, as they adapt bit by bit. For Oliver, the change was so sudden, he felt he stood out too much, that he looked ridiculous and he was going to fall over all the time. Quietly, when they were alone, Thomas said he felt the same. There were so many teen bodies in that warehouse, so how were they meant to know which one was right? He chose one that looked a bit like him, had all the traits his mother loved so much. Now Oliver looks at some of the other teen boys and wishes he chose theirs or had bits of theirs. When he gets uploaded into a man's body, he'll remember to look for bigger hands, maybe a bit taller, hair that doesn't muss up so easily. George always has tidy hair whatever he does, and he can lift heavier things. It seems all the skills Oliver learned as a kid are useless here.

At least he has Thomas to confide in. They discuss it quietly, sometimes, how much harder everything is here, how stressful and lonely.

Evie's charging port is next to Oliver's. She's one of the nicer girls, quiet like Thomas, with bouncy brown ringlets that remind him of his mum, although Evie's ringlets look more organised. Evie often says to Oliver and Thomas she doesn't like some of her classes much either, though she never goes into detail about what they do. Whatever they do, it doesn't usually involve the bruises and muck the boys have to put up with, so Oliver thinks it can't be that bad.

Evie's friend, Mia, keeps telling Evie to relax, to go along with it, get it over with, but Evie says she struggles to get it done faster or slower. What *it* is Oliver can't imagine. The girls go to their lessons in a different part of the Institute and never talk about it. That's the thing about girls. They can keep secrets.

Evie has a caring way about her, like Oliver's mum, and a pleasant smile, like nothing is ever too much trouble. She doesn't have the piercing laugh that Mia and some of the girls do, and she dislikes the boy's brash jokes as much as Oliver. Evie is peaceful to be around. Sometimes, when no one is watching, they hold hands. When they do, Oliver's internal temperature heats up, and he has a fluttering feeling in his chest. It's not unpleasant.

The noise is what Oliver often struggles with the most at the Institute. A lot of the teens are so noisy. They laugh so loud Oliver thinks if there were any windows, they would rattle. The communal room echoes. Even the large room where they work makes their shouting voices bounce around. And the work is noisy too. It's so rarely calm. Nighttime, when he's meant to be on standby, is the only time it's peaceful enough to think. Perhaps if everyone was quieter, more insects and bugs would come to visit. The din would be enough to scare off Oliver, let alone a little creepy crawly.

Some of the teens have gone on work placement. Oliver had a little tug of jealousy. He'd love to get out in the real world again, to be able to watch all the other people going about their business. He wasn't chosen, though. None of the boys were. Evie and Mia weren't either. They said none from their classes were. Rumour has it, there's going to be a second lot sent out soon. Oliver wonders where these rumours come from, since none of the staff ever seem to tell them anything. He asks Josie sometimes, and she'd say if she knew.

Josie seems upset this evening. Her hands shake as she helps them plug in. There was someone else around the communal area earlier, fitting red lights and speakers that he says is an alarm system.

'Are you okay, Josie?' Oliver asks.

She always turns all the other teens on standby first, so it's just Oliver and Thomas with her at the end. 'I'm fine, Oliver. Don't you worry about me.'

'What's the alarm for?'

'They're just sensors in case there's a problem.'

'Like what?'

'Nothing you need to worry about.'

But Oliver does worry. He always worries. 'Thank you for sending my letter. Did you see my mum?'

'No. Sorry. I only dropped it off at the house.'

'Maybe if we find some more paper, I could write another one?'

Josie smiles. She has a sheen in her eyes, as if she's about to cry. 'I'm sure she'd like that.'

'Do you think you could try to see her? Just for a moment? I worry about her all the time. I just want to know she's okay.'

'No promises, but I'll try.'

Josie and Thomas spend some time together now, as they do every night. Oliver doesn't interfere. He keeps his distance, as much as he can in the small space. They go into the office which is behind a mirror and Oliver can't hear or see them.

It's hard for Oliver not to be jealous. Thomas is his best friend, and he still gets to see his mum almost every night. So many times Oliver has asked Josie about bringing his mum to the Institute but he knows it would be impossible. She's not going to risk her contact with Thomas by breaking rules. Taking the letter for Oliver was risky enough. He begged her for years to send a letter but she kept saying she wouldn't be able to. Then the other day, she gave him some paper and said to be quick.

It's silly. He's a teen now. He doesn't need his mum anymore. Lots of the teens here never even mention their families. But he tells himself they probably didn't have mums as great as his.

Josie puts Thomas on standby and gives him a peck on the forehead, then says goodnight to Oliver. She's still all wobbly, like she's afraid. She supports herself against the wall for a moment before she sniffs, then wraps her coat tightly around her. Oliver watches her face, tilts his head, and blinks a few times. He notices her face is a little tighter, her brow lower.

When Oliver's alone, he worries some more. No one ever tells Oliver and the other teens what's going on in the world outside. They've no TV, no newspapers, no one from the outside to talk to. All they have is their mundane work.

Josie seems upset even though she says she's fine. There's a new alarm. Those two things are odd. Things have been the same for so long, but all of a sudden, there's change in the air. And Oliver knows change can be either good or bad. He knows there are many people out there in the world, and plenty of them are evil, like Anthony. His fists clench when he thinks of

Anthony, though he tries to stay calm. He needs to stay relaxed if he's going to charge properly while not on standby. But he can't relax. Without knowing, he can only dread. A hundred reasons for an alarm come to him and none of them are good. And Josie being upset—maybe someone has hurt her. Maybe the world is collapsing outside. In here, Oliver would never even know.

His thoughts spiral now. Of bad things, of hurt people, of his mother in pain. He's useless in the Institute. The staff here need to see he's ready for the real world, that he's ready to do some good.

He taps his foot, restless, the space shrinking as his desire to get out increases. If Josie can't see his mum soon and let him know she's okay, he'll need to find another way to check. He glances around the darkness, as if somewhere he'll spot a phone he can use with his mum's number written on it. That's obviously a stupid idea, but all he knows is two more years is way too long if people out there are in peril. If he doesn't get selected for work experience soon, and if Josie can't confirm his mum is okay, he'll need to find a way to leave. If there's a hint of danger outside, he needs to be there to make sure his mum is okay.

Chapter 6

The explosion and news reports have only added to the number of people protesting about the bots. When the choice is so binary, bots or none, the population rips down the middle. On their way to work, wrapped up to fight off the chilly air, Harriet and Theo dodge several gatherings of union speakers. What began with concerns about electricity supply has now morphed into something bordering on bonkers. Up on their soapboxes, the speakers hardly resemble the employee rights groups that founded the unions. They're more like preachers, shouting through megaphones to be heard over the constant noise of the trash falling down, prophesying the end is nigh if bots become the norm, that bots are the second Great Flood, that judgement day is coming. Through a megaphone they shout to be heard over the hubbub of rush hour, over the constant crashing of rubbish beyond the walkways from the upper levels. It's the kind of volume that rings in Harriet's ears, a tinnitus of hate.

'Bloody hell,' Harriet says as they stop to listen to one. Their message has ramped up several gears, from impassioned to lunacy. At least such a dense gathering makes the cold air bite less, despite the icy atmosphere from the crowd.

'All these people listening and not a single sensible word has been said,' Harriet says.

'We are the Flesh Fraternity, and mark my words, these bots will mean the end of humanity! The Devil is a bot!'

The Flesh Fraternity, like the guy on the evening news. Fear of some Devil problem has infected what used to be a sensible group. Harriet tuts and they walk away, not too far before they have another gathering to step around, much the same messages being shouted.

As Harriet and Theo find some space away from preachers, the din from the rubbish gets louder and the lights dimmer. They keep to the centre of the walkway as several items of trash manage to bounce over the fence and scatter across the walkway perimeter. It's particularly noisy today. There must be a demolition job going on a few levels up. When married to Anthony, Harriet got used to living on the top levels. The lack of crashing rubbish was bliss, like getting rid of a headache. Adjusting to the headache again, though, is taking years.

'Can you believe they've made up a whole new religion for this bullshit?' Harriet says. 'All this attention and you'd think they'd use it to make a point about something useful. We're drowning in upper-level rubbish and they blame a few bots for the end of days.'

'I don't think there's any point making common sense arguments to people who think that the Devil is a robot,' Theo says.

Dexter is already in and roaming the halls when they arrive. Harriet walks to her classroom, a cup of coffee from the staff room still hot in her hands when he confronts her.

'This MechaniTeen is assigned to your class for now,' Dexter says, presenting her with one of the MechaniTeens. She has sleek black hair and a smile enigmatic enough to outshine the Mona Lisa. 'We may rotate at some point, but for now, you'll be working with Beatrice. Say hello to Ms Chapel.'

'Oh, Harriet's fine.' She waves her hand at the formalities.

The glare Harriet receives from Dexter tells her using first names is definitely not fine.

Beatrice has the kind of breathtaking beauty Harriet used to envy when she worked in the movies. High cheekbones, large green eyes, a delicate nose, and shiny hair that does what it's told without an hour of styling and bribery. Photo quality. Harriet wonders if all the teens are this attractive.

When Dexter is gone, Harriet relaxes a little, and as they wait for the morning bell, Harriet gestures for Beatrice to sit at the desk with her.

'Welcome, Beatrice. It's lovely to have you with us.'

'Thank you. I am really excited to be here.' She avoids eye contact, looking anywhere but at Harriet. Her hands on her lap are clasped so tightly together, her fingers blanch. Her skin pinkens around her cheeks, showing the bioluminescence Harriet found so fascinating when she first took Oliver home.

'You can relax, Beatrice,' Harriet says, keeping her voice soft. 'First days can be nerve-racking, but you're going to be fine.'

Beatrice looks up and, after a second of eye contact, her enigmatic smile twitches to appear a tad more genuine. 'My body is struggling to relax. I'm sorry. I don't know why. I just think I'm going to mess everything up and make a bad impression.'

'You're just nervous. It's normal. Don't worry, you'll settle soon enough.'

Harriet sits upright, takes a big, lung-inflating breath followed by a slow exhale, and Beatrice watches and copies. It's a trick Harriet has learned from the MechaniKids she teaches. They copy so well, so she gives them the right sort of action to replicate.

Beatrice sits back in her chair, a little less rigid.

'So, tell me about the Institute. It must be quite different from being here?' Harriet sips her coffee, savouring each mouthful.

'It was fine, but I am pleased to have a change. I was hoping for art class, but drama is a close second.' Her voice is like she's in a job interview, very formal and lacking emotion, not at all like the kid's Harriet's known, as if being away from the real world means she's forgotten about intonation. Drama will be good for her, Harriet concludes. It should help her let her guard down.

'Do you do much art at the Institute?' Harriet asks.

'No, but I did when I was a kid with my family.'

'Were they nice to you, your family?'

Beatrice pauses a while before answering, her smile curling up at the corners a little more, her gaze somewhere in the mid-distance. 'They were. They gave me lots of books and taught me to read, so that was nice. And I had a television that usually worked.'

'So, lower levels then?'

'Yes. On six.'

Harriet shouldn't badger her with too many questions on day one, though she's dying to ask the one question.

The class piles in then, loud and boisterous. The noise of them makes Beatrice jump, but as she watches the class play and laugh and demonstrate their high energy levels, her face softens, her eyes sparkle, and that enigmatic smile breaks into a full joyful grin.

'Right away, class,' Harriet says, raising her voice to be heard over them. 'Hang up your coats and I want you to do your warm-up drills. Today, for a warm-up, you're going to be jungle animals.'

The class begins straight away. Harriet gives Beatrice a nod as she stands, and she glides between the group, delighting in their performances. She laughs at the cheeky ones and cowers from the predators, and her interaction makes the children work even harder. Any shyness and anxiety she had a moment ago disappears when she hears the children's laughter.

They're mostly lions and tigers, as always. There's one boy who's a snake slithering around on the floor, and a couple of jumping creatures Harriet assumes are gazelles, though couldn't say for certain. One pupil, Pavi, takes his role as a lion a little too seriously with Vera, who's doing her best not to be prey. Harriet walks over to put an end to the hunt and to remind the children to play nice.

'She doesn't care,' Pavi says. 'She's just a bot.' He puffs his cheeks out and blows a raspberry at Vera.

'Enough of that!' Harriet says, raising her voice to a volume she reaches so rarely. 'You are all children in this class, so you must all behave and be kind.'

Pavi folds his arms and squints his eyes. It takes more than a telling off to undo childhood prejudices. Harriet has had this discussion with some children multiple times over the last few years. It's even more concerning when, like Pavi, that child has a MechaniKid in their household.

Harriet stands at the back with Beatrice and apologises, though Beatrice doesn't seem to have taken any offence.

'Watching the television made me love movies,' Beatrice says. 'I am so excited to be helping teach drama.'

'We're delighted to have you. Do you know the rest of the teens on work experience?'

'Yes. Some more than others. Let me see, there's Mary and Lucy at this school, then from my class working elsewhere there's also Clare, Connie, Monica and Beth—'

'Any boys?' Harriet interrupts.

'No. All girls. In our class, we learn skills for female roles. And teaching is for the girls only.'

Harriet bristles at that comment, knitting her brows. 'Oh. Says who?'

'It's just the proper way, is it not? Although Mr Eamon is a man, so I suppose the headteacher is in charge and so is more suitable for males.'

Harriet doesn't answer, pursing her lips instead, that TRI man from the TV last night repeating on her like a burp. Beatrice says this without an air of prejudice, more like she's just dropped in from over a hundred years ago and knows her options are limited. Harriet reminds herself of the sheltered teaching Beatrice would have had at the Institute. Without any outside influences, it would only take one teacher to instil such thoughts into impressionable minds. At least Beatrice is here now, and Harriet is going to be able to open her eyes a bit.

She has another sip of coffee, and she wonders if Oliver would have been taught the same attitudes as Beatrice. 'When you were at the Institute, did you spend time with boys and girls?'

'Oh, yes. Of course. I am quite familiar with boys. Our recreation time we could spend together.'

She can resist asking no longer, and the class all seem happy enough in their make-believe jungle. 'Did you know a boy teen named Oliver?'

Beatrice ponders for a moment. 'No. I don't remember an Oliver. There were a lot of us, though. I only ever spoke to a few others.'

Of course she doesn't know Oliver. That would take an element of luck Harriet never seems to have.

'Beatrice?' Dexter's big red face appears in the doorway and Harriet jumps. 'Some kid has been sick just outside the toilets. Go clean it up.'

'Of course.' Beatrice stands, still smiling. 'I'll be back as soon as I can, Ms Chapel.'

Harriet nods as she leaves, walking with fluid movement just like a human. She wonders if the teens take a while to get used to their new bodies. When she first took Oliver home, even sitting down was something he had to learn.

For the rest of the day, she finds it hard to concentrate, coffee or tea unable to keep her mind on the here and now. Whenever she's not talking, her mind drifts to Oliver.

She needs to believe he's somewhere he can read books and delight in the birds and insects, that he can fuel his imagination like the children in her class, can access a climbing frame and use his body in ways he enjoys. But she's imagining her little boy Oliver, who liked little boy things and, as Theo said, he's a teen now. She doesn't know what sort of things he'll enjoy these days.

Maybe there's a girl, or boy, his first crush. Is that too human? Perhaps she can ask Beatrice about such emotions. Oliver loved Harriet. Loves—he still does. He can't switch off love for his mother so easily. If he can love a mother, then he must be capable of the other kind of love too. She imagines him doing what teenagers do: stealing glances, holding hands, the embarrassment of his first kiss.

Sometimes Harriet imagines him as a robot. Metallic and inanimate, a part in a factory, mute, a machine. He exists like that momentarily in her mind and she thinks, what would be the point? Why give him so much experience and feeling just to strip it all away?

Instead, she imagines him again as a teenage boy, cheeky, mischievous. A fumble, a kiss, that first broken heart. A telling off from the teacher and giggles with friends in the evenings. The kind of trouble she was never able to get into. Because that's all anyone wants for their children, to have what they never did and to have whatever they were denied. A better life. A happier one. A degree of freedom more.

Chapter 7

Harriet should go straight home after work, veg out on the sofa and rest her tired body. She's so often tired these days. She recalls with more than a smidgen of nostalgia life in her twenties, filming all day, then going out after work, even exercising, visiting an accent coach, combat coach, singing coach, each day jam-packed from waking to sleeping. Being on the wrong side of forty is most noticeable in her energy levels. But going home always feels empty. It doesn't matter how caring Theo is, how eccentric and bubbly Monty is, how beautifully they've decorated. She loves living with them. It feels like home, but the place can never be full without her son. Children grow up and leave home all the time, but the lack of contact for Harriet is the worst. It's like empty nest syndrome on steroids.

So, instead of basking in her woes in her never-full house, she meets Theo and Monty at a bar after work. They already have the drinks in when she arrives. The beer on level 5 isn't a patch on the wine from the upper levels, but it's a hell of a lot better than the cabbage wine her mother used to brew below ground.

The bar is the kind of cosy place that always has the ambience of drama, like everyone's had the most exciting day. Grubby carpet coated in dust and stains, the walls chock-a-block with picture frames displaying antique pictures of Reading town when people lived at ground level. There's a river in some pictures, a train line in some others, all with a view of the sky. And not a piece of litter in sight.

'I shouldn't have got my hopes up. I didn't, not really. Well, a bit. I just really, really wanted it to be him.' Harriet sniffs and blinks away the mist that's forming. 'Sorry to keep going on about it.'

Theo dismisses that apology with a wave of his hand.

'The teen girl I have in my class, Beatrice, seems great. I asked her if she knew Oliver and she said no. So, there's that.' She takes a large sip of her drink.

Monty grunts and cracks his neck.

'You okay?' Theo asks and rubs his arm.

'Yeah, just frustrated. Electricity has been shit all over our end of town today. I have to finish this bedroom set for this order from 70, and I've had to do everything without power tools today. My arms are knackered.'

'Come to school and do what you need there,' Theo says. 'Our electricity is always fine.'

'TRI isn't going to be happy until the entire country is in blackout except for them and whoever has a bot. Someone really needs to do something about it,' Monty says. 'Electricity is power.'

Theo nods and they all sip their drinks in silence for a moment.

There are no words of consolation Harriet can offer Monty. The electricity availability has been awful, everyone says so. They'll likely go back to a dark house later, and they'll need to budget for the extra expense of gas to keep the place warm. It's still freezing on this level, despite the news saying it's a pleasant day up top. The TV and radio giving weather reports this low down always seems daft. The sunshine doesn't warm the lower levels. They're always in the shade.

Harriet finishes her drink and stares into the foam at the bottom of the glass. In hindsight, perhaps a night in would have been better. She could sit in her room alone and mope, instead of making faux-cheery conversation and attempt to drink her sadness away. She could read Oliver's letter again. She has one letter to cherish. That's it after three years. Why not regular letters? Just an occasional visit would be nice. The letter confirmed visiting must be possible, since Oliver is still friends with Thomas. Josie handed Oliver back to TRI to keep access to her son, so Josie must be visiting. Josie broke Harriet's heart. It's not fair she can see her son and Harriet can't.

The bar is heaving. That's always a sign the electricity for residences has been iffy. Everyone flocks to the bars in search of lighting and heating. Harriet used to come to this bar a lot a few years ago with Theo and Monty when she first moved in. Get out and meet someone, they said, as if a new partner would take all her hurt away. There was a man for a while, Yanis. But where Harriet wanted mere escapism, he wanted connection.

That ended the way these things usually do for Harriet—him calling her distant and cold, and her not arguing otherwise.

There'll be someone else, Theo and Monty have told her so many times as they seem determined to marry her off. Out of love rather than a desire to get rid of her. In this day and age, being single is still a dirty word. A woman in her forties must surely be gagging to be rescued from her all-encompassing misery, everyone seems to think. Surely, any woman can only feel complete when a partner is shoehorned into her life.

Harriet puts up with their comments and doesn't argue, but also doesn't action their suggestions. She's happy single. Well, as happy as she'll ever be. She's not just single anyway. She's a single mother with absent sons, one still living somewhere out of reach. No new partner will be able to complete her.

The gossip on everyone's lips in the bar tonight is the bots. It's still the hot news article of the day. Monty says *Get Level* is filled with it, people debating whether or not bots should exist, the damage they're doing, or the benefits. Harriet has read the highlights, though has been too busy to engage much. Besides *Shamed Parents,* she avoids most of it, though she's been skimming articles to check for any more explosions from the Human Front. If it weren't for *Shamed Parents,* she probably wouldn't log on at all. She spent far too much time on social media when she was acting. Her photo was often sprawled across pages with people rating her looks, her performance, everything about her as if she was inanimate and had no feelings. She learned to stay away for her own sanity.

Harriet's eyes bulge when she overhears one conversation. She locks her gaze with Theo and Monty, the three of them silent as they listen in.

'I've heard there's a bar down on 3 that will have those MechaniTeens in, you know, for pleasure.'

'Really?'

'Yep. My, erm, friend, goes to that bar a lot. Their girls are nice, but you can't ask them to do everything you want. The bots though, they'll be up for anything.'

Harriet's jaw drops. Teens. That's all they'll have to staff the bars with. The first generation fully grown MechaniBots are still two years away from production. The bots they'll be hiring will be children on work experience. She tastes bile, a simmering anger threatening to bubble over. Those MechaniTeens will have bodies and mental ages of sixteen-year-olds. Far too young to be lured into such a job. Her stomach knots more when she recalls she was a similar age when she found herself in such roles. If anyone knows that's too young, she does.

She leans into Monty and Theo. 'I don't think I can stand listening to this any longer.'

'Me neither,' Theo says. 'Let's go home.'

On 5, the dark night is as dark as ever. Particulate matter clogs the air, raining down from the underside of the walkway above. When she stayed at the women's refuge on 4 with Oliver, the stagnant sooty air never bothered her. She was so enchanted by her little boy it wasn't possible to be annoyed. As she walks now in the pitch blackness, everything about the lower levels annoys her. The levels above block out the view of the sky above, obstructing even the moon. It just seems so unfair the likes of her ex-husband is gifted with a view of the sky, to see the stars and feel the sunshine, whereas she and her wonderful friends have to scrounge out a living in his shadow.

Some streetlights flicker on for a moment, then switch off again. The large advertising billboard stays lit, and that stops it being pitch black. Some new kitchen implement is the must-buy of the minute. They all laugh at that. The thing requires electricity, so it seems quite pointless down this low.

They round a corner and walk past the seedier end of town. Here, the bars are more like the venues where Harriet used to work. Tips get higher for more flesh on show, even higher still for a grope. She worked a couple of levels lower, where the floors were stickier and clientele even less polite. They continue to walk away from the strip where it's darker. No advertising billboards function in this part of town, not at the moment. The sporadic electric favours the billboards, so it's a bad sign when even they aren't lit. Monty isn't going to be using his power tools any time soon. The air purifiers that Theo fixed will be useless for a while.

They light torches to cast a beam across the walkway. This part of town isn't too busy. Most people are either home already or staying out in the clubs till closing. Harriet often feels like an anomaly, stuck in the middle between the two groups of hermits and late-nighters. The occasional drink after work is becoming a rare thing in the all-or-nothing culture of the lower levels.

From somewhere ahead, cutting through the darkness, comes a scream, muffled. The three of them pause a moment, strain to listen again, wondering if it's children playing or cats. The scuffing footsteps around them also slow, the general hubbub of the evening quieting to almost silence. There's a break in the cascade of trash, a few seconds, and they hear it again.

Another scream.

They run towards the scream, whereas so many run away from it. A scream is either a cry for help or a warning, and they are driven only by instinct. A scream like that is female, young, and on the dark streets there's little doubt as to what that means.

Harriet stumbles over a pothole, hanging off Monty's arm, keeping her upright. The walkway surface is getting worse and the torches only pick up the biggest holes.

Their torch beams capture the silhouette of a man pushing a woman up against a building. Her flailing arms are nothing against the might of him as he pins her to the wall, forcing himself upon her.

'Hey!' they all shout and the man whips his head around, his angry face highlighted in the torchlight. He growls like a dog as they run at him, pushing him to the ground, Monty doing the lion's share of the restraining. Theo and Harriet stand in front of the woman as Monty crouches, flexing his muscles, ready to pounce. The man pulls up his trousers, charges at Monty who stays upright though grunts as he's winded, the man landing a punch to his face.

Theo gasps and steps forward, but Harriet holds him back. Monty can handle himself a lot better if he's not worried about Theo.

Blood gushes from Monty's nose, shining crimson in the torchlight and Monty screams his battle cry. He punches the man back, once in the face and twice in the gut before the man falls to the ground. Monty hovers over him, his foot raised, one heavy boot about to land on the man's neck.

The man holds his hands up, a pleading beg for mercy, and Monty lowers his foot to the ground.

The man stands. 'It was just a bit of fun. She asked for it.' His voice is higher pitched than Harriet expects. With his squeaky beg for mercy, she sees him for the coward he is.

She steps forward next to Monty who flexes his biceps, blood pouring down his nose and he makes no attempt to stem its flow. He glares at the man as he bares his teeth, blood pooling in the gaps. Harriet steps closer still, ready to spit in the arsehole's face. The prick stands, his eyes bulge, then he scarpers into the night.

Harriet and Monty both exhale a shuddering breath.

'Are you okay?' Theo asks, finding a tissue in his pocket to hold to Monty's face.

'I'm fine,' Monty says, his voice stuffy as he pinches his nose.

Harriet approaches the woman with tiny steps, holding her arms up. She's still got her back pressed against the wall, her whole body trembling.

'Hey,' Harriet says gently. 'You're safe now. We're not going to hurt you.' The woman's hair is in disarray over her face, and she pushes it away.

Harriet's jaw drops when she realises it's Beatrice.

Chapter 8

'Beatrice! My God. Are you okay?' It's a stupid question. She's clearly not.

Harriet supports Beatrice, her arm around her, and helps to straighten her clothes. She brushes her hair back and feels a spongy spot in the back of her head. She inspects her clothes. Her jacket is torn at the back, the button ripped off her trousers. 'Where else did he hurt you?'

'I . . .' Beatrice's tremulous voice trails off, and she covers her face with her hands, curling forward and tucking her elbows in, shielding her body.

'Where were you going?' Theo asks. His voice is calm and concerned, though Harriet bristles. It's irrelevant where Beatrice was going. She shouldn't be attacked anywhere. 'It's late and dark,' he says.

'I . . .' Her eyes are still on the ground, her chin in. Even with the dimness of the streetlights, the reddening of her cheeks is noticeable. 'I just went for a walk. To get some air.'

'Alone?' Harriet asks.

'I had no one else to walk with. The place where I stayed on 6 was fine. I never had any trouble. I only smiled at that man, to be polite. I didn't mean anything by it.'

Smiling at a stranger, alone at night, it's like the Institute has taught these teens nothing. Beatrice is too pretty and too naive to navigate the lower levels alone.

'We need to report this,' Theo says as he checks Monty over. 'We can't let him get away with it. I think your nose is broken.'

'How do you know each other?' Monty asks Harriet, consonants soft and congested as he continues to try to stem the bleeding from his nose.

'This is Beatrice,' Harriet says. 'The MechaniTeen from school.'

Monty's eyebrows shoot up. He drops the tissue covering his nose for a moment, then as the blood starts to flow again, he tilts his head forwards.

'The police down here are useless, Harriet,' Theo says, then to Beatrice, 'Did you get a good look at him?'

She nods. 'I think so.'

Harriet's eyes are still on Monty. She can't imagine how painful his nose must be. Theo is rubbing his back, but Monty steps away. He likes to act the tough guy, invincible and protective. Harriet notices his biceps tighten, his red and streaming eyes narrowing as he looks in the direction the man went. 'Anything you noticed, Monty?'

'Yeah, that he got away with barely a scratch on him. I should have kicked him in the nuts. The pervert.'

Beatrice steps away from the wall and stands a little more upright. 'Thank you so much for saving me. I don't know what would have happened if you hadn't come along.'

Monty's shoulders drop a little, and his eyes soften. 'He had a scar down his right cheek. I got a pretty good look. I'd definitely recognise him.'

'I should have grabbed him, marched him down to the bars and had the community dole out some justice,' Theo says, his arms tense at his sides, though Harriet is pleased he didn't try. Theo isn't a fighter. On the coldest days, he walks with a limp and has never been able to put weight on. Monty is strong enough for the two of them.

Monty steps closer to Theo, as if worried he's going to go chasing after the creep now. 'Theo's right. The police are useless.'

'Well,' Harriet says, 'it's the best chance we have at getting any sort of punishment. Are you okay, Beatrice? If we go and report it?'

'I . . . I think so. I'm sorry to be so much trouble. They never covered what to do in these situations at the Institute.'

'It's okay and don't apologise. You have nothing to be sorry for.' Harriet wraps her coat around Beatrice. It's silly as she won't feel the cold, but with the back of her clothing ripped and Beatrice still shaking with shock, it seems like the right thing to do.

They walk for half an hour to a part of town with working streetlights and not a bar in sight. It would be a lot more practical if the police station were located where most of the trouble was. Theo describing them as useless sounds about right. Down here, people rely on community justice and bounty hunters more than the real police.

Inside, the high wattage lights glare off the white walls. Sitting behind a desk is a single officer, engaged in a game on his computer. They approach the desk and Harriet clears her throat.

Without looking up from his screen and still cheering himself on when he completes a stage, the officer says, 'Yes?'

'We're here to report a sexual assault.'

The officer's shoulders slouch, and he exhales a sigh. Looking up at Harriet, he wrinkles his brow and pulls his chin in. 'You?'

She should be more offended at his surprise, but she's too annoyed to care about that. 'No. This girl. Beatrice.'

As if his arm weighs a ton, the officer reaches for a clipboard and a sheet of paper, then tells them to fill it in.

There are no chairs to sit on, so Harriet rests the clipboard against the desk and takes the pen. 'What's your address, Beatrice? Where are you staying?'

'At the school.'

'Overnight?'

Beatrice's voice is small as she talks to the floor. 'I was told to stay at the school, and charge my battery there every two days. TRI makes sure the school has electricity.'

The police officer sits upright now and holds his hands up. 'Hold on a moment. She's a bot?'

'Yes,' Harriet says. 'A MechaniTeen.'

He folds his arms, one side of his mouth curling up. 'So why are you wasting my time? There's no crime here.'

'She told him no!' Harriet says, her voice shrieking with rage. 'He didn't even know she's a bot.'

'Yeah. That's exactly what he'll say.' He snorts a laugh. 'I don't reckon the vacuum cleaner nozzle is that willing, but when a lad wanks into that, it's not rape.'

Harriet slams her fists down on the desk, as Theo and Monty grab one of her arms each.

'Just leave it,' Theo says. 'It's not worth it. I told you the police are useless.'

Harriet's heart pounds in her ears. Her tense muscles won't relax even as Theo and Monty gently tug her away, her wide eyes remaining on the officer.

'What about you, Monty?' she asks. 'He broke your nose!'

The officer laughs some more and Harriet has a good mind to break his nose too. 'Lemme guess, he punched you after you interrupted his wank? And I'll bet you punched him a few times?'

Monty huffs, shakes his head, then walks away.

'Indecent exposure, then,' Harriet says. 'At least he shouldn't be doing that sort of thing in public.'

'Seriously?' the officer says, his face a picture of mockery. 'That's what you want me to investigate? Stop wasting my time and perhaps mind your own business in future.'

Harriet's nostrils flare, and her temples ache from her clenched jaw.

'Ms Chapel?' Beatrice's voice is soft in Harriet's ear. 'It's fine. Come on.'

They exit the police station, standing outside where the lights are dimmer. Harriet welcomes the cool night air. She turns her head side to side, searching the shadows for a man with a scar. If the police won't do anything, she'll serve up her own justice. Maybe they can get a sketch done and pay a bounty hunter.

'I'm sorry,' Beatrice says. 'I really don't want a fuss.'

'We can't have you staying at the school,' Harriet says. She glances at Theo and Monty and they give her a nod. 'You can stay at ours. I'll walk you to school in the morning.'

A hint of a smile forms on Beatrice's face, and they start walking home, Beatrice and Harriet a few paces behind Monty and Theo. The streets are still quiet here and over the constant percussion of falling rubbish from the higher levels, Harriet can make out bits of the whispers between Monty and Theo.

One sentence Monty says chills her bones. 'Fuck the justice system. I'll sort it myself.'

Harriet glances at Beatrice, whose stoic expression remains fixed.

A chill creeps over Harriet at his words. She presses her lips together and shakes her head, sifting out her doubts. Monty's just been injured. He's not thinking clearly. He's probably in shock. He won't do anything stupid.

Though she can't rid herself of all her fears. Hate is contagious and there's so much of it around at the moment. She shivers to think how readily it spreads and what it can make people do. It's like some pressure cooker, and all the animosity is ready to burst out.

Chapter 9

Today, Oliver and his class are learning to use huge diggers and trucks. It's all indoors in a space where the ceiling is vaulted so high even with the telehandler arm extended all the way, it's still not that close. Bright spotlights shine in the space that dazzle if he looks straight at them. As always, there are no windows. There are six different machines, and all the teen boys in his class get to use them.

Oliver's using the yellow truck first. The colour makes it more appealing somehow. It reminds him of flowers he used to see around the parks. He hasn't seen a flower since he got to the Institute, but he can still picture them.

He concentrates and tries really hard, though learning the controls isn't that difficult. He doesn't want to suck at this as badly as he sucks at all the lifting and carrying they often do, and he doesn't want to make the staff angry.

When he was a kid, he never doubted whether he was good enough. His mum always said he did well, his tests at TRI were easy. It was all the reading and thinking tasks he could do well. Now, he always feels out of his depth.

He has to use the prongs on the telehandler to pick up big sacks and it takes him a little while to learn to aim. He tilts his head one way, then the other to gauge the angle and after a couple of attempts, he gets it. It's certainly much easier than lifting the heavy bags by hand. If he does well, maybe he'll be chosen in the next group who get to leave on work experience. Although Thomas also needs to get chosen. He wouldn't want to be separated from him. Some of the other teens are mean to Thomas. They're mean to Oliver too, but he can handle it. Thomas is quieter and doesn't stand up for himself.

It's Thomas's turn, and he takes a little longer to master the controls, swinging the arm out by mistake at least once.

'It's all right,' Oliver says. 'You'll get it next time.'

Like Oliver, Thomas would be much happier in a quieter job with more reading and fewer big machines.

George, the tallest and strongest, laughs when Thomas messes it up. 'Useless. You should go join the girls with their lessons.'

Oliver tuts and keeps encouraging Thomas. 'Ignore George. He's an arsehole.' Why do they always end up in a group with George? There are over a hundred boys at the Institute and George is the worst.

Thomas tries to extend the telehandler and misses the sack again. He curses. His blush reaches even the tips of his ears and his head hangs low.

'Just quit already and let everyone else have a go on that one. You're crap, you're never going to get it. Sissy bots raised by sissy mums.' George sniggers and some of the other boys join in too.

Oliver sees red as rage fills his body, and his hands curl into fists. 'Don't say things like that.'

'Oh, what are you going to do? Read a book to me?' George rubs his eyes in a teasing way, like a baby crying.

'Shut up, George!' Oliver yells so loud, he startles himself. He stands straight, shoulders back, puffing his chest out, trying to look bigger, though he's still much smaller than George. He can posture like George, though. He can make a noise and seem bigger. Like a little wren. That's a tiny bird but sounds big because of its loud song.

Everyone is watching now. None of the diggers or trucks are moving. Oliver feels twenty pairs of eyes on him and his inner temperature dial turns up a few degrees.

'Or what, sissy boy?' George steps closer, his T-shirt twitching over his flexing muscles. He's such a show-off.

Thomas is out of the truck now and tugs on Oliver's arm. 'Just leave it, Oliver. The boy's a jerk.'

'What did you call me?' George says, narrowing the gap between them. From this distance, he looks so much taller, and Oliver tenses and straightens as much as he can. In George, he sees his mum's ex-husband, Anthony. He sees that innate cruelty and desire to belittle. Oliver will never put up with a bully. Not when they're insulting his friend and his mum.

'He called you a jerk.' Oliver takes another step towards George. No one picks on his best friend like that. Thomas is the kindest person he knows and Oliver won't stand for people picking on him just because they feel they can. George's tough guy attitude is pathetic, and Oliver takes another step forward. 'You hear that? You want to be mean to Thomas, well, you'll have to be mean to me, too.'

George's lips curl up into a snarl, just like Anthony's used to. He must have had a horrible family as a kid. A whole household of Anthonys. But Oliver refuses to allow that to be an excuse, refuses to pity him. Oliver lived with Anthony, and he didn't turn out to be a horrible bully.

George's torso grazes Oliver's, and he looks down his nose at Oliver. 'Fine,' he says. 'You're a pair of useless sissies.' George reaches back with both arms, then pushes Oliver and he stumbles backwards.

Oliver loses his footing on some stones and he falls, landing on his backside. His hands go down and he can feel where his skin has bunched up. His hands were already tired and now they're going to be even worse. The rest of the room disappears. He has tunnel vision with George's sneering face the only visible thing. Oliver jumps back to his feet and charges at him, his shoulders ploughing into George's chest.

They roll around on the gravelly floor, Oliver swiping at George when he can, but George is far stronger. Somehow, Oliver forces his way on top and lands another blow to George's face, right on his nose.

Then, hands clutch him by the armpits and pull him off. His legs continue to kick.

'One more punch!' Oliver shouts. 'I'll finish the prick.'

George is standing. There's no one restraining him. His face is damaged, blue-black bruising around his temple and nose, and that snarl morphs into a smug grin.

Oliver looks behind him. It's one of the staff who's restrained him. The big bald guy with the crooked nose and one ear that looks like it's been half bitten off. He's fumbling for Oliver's standby button but Oliver flinches and snaps round. 'No!' He spits. 'Don't do that.'

'Are you going to behave?'

Oliver shakes himself free, then stretches his neck. 'Yes. George was just—'

The staff holds up his hand. 'I don't want to hear it. Just don't damage each other, okay?'

Oliver's gaze drops to the floor, his bottom lip sticking out in a sulk, and he nods. It's one of his least favourite staff. It's the one who's always trying to tell them to work harder and be better, not caring at all that Oliver and Thomas are perfectly good at lots of things, just not always heaving heavy sacks around and using diggers. The staff think they're all the same because they're all MechaniTeens. They don't seem to understand they come from different families and are in different bodies.

'Right,' the staff says. 'We'll just let your battery run down a bit. Go and play some mind games on the tablet.' He hands a computer to Oliver.

The mind games wear their batteries out more than anything. Their battery lasts two days in the teen bodies, as opposed to one when he was a kid, but these games are addictive and so enthralling, it eats up their battery like nothing else.

'We'll keep you on partial charge for a day or two,' the staff says.

Oliver gasps. That's the worst kind of punishment. Being low on charge makes everything take so much effort and he feels so tired. 'But, George—'

'George has a broken face and needs to go and get repaired. That's punishment enough, don't you think?'

The staff never say what their names are, as if names would make them seem friendly. They're not. None of them are. Perhaps their lack of names is to stop them establishing any form of attachment, since they seem to think bots aren't worthy of friendship. Bots are so incredibly un-human to them. That's how Oliver feels sometimes. That he is lesser. He never felt like that in the real world, with his mum as a kid. He knew he was different, but never less important. Here, he's bottom of the food chain.

Oliver scowls, snatching the tablet, then sits on the floor in a corner. Perhaps he can only half engage with the game and conserve some battery. As soon as it starts, it's impossible. The bright lights and tinny music capture all of his attention and he's instantly engrossed.

Oliver loses track of time. It's only when another staff member takes the tablet off him, he stops playing, instantly feeling crestfallen without it. He looks around. All of his classmates have gone, and he didn't even notice them leave. He's alone in the room with the trucks. He walks back to the communal area, dragging his feet.

George is talking loudly, as he always does. He has a patch on his face to keep his repair in place while it heals. His friends are crowded around him and they all glare at Oliver as he walks in. Oliver keeps his head down and goes to stand in his usual charging area.

George says that when he was a kid, he dug some tunnels below ground. Oliver knows he's talking nonsense. Bots can't live below ground as they can't charge. Maybe he visited there, like Oliver did. He's sure George's just saying this to impress Mia and Evie and the other girls. He's always boasting in front of the girls.

Usually when George starts talking such crap, Oliver tightens his fists and grits his teeth, but he's too tired even for that.

Thomas is waiting for him in the adjacent charging port, offering Oliver a small smile.

'Hey,' Thomas says. 'Thanks for standing up for me. You shouldn't, though. It's not worth getting in trouble.'

'Well, that's gratitude for you.' He spits and regrets it, though doesn't apologise. He's too tired and cranky to watch his manners.

Thomas's cheeks redden. He's always blushing and sometimes it's hard for Oliver to know why. He can tell Thomas is sad now. Probably since Oliver has been mean. Oliver leans back against the wall, staring at nothing.

The communal area is as bleak as the room he just came from. When they first arrived, Oliver thought maybe they'd put some pictures on the wall, but they've never been allowed. There's a long mirror that covers one wall, which they all suspect is actually a window for the staff to watch them. Besides that, the only furniture is the charging ports. The brown walls are smooth and featureless, and the only other sound is a hum of a dehumidifier.

Evie stands to the other side of Oliver but doesn't say anything, though she has that same sympathetic face Thomas wore a moment ago. He knows she's probably had a horrible day too doing whatever it is the girls do, so he makes an effort not to snap at her. Mia is standing on the other side of the room, swooning at George. Mia's friendships always seem fickle. She likes to impress and be admired, like George does, and also likes to laugh even when it's not appropriate. Oliver is too drained to be annoyed.

One of the staff comes over, the same one who took the tablet from Oliver. He's usually less mean than the other one, doesn't push them around or yell at them. He's skinny with patchy black hair and a head with moles on it that look unhealthy.

The staff has a tablet and reads from it. 'The next wave of work experience teens leave tomorrow.'

Despite being so tired, Oliver stands a little straighter, and so does Thomas. Oliver hopes he doesn't fall asleep before all the names have been called. If they could have a break from the Institute for just a few days, that would make the next two years so much easier to bear. His whole body tingles, excitement whipping away the last of his battery rapidly, and he yawns.

The staff clears his throat, then reads the list of names. Oliver's tingling sensation dissipates as the list goes on, and his back rounds as his insides hollow. They're all girls' names. Including the final two on his list. 'Mia and Evie.'

Oliver looks at them. Mia smiles, flicks her pale blonde hair over her shoulder, and she looks genuinely happy. Evie doesn't, though. Her mouth is downturned, her eyes stare nowhere as if she's looking into a dark pit. She looks how Oliver's mum used to look when Anthony was due home.

When the staff member leaves, Oliver summons a bit of energy to have a quiet word with her.

'Are you okay? It's exciting to be going out into the real world.'

Evie shakes her head and folds her arms over her body. 'I shouldn't feel scared, but I do.'

'What sort of work will they have you do?'

'Probably what they've been training us for.' She shudders a little as she says this, and looks at the floor.

He nods, then resumes his position staring at the wall. He wishes he had the energy to talk to her for longer, to hold her hand. If he was sent out to do the same work, maybe he wouldn't be that thrilled, since he hates the work they've done so far. But at least he'd be away from this place, would have some fresh faces to see and talk to, would hopefully be somewhere where they can at least see outside. Really, the reason he would be happy is because he thinks, perhaps, he'd be able to see his mum.

Is that possible? Do the teens get to visit home? When the girls come back that's the first question he'll ask.

He glances at Thomas, who looks between him and Evie, a face full of fear for her. Oliver wants to reassure him, but his battery is down to almost nothing now and he has no energy even to open his mouth.

Josie comes round and puts them on standby. She's still wobbly and has to stop to catch her breath after each teen. Oliver wonders if the air is bad down here and that's making her breathless. He wouldn't know, but Josie doesn't seem comfortable. She does the rounds and one by one, the teens fall silent. Oliver takes a breath and welcomes his lack of energy then, as he can enjoy a few moments of peace.

Josie chats to Thomas for a while, and his face lights up when he sees her. Oliver can't hear, can barely see anything now with his battery so low, but he wonders if Thomas appreciates how lucky he is. He also wonders if Thomas would learn to stand up for himself a little better if his mum wasn't around nearly every evening.

Josie doesn't turn Oliver on standby, as per his request every night. She's not even meant to charge him fully tonight for his punishment, but she plugs him in just the same. Being so depleted, the surge of electricity is like a high. He has enough energy to speak to Evie more, to reassure her, but she's on standby so, instead, he watches her sleep. She has long eyelashes and pretty pink lips. He doesn't hold her hand while she's sleeping; that wouldn't be right. She looks peaceful, but they all look like that when they're sleeping, and he wonders if she has nightmares too.

With Evie leaving the Institute, that's another person he has to worry about and can't look after. He faces the wall ahead again, staring into the blackness, picturing all the dangers in the world and Evie and his mum coming to harm. He folds his arms, stamps his foot, useless and frustrated. He needs to be free of this place, even just for a little while, so he can know for certain the world isn't as dangerous as he's imagining.

Chapter 10

The only way for Harriet to know for certain Oliver is okay is if, by chance, she gets another letter. Still no one on *Shamed Parents* has received one, but then Harriet hasn't openly admitted she's had a letter either. They're all anonymous on that forum. She goes by her initials, HC. It's stupid. They should be proud parents. They are, inwardly, but their pride is a secret, hidden from view.

She checks the letter box every day now, often twice. She's the only one who does, since mail is so rare. Snail mail, so Monty calls it. The neighbours probably think Harriet is due a lawsuit when they catch her checking. She always smiles, says good morning and hopes her pleasantries will make her seem less like someone about to be evicted. She checks this morning and her shoulders hunch. Any hint of morning cheer morphs to disappointment as there are no more letters from Oliver.

'Is everything all right?' Beatrice asks when Harriet walks back through to the kitchen and sits next to her. Beatrice is still in the ripped clothes she was wearing the night before. There's some bruising around one of her arms and across her neck, the telltale blue-black smudge that occurs when a bot is damaged.

'Yes, thank you, Beatrice.' She tries to smile. 'How are you?'

'Fine. I have sixty per cent battery remaining.'

Harriet's forced smile tightens at Beatrice's response. There's no way Beatrice is fine. She just doesn't want to talk about it. Is this what happens with the teens? Shut away and in new bodies they become less able to communicate?

'If you need to talk about last night?'

'No. I'm fine.'

She can't force Beatrice to talk. She just hopes she knows she's here for her whenever she's ready. Harriet is hardly one to consider someone else a closed book. She should practise what she preaches.

When they got back last night, Beatrice sat at the kitchen table and it looks like she hasn't moved since. The books Harriet gave her to read are unopened. Harriet thought she might like to draw, since she was hoping to help in art class, but the pen and paper she left out for her are unused.

Theo is making tea and there's no sign of Monty yet. Harriet doesn't want to ask. Theo is quieter than normal, hasn't uttered a word, and sits staring into the mid-distance. There's clutter all over the table—there always is—and he brushes a little to the side to make space for his cup.

When Harriet lived in Anthony's top-level penthouse, she was bored so often the place was immaculate, and huge enough that it never seemed cluttered. Here, crammed into this little apartment, the detritus of life and work covers every surface and Harriet loves the disorder. It's home.

Harriet looks at Theo, her mouth twisting with worry. She gives him a strained gaze, willing him to look her way. A moment of eye contact is usually all they need to convey what they're trying to say. But he doesn't look at her and only stares into his cup. Harriet bites her lip as she worries. She didn't hear any yelling between them last night, but she knew they had an exchange they didn't invite her into. It's the hushed words behind closed doors she worries about: Monty's words of anger, threats of justice. Monty has a colourful past, of which Harriet only knows tidbits of information. His distrust of the police comes with personal experience. Like so many below ground, he didn't escape the darkness unscathed.

Harriet's phone rings and it makes her jump so much, she almost knocks over every item on the table in answering it. She stares at the screen for a moment. An anonymous number. Could it be news from the Institute?

'Hello?'

'Harriet Chapel?' The voice sounds like he's from the top levels, clear and enunciated.

'Yes, speaking.'

'It's Simon Keller from the BBC, wondering if you'd like to comment on the video on our news site?'

Harriet's brows knit. 'Video? Excuse me?'

'I'll send you a link now.'

Her phone pings again and on her screen is a video, unflattering and jerky, but in the low light, it's undeniably her. A torch beam highlights her face, upping the contrast between the dark shadows under her eyes and the pallor of her cheeks as she tells the Ban the Bot protestors to piss off outside the school gate.

Harriet's stomach drops. Shit. Some arsehole actually filmed that.

'We also have a witness statement from the school which says you favour bots over children.'

Harriet's palm goes to her forehead, and she stifles a groan. 'The school has an inclusivity policy, an obligation to make sure the MechaniKids are safe, same as every school in the country. There is no favouring the bots over children.'

'But outside the school gate, you obviously have little empathy with the Human Front group.'

She grits her teeth and takes a breath, considering her next words before they blurt out uncensored. 'The Human Front has been causing explosions. It's difficult to have empathy with that.'

'What about the Flesh Fraternity? Can we get a statement regarding your opinion on them?'

'They are two sides of the same coin,' she says, sounding more riled than she intends, then with a little more clarity, continues. 'The anti-bot brigade blocks the school exit every day, not letting us pass. They are an aggressive group that should not be interfering with teachers going about their job. And that's all I have to say.'

She hangs up.

'Was that—?' Theo asks.

'Yep. Yes, it was.' So much for staying anonymous. Her back hunches. Her elbows land on the table, and she puts her forehead in her hands. Any enthusiasm for her day at school completely vanishes.

Monty appears in the doorway, his face purple and bruised, his nose swollen. Harriet gasps.

'I know I look awful. You don't have to say it.'

'Oh, Monty—'

'Was that phone call what I think it is?' He interrupts before Harriet can offer any sympathy. 'I've just seen a video of you telling the Human Front to piss off.'

She winces at his language. In front of Beatrice, it seems crass. 'The news, yep.'

He tuts, and shakes his head. 'It's way too easy to get sucked into all the bot-hating crap,' Monty says. 'You know we love Oliver. So many others care too.'

Harriet knows this. Monty and Theo both adored Oliver when he was a kid. Monty made him a little dinosaur toy once.

She stands to give him a hug, her relief at his support taking some of her unease away. 'I know so many love the bots,' she says, not mentioning her fear of the many that don't. Beatrice doesn't need to hear her worries right now. She needs reassurance and comfort. Perhaps cleaning up will make her feel a little better. 'We should tidy your hair a bit, Beatrice. Would that be okay?'

Beatrice takes some strands of her hair in her hands, inspects it, some dust falling out as she does. 'Yes. It does need sorting.'

Harriet picks out bits of brick debris from the night before and combs out some dust. She should have done that as soon as they got home. It was unfair to leave Beatrice in that state, but she seemed shut off, still does. The soft lump on the back of her head is still there, though reduced. Beatrice accepts this level of grooming for a few moments, then huffs and shrugs herself free.

'You can rinse off in the shower, if you like,' Harriet says. 'A bit of water won't hurt.'

Beatrice nods, her smile appears strained.

'Have you any other clothes? We can fix these, but you might need to wear something else today.'

'My bag is at school. I guess I have to walk there wearing this.' Beatrice's gaze goes to the floor and a blush creeps up her neck.

'I might have something you can borrow.'

Beatrice's head turns Harriet's way, and she takes in her attire. 'No, it's fine.'

Theo snorts out a laugh at that, while Harriet stifles her own chuckle. Monty's hand covers his mouth, and he leaves the room rather than laugh in her face. If insulting her dress sense is what's needed to lighten the mood around the apartment, she'll take one for the team.

'You working today?' she asks Theo.

'Later. Gordon is going to call me when the scavenger haul comes in.'

'You're not going to be there when I have to walk past the anti-bot brigade this morning?' She makes sad eyes at him and he laughs.

'Sorry. Hopefully they're not too bad today.'

Harriet exhales, then walks to her room. Her legs are already sluggish and the day has hardly begun. She could do with some sunshine, a kick to her circadian rhythm, or at least an assurance her walk to work won't involve wading through people who hate and threaten her son.

Harriet spends a little longer tidying herself for work. God knows what shit she's going to walk into with that video of her online. She swallows her anger. She should have known better than to lose her temper outside the school. It's all a game. She should know that by now. She has to play every day, every walk and every lesson and every interaction. With cameras everywhere, she's always on stage. Lights, camera, action. Hair and makeup done, sucking in her gut. Play the part, remember her lines, give the audience what they expect. A polite woman, meek and demure. From the period dramas, nothing without a rich man to bolster her up.

She's let her movie accent slip, since living down on 5. Her accent now has a below ground roughness, a twang of shortened consonants, a tell that her opinions don't matter, but her actions do. If she'd said piss off with all the plummyness of the top levels, she'd probably attract more support.

As Harriet and Beatrice walk to school, Harriet attempts some small talk about the children, the busy streets, the classes they'll have at school today. Beatrice is nothing like the chatty classroom assistant she was yesterday, but a shell of that girl. She has every right to be withdrawn. What is there to say after the traumatic night Beatrice had?

Somehow, the walk is a mixture of cold yet humid, and a trickle of sweat traces its way down Harriet's spine. Walking up on 99, the wind took getting used to. It cut through the top levels most days. Her top would billow out, a pocket of fresh air cushioning her skin. She craves that some days. The freshness. The comfort of being cool, yet not freezing.

They should have left earlier, Harriet realises when they hit a wall of people. There's a union guy on the corner and the gathering around him is thick and animated, although they don't go by union anymore. Harriet had forgotten their new brand, but Flesh Fraternity is written on a sign in front of him. Harriet wants to grab Beatrice's hand and drag her away from this nonsense, but Beatrice isn't a kid and probably wouldn't like that. When she had Oliver, she'd stand in front to shield him. But Beatrice is only just a shade shorter than Harriet. Protecting a teen is a much harder task.

The crowd cheers and this speaker sounds like a fully fledged preacher. The speeches of the Flesh Fraternity are becoming even more ludicrous. He shouts his prophecies, standing up on a wall, a stage, as he entices his audience. Harriet has worked with people like him before, those who think their minor part is actually the lead. He gestures, throws his limbs about as he cites some rehearsed drivel that the crowd seem to be lapping up.

'The Testaments are ancient. We are writing another chapter. The Modern Testament will guide us through modern issues. While the churches wait for the son of God to come back to us, we must fear the Devil! You do not need to have faith in God to fear the Devil! Man who is born of woman is short-lived and full of turmoil. But that who is born machine will inflict the turmoil!'

Harriet groans and pushes harder to get through the crowd. There's a biting chill in the air, the constant shade from the upper levels ridding the walkways of any warmth. People are probably there for the cumulative body heat, Harriet assumes. Surely, no one believes this crap.

'He's obviously talking nonsense,' Harriet says to Beatrice.

'Free speech is important for humans,' Beatrice says, with little intonation Her expression remains stoic, unrattled and unriled by the speech.

She has a point. Harriet was always taught to stay quiet as a child, and then spent years with her ex-husband where she didn't dare speak her mind for fear of his violent rages. Even in her movie roles, she largely played a meek damsel being rescued by a brave man.

But why should she be so silenced?

No one is speaking up for the bots, and the realisation constricts her throat. She should say something now, push forward and commandeer that wall, shout in the face of him, but she has stage fright. She's not ready. It's been too long. Whatever words come to mind, whenever she thinks about speaking, she can feel

Anthony's arm pressing into her neck, can still smell him, still hear the rattle in his voice. The pain from the arm he broke is still raw after all these years. That's what her marriage did to her. It made her afraid forever.

They walk on and the crowd thins. The Flesh Fraternity nutter has had the effect of drawing the protestors away from the school, the thinnest of silver linings, but she'll take it. With some space around them, Harriet can take longer strides, hold her head up a bit more. With a little more air around her, she can imagine herself fighting properly for the bots. She's never had much courage, but now, surely, she should be able to muster some and fight for what she believes in. She can fight to make the world safer for her son. That makes her more afraid than speaking out, that Oliver will be in the real world again, and the real world will be dangerous. She's not some young pushover anymore, she's not . . .

Harriet gasps. Beatrice freezes. The two of them stand still just outside the school fence, staring at the scene in front of them.

'Go inside, Beatrice.'

Beatrice doesn't move. Her entire body shakes.

Harriet faces Beatrice now, her head blocking Beatrice's view and she puts her hand on her shoulders. 'Beatrice. Look at me. Don't look at that, look right at me.'

Beatrice's wide eyes meet Harriet's. There's so much fear in her face. All colour has drained from her cheeks leaving them ashen and her limbs have an uncontrollable tremor.

'Now, I want you to look at the ground. Nowhere else, okay? Go inside, change your clothes and charge. Don't speak to anyone or do anything else. Do you understand?'

Harriet thinks she sees a nod, though it's hard to discern from the rest of Beatrice's shaking. She'll have to assume it's a nod.

'Okay. Now, go, go.'

Harriet releases Beatrice's shoulders and watches her do exactly as instructed, her head low, walking with quick footsteps as she goes into the school. Harriet is left alone, and she has to look straight ahead and take in the sight again. A sob erupts from her, and she puts both hands over her mouth. Her stomach twists, then caves in and she bends double for a moment before squeezing her eyes shut and righting herself.

She can't go to pieces now. The children will be arriving soon. She can't let them see.

She removes her jacket and walks towards the fence, then begins to untie the ropes that pin the little MechaniKid boy to the fence. She starts with his torso; his dismembered arms can wait. His eyes are still open, though dull and unseeing. There's a hole in his chest where his battery should be. Harriet sniffs as she releases his head and his little body, then lies him on the ground. The back of his head is so dented, wires and bits of his inner workings hang out like entrails. She covers him with her jacket as she works on untying his limbs.

His name is—was—Joshua. She didn't know him well. He's young, and only just started at the school. She met his mother once. She seemed fair, the practical sort, not unkind. Harriet can't fathom how Joshua has ended up here, in this state, though she knows who is responsible. The sign pinned to the fence above leaves no ambiguity. *Flesh First* is scrawled on a sheet of cardboard. She takes that down and strides to the walkway fence and throws it over, then bundles up Joshua. When she lifts him, it's like carrying her Oliver again when he was little, the same weight in her arms. She chokes back a sob as she takes him inside.

She places him on the table in the workshop, then sits, exhausted and spent. Her body's done and the day hasn't even started. Evil does that. It sucks the life force from every pore. It's so much easier to be pleasant, accepting, simply nice. This level of malice requires an energy and lust for wickedness that Harriet can't imagine. How can someone be so enthusiastic to cause harm?

At least it wasn't Oliver, as much as it pains her to admit such a thought. No life deserves to be stripped from this world so early, in such a brutal way. Harriet has been afraid of something or other her entire life. Her parents, her brother's wellbeing, Anthony. But a mother's fear for her son's safety is something more terrifying that she's ever known. It's as if kindness is the more oppressive force and hate is about to break free. It's dawning on her more and more, that the world is not safe for her son, that the world needs fixing somehow.

Chapter 11

Dexter doesn't care. Of course he doesn't.

'Well, TRI will be annoyed their property is damaged,' is all he says. He'll get a receptionist to call Joshua's mother and inform her. 'It's up to her what she wants to do about it. Well done for taking it down.' *It.* Harriet's teeth grit at the word. 'Be terrible if the other children were to see that,' he says, his tone a few notches off genuine.

Still, it's maybe the nicest thing Dexter has ever said to her. Does she detect a trace of empathy?

'Make sure the workshop doesn't waste any electricity sticking it all back together for the sake of aesthetics,' he says as he leaves.

Definitely no empathy.

It. Harriet's always loathed that pronoun.

Beatrice is still charging. She has her eyes closed and head down, her face drawn and pale. What an introduction back to the real world away from the Institute! She's supposed to be on *work* experience, not *learning how shit the world is* experience. Harriet rubs the back of her neck as she sits, wondering if TRI will deem work experience too dangerous for the teens and cancel the program. Any slight chance of seeing Oliver again would completely disappear then.

She should have stood up to Dexter more, should have told him that the MechaniKids are more than just property and they should send letters home to the parents, to offer some sympathy to Joshua's mum. Yet when she even thinks about being confrontational, her chest constricts and beads of sweat collect across her hairline. Anthony's voice still sounds in her head, as if he's saying it right now.

You're useless, you slut, you whore.

She can see him and smell him as every dark moment catches up with her. That scar on her memory never healed. He's right. She's useless. She can't do anything. She's not strong or influential. Her lungs struggle for breath as his voice repeats over and over.

You bitch. That fucking toaster is not our son.

She sits in her classroom now, and she can feel the wall pressed into her back as Anthony's hand pushes on her neck.

She can't breathe, her vision greys, and nausea grips her stomach.

No. She escaped. She got away. She's free of him.

But as she wills her heart to steady and her lungs to inflate, she knows however much distance is between them, she'll never be free of him. He's left too many marks.

It takes a few minutes for her to regain control of her body. Her vision restores and her sweat dries. One more attack done.

She's had plenty over the years. It's not him; it's her memory of him.

The sound of running feet down the hallway snaps her attention. They're too light and rapid to be Dexter. She looks at the door and her face twists with surprise when Theo arrives.

'Thought you weren't in till later?'

His face is red, and he holds a hand against his chest as he catches his breath. 'I got here . . . as fast . . .' he speaks between panting breaths. Theo's childhood limp makes running a lot harder for him. It's barely noticeable most days, though he uses too much energy to conceal it. Having such a weakness on the lower levels makes him a target and he winces it away, hiding it usually.

'What is it?' Harriet stands, then walks over. His forehead shines with sweat, and damp patches soak through his shirt. She waits for him to be able to speak.

'Gordon, the other workshop tech, called me.'

'And?'

He manages a deeper breath and looks her straight in the eyes. 'It's Oliver. He's found him.'

Harriet's breath stalls in her lungs, her heart skipping several beats. 'What do you mean he's found him?'

Theo's face is still red, and he wipes his hairline with his sleeve. 'I told you we were waiting for parts. Well, they bring up kids, sometimes.'

Harriet's eyes widen. 'Oliver's MechaniKid body? So, not Oliver now?'

'Yeah.' He puffs his cheeks out and exhales. 'I don't know if you want to see him? I just heard and raced here and . . .' He bites his bottom lip before continuing. 'I didn't think actually it might be weird.'

Harriet leans against the wall in the same way Theo is. Finding Oliver to her means finding Oliver's soul, his personality module. His MechaniKid body is just what Theo was waiting for: parts. She swallows, presses her lips together and blinks as her eyes mist over. 'He's definitely not in there?'

Theo slouches more, his chin dipping. 'No. Sorry. His personality module is cut out. His battery, too. It's good his personality module is gone, as taking the battery out basically short circuits everything and would have fried it. They found a pile of MechaniKids. They're worth keeping in case any of the kids here need donor parts.' He takes a step closer to Harriet and puts his arm around her. He's still clammy from his run. 'Do you want to see him?'

She holds her stomach and exhales as her gut caves in. 'I . . . I don't know. It's not Oliver anymore.'

'Did you want us to keep him for parts? We could bury him or something instead.'

Bury. Like below ground. She shakes her head. Being below ground is what she definitely doesn't want for Oliver. Her brother, her baby Freddie, they all share the same grave, their tiny caskets thrown over the walkway fence. Out of sight, out of mind. But of course it doesn't work like that.

'No. No, he'd want to help. He'd want to be a donor. That's who he was. *Is*. He's so caring and giving. And yes.' She takes a breath, then stands straighter. 'I'd like to see him.'

With Beatrice on charge and still an hour before classes start, Harriet and Theo walk through to the workshop. Slow footsteps, which she tells herself is so Theo can manage but, really, her emotions are in turmoil. It's been three years since she saw her son's face. The only picture she has of him is the wanted poster her ex-husband gave the bounty hunters. In her mind, he's always smiling, always curious, always laughing. His dark blonde hair is never tidy and his eyes are so blue they could shine in the darkest night. Her chest aches, her heart crushed as it has been since her brother died, since her newborn baby Freddie died, and since Oliver left her life. Grief never goes away, not really. It's an ocean. When fresh, the waves are turbulent and massive, then they calm, mere ripples that catch her off guard occasionally. Then, years later, a rogue wave appears from nowhere, just as she's experiencing now. It's the permanence that's so hard to grasp. Her losses before Oliver were forever. But when Oliver was taken, she never lost hope, never stopped imagining she'd see him again sometime. Hopeful but not certain. There's pain in the ambiguity of his absence.

The workshop is furnished with wooden tables and all manner of tools. Several crates overflow with parts yet to be sorted. It smells like sawdust and solder. Theo walks to the middle table and Harriet pauses a moment and braces herself. On the table, there's the shape of a small body draped in a sheet.

Such a tiny thing. Her little boy. A duckling still imprinted on its mother. Even though he was always that size, she'd forgotten how small. She steps closer, her body tingling. She wants nothing more in the world than to pull that sheet back and have him sit upright and call her mum.

'Shall I leave you alone?' Theo asks.

'No. He loved you too.' It's a good excuse. Really, she thinks she'll go to pieces alone. Theo steps next to her, and the warmth coming from him is more supportive than he can know.

She's alongside the table now, the top pressing into her waist as she leans on it. She gazes over the whole sheet, the shape of his body, his head, shoulders, down to his perfect chubby feet. He looks intact, all his limbs present, and she touches his hand through the sheet, feeling his individual fingers.

Her hands, cold and trembling, reach for the edge of the sheet and after a steadying breath, she pulls it back.

When she exhales, it comes out as a whimper. She wipes her eyes on her hand as they blur with tears and she wants to see her little boy in perfect clarity. His face is still perfect, his eyes closed. He could be sleeping. He doesn't rot like the other boys she's lost. Greedy gulls would never peck at him. His hair is a mess—it always was—but there's some dust and debris knotted through the ends. She runs her hand over his cheeks, stained with blue-black bruising. Her thumb strokes his eyebrows, his eyelids, the dimples in his cheeks. She ruffles his hair. When she cups his head, she finds the gap in the back where his personality module has been cut out. Her eyes go further down to his battered and broken torso, the dent in his front where the battery was removed. He still wears his dinosaur T-shirt.

'Can you be sure they took the personality module out first so it didn't fry?' she asks Theo.

'No. But they would have. Or else why take the module out?'

Somewhere out there, her little boy lives on. More grown up, taller, living his life without her.

Her chest shudders, and her cry comes from somewhere deep, a choking wail. It's harder than she thought it would be to stay standing. It's been three years, but that's nothing in a lifetime of hurt. She misses his voice, his laugh, his facts about spiders and birds. The way he asked if she was okay.

She bends double and cries into his perfect hand, her tears pooling in his palm. She's cried so much over the years she's like a dripping tap. As Theo's hand rubs her back, there's the sound of him sniffing too.

What a waste, to throw away a body like this. The company that made him tossed him away onto the garbage pile with old clothes and furniture, as if that's all he ever was. He really meant nothing to them. As disposable as last week's fashion.

'I want to ask,' Theo says, 'say no if you want, but there's some programming still inside, separate to the personality modules. His original programming. I've been doing some investigating, and it would be good to see how they start.'

'It won't turn him back on?'

'No. Not at all, sadly. We think when they're first made, they have a little innate programming, so it's not personality, it's unchangeable. The nature of the nature-nurture debate. He won't wake up, but it might be good to see what TRI does for the original programming. There are rumours that some of the kids are wired differently like that.' Theo looks over at a table at the far end of the workshop.

Harriet hadn't noticed before, but she follows his gaze. There's another sheet, though only half-covering what's underneath. Her breath catches when she sees who it is. The ribbons in her hair are the first giveaway. Her head is still as smashed in as it was the night she was killed. Delilah.

Harriet approaches the workbench and looks at her sweet face, taking some of her hair in her hands. It's only her head and torso. Her limbs were ripped from her when she was murdered. 'You were talking about the original programming being different,' Harriet says to Theo. 'Amber, her mum, always suspected she was different. Her initial tests at TRI were done in private, without Amber present. She was always a bit too keen to please.'

'Right. Okay, if you're happy and Amber will be, then I'll check that out.'

Harriet bends to place a kiss on Delilah's forehead. She'll go visit Amber and tell her. Amber's been in prison since the attack, but she's due to be released soon. She'll want to know her daughter has been found.

Harriet remembers how worried Amber was about her daughter. Whenever Harriet visits her, she still insists she thought Delilah's original programming was something awful, that they'd made her to be submissive rather than empathetic like Oliver. Harriet remembers when Delilah first said no and started asking questions. Amber was so proud. Whatever programming TRI tried to enforce, a mother's love and influence is more powerful.

'I'll upload their base programming onto some software,' Theo says. 'We'll see how they start these kids. If we suspect they're being raised for different purposes, that may give us a clue. It won't disturb Oliver at all.'

Harriet walks back to Oliver, kisses his hand, then replaces the sheet covering him. 'He'd want to help. You know he would.'

Joshua's mum comes in to collect his body or what's left of it. His battery had been torn out, probably to sell on for the lithium, Theo thinks. His personality module, if not dented enough, would have been fried.

Theo found a nice enough box and sheet to wrap him in. Harriet notes her glint of tears, a red rim to her eyes, her words punctuated by swallows. She's sad and trying to hide it, worried how it'll look to be upset over the death of a robot. Harriet wants to hug her, to empathise and console. When she leaves through the doors, Harriet chases after her.

'Excuse me. I just want to say, I'm really sorry for your loss.'

She gives a small nod. 'You're Ms Chapel? The one who took him down?'

'Yes.'

She steps closer, another sniff, some blinks. She can't wipe her eye as she's carrying the box. 'Thank you for treating him with dignity,' she says in a whisper. 'The world needs more of you.'

She walks away, and Harriet is left dumbfounded but invigorated. She is not ashamed. Not now.

Harriet dodges Dexter for the rest of the day, and by some miracle there's no more animosity from parents, which is a shame, she thinks. Seeing Oliver, his battered little body has lit something inside her. Her anonymity isn't important now. The bots need protecting, and that cause needs a voice. It's time to step up. She's done being silent, a pacifist, some extra in the stage show that's this shitshow of a performance. She's not going to wait in the wings for her chance to shine. She's a star, a director, and she will take centre stage and stop this.

Chapter 12

The Institute isn't the same without Evie and the others. Oliver hates it even more. Just all boys together makes the atmosphere louder and more bolshy. Oliver worries about the girls, but he worries about everything. He spends his days with the boys, heaving bags of gravel around and learning how to mix cement. He's mastered the diggers and trucks now, but the staff haven't announced work experience placements for any of them yet.

He tries to prove himself, but the lack of mental stimulation tumbles his mind into worry territory often. Without windows, he never knows what time of day it is. His memories of living up high and seeing the sun are fading. The heat, the glare, seems like so long ago. The sky appeared different at night, filled with little lights. What were they called again? He can't remember. It doesn't seem important to know such things now, since he's resigning himself more and more to the certainty he'll never see the sky again.

Once charged, they work non-stop until their batteries are down to ten per cent. His cement yesterday dried too quickly, his bricks were uneven, but he didn't care. It seems a stupid thing to be concerned about. People, the animals, and insects.

Those are the things that concern him, but the staff here never listen when he says he wants another job. He hasn't mentioned that in a while now, and it seems pointless to keep on at them. But his mind boggles as to why life in the Institute should have to be so different. Why did they tell his mum to teach him empathy when here, they just teach him how to do manual labour?

Maybe it's just for a little while, he tells himself often. Maybe they're going to try out all sorts of jobs. But it's been years, and nothing's changed.

This morning, he waits in the communal room with the other boys. Some of them are hurling insults at each other, a lot of it in jest, but it's the kind of banter Oliver has never understood. He stands next to Thomas, the two of them alone in their corner.

Last night, Oliver wrote a letter to his mum again and gave it to Josie. He couldn't believe his luck when she said he could send one more. He wishes he could hear from his mum, to know what she's up to these days, if she's happy and healthy. He wrote quickly, not wanting to delay Josie, and when he gave it to her, he was sure he saw a glint of tears.

Josie gave him a hug, something she rarely does because she reserves all her affection for Thomas. But she hugged Oliver and gave him a kiss on his forehead. It was nice. It reminded him of his own mum. She didn't say goodnight like she usually does, though. She just left and zigzagged a bit as she walked away, like she couldn't balance properly. Anthony used to walk like that when he'd been drinking, but Josie didn't seem drunk. When they woke up, it was someone else who turned them back on.

'Mum was weird last night, didn't you think so?' Thomas asks.

Oliver's glad Thomas noticed. He didn't want to bring it up and upset him. He nods. 'Yeah. She seemed . . . I dunno . . . worried.'

'When we were chatting, I kept asking what's wrong but she wouldn't say. She just hugged me and told me she loved me, like she always does, but she seemed different. Like she didn't want to let go.'

'You don't think she's in trouble, that my letters have been spotted?'

'She still took it, didn't she?'

'Yes. She offered. I didn't even have to ask.'

'Well, it can't be that then.' Thomas rubs his temples. 'I'm worried, though. She kept coughing. Maybe she's sick. Humans get sick a lot, I think.'

'Probably a little illness then,' Oliver says, an attempt to reassure. 'She'll be fine. She'll be back when she's had some medicine and is better.'

The staff member walks in and the conversations hush. Oliver and Thomas press their backs into the wall as the staff clears his throat. It's the one with the bald head and wonky nose. He always has a half sneer on his face. Oliver doesn't want to anger him again. There are qualities he shares with Anthony. He starts off all nice, but then shouts and screams if the tiniest thing doesn't please him. Oliver watches him flex and clench his fingers as he stands before them, that sneer getting bigger.

'Today, you are going to watch some television,' he says.

There are a few cheers and air punches from the boys, including Oliver, as his tension dissolves. Watching TV sounds much better than all the manual work they've been doing.

They follow the staff through to the usual room where they make cement, only this time there are rows of seats. It's the first time Oliver has sat on a chair in a long time, besides in trucks. He hadn't realised how worn out his feet had become. When they go for checkups with an engineer, the engineer asks if they feel any snagging or rubbing, Oliver always says no, yet his body is tired, but if he says this, then the engineer checks his battery and says he's not tired. All he does is dot a little oil on his joints.

Tired is a thing he has learned to mimic, the engineer says, and reminds him he's a robot, as if Oliver didn't already know. Here in the Institute, they seem to delight in reminding them they're robots. Oliver doesn't get upset like he used to as a kid. He never feels the need to cry, but he gets cross and confused. Why did they send him out into the real world with a loving mother if they didn't want him to learn human emotions like tiredness?

Last check up, when Oliver said he felt tired and lonely sometimes, the engineer reminded Oliver he only needs this body for another two years so it's fine to wear it out. Oliver asked why they don't just put them in full-grown man bodies straight away. The engineer said it's because they're learning and have to know how to use a different sized body, and the full-grown ones would be too much of a jump. He also said parts are more expensive and the adult bodies have to last longer.

Oliver wondered if he was telling the whole truth. He likes the engineer more than the other staff. But the engineer didn't make eye contact then.

So, sitting and watching TV sounds like a good day. His knees bend exactly as they should to sit, which shows how much Oliver has retained that information from his kid body. Perhaps if they sit nicely, they'll get to use chairs more often.

The staff pulls a screen down, a big white thing that stays hanging even when he lets go. He then walks behind the chairs, to a machine thing and turns it on. Oliver and the other boys gasp in awe. It's nothing like the little telly Oliver watched at the refuge. The screen fills the whole wall and is so clear, it's like real life. It's better than any telly Oliver has seen before. He never got to watch the one at Anthony's and in the refuge it was a crackly little thing. This one is so real, it could be a window. There are speakers all around the room making Oliver feel like he is in the movie as the sounds come from everywhere. His mum used to be in the movies, and he wonders if this movie will be hers.

There are no opening credits, no song or title. The movie starts straight away and it's not the happy, colourful sort of movie Oliver has seen before. It's just awful. There's image after image of people suffering and screaming like they're in a landslide. Oliver saw one of those below ground years ago and his mum got stuck. This one, if possible, is even worse than that.

His hands go to his chest, the place where pain comes from. When he tries to cover his eyes, the staff shout at him not to. He's told to sit on his hands, to not even blink.

It goes on for hours. His battery was a hundred per cent when they started and he longs for it to deplete so he can go to sleep and not watch this anymore.

There are children, human children, hurt and suffering, bleeding, crying out for help. Their hands reach forwards, like they are trying to grab for help and Oliver needs to reach back, to pull them from the rubble and look after them. Their limbs ooze blood, some limbs fall off altogether. The screams come from all around, the surround sound speakers making it too real.

This is worse than the usual manual labour. Oliver wants to go back to hauling sacks and gravel, anything but this. Crushed bodies and pain and death. Blood and spilled organs. People crying, grieving, suffocating and suffering.

Oliver's suffocating with them. That's how it feels. Like his life is being drained from him as it is theirs.

He holds Thomas's hand. If the other boys saw, they'd probably be cruel, but he doesn't care about that right now. When he looks over at Thomas, his bottom lip quivers and his head jolts back with each new injury and horror.

Oliver peers around the rows of seats. Some of the boys hardly react. Some even laugh. How can they have been raised so badly, to laugh at human suffering!

And still it carries on. More wails, more injuries. At one point he and Thomas lock eyes, holding each other's gaze, like looking into each other's eyes can undo what they've seen. All the while, the staff shout and tell them to look, tell them they must keep watching.

Oliver wishes he could cry real tears, perhaps the staff would see how upset they are then.

His battery runs down but not quickly enough. He knows if he pays more attention, it'll run down faster, so he resolves to do that, to increase the torture now to make it shorter. He stares at each videoclip and image intently, searching every corner of the screen for the details, trying to commit it all to memory. His free hand holds his stomach, the other not wanting to let go of Thomas's. He feels he will be sick, if that's possible for a MechaniTeen, but his insides roll and lurch as he continues to watch.

Eventually, his battery reaches ten per cent.

The screen dims, and the sound goes away. When they are allowed to move, he hugs Thomas and the two of them shake in an embrace for a moment.

'Off to your charging ports,' the staff says, as abruptly as that.

Oliver's legs don't want to work properly. When he tries to walk it's as if the floor is wobbling.

'Why did we have to watch that?' Oliver asks the staff when they're walking to the communal area.

'Jobs requiring empathy are not in demand. Some of you are too soft. There were too many empath bots made. You need to be hardened up.'

'I can't imagine ever being hardened to that.'

'We'll see. Once you've had a hundred sessions watching that, I'm sure you'll cope much better. New things are always difficult.' He says this without a hint of emotion or sympathy.

A hundred sessions. Those words make Oliver's limbs feel heavy. He has an urge to go on standby and never wake up.

When they get back to their charging ports, Oliver leans over and whispers to Thomas, 'I can't handle another day like that. Not another day.'

Maybe that's the sort of work Evie's been doing, and that's why she hates it so much. He has a longing for Evie then, and he thinks he'd hold her hand even if other people could see. He misses her quiet ways, her sympathetic smile, and hopes wherever she is, she's happy. He's never hugged Evie before, but after today, he'd really like to.

Perhaps this is why Josie was upset. She knew what was coming and was sad for them. Oliver wonders this as someone else comes to put them on standby, someone who is not Josie. He looks at Thomas who fidgets, his eyebrows drawing in as someone other than his mother circles the room. Josie's never missed two visits in a row before. This new staff is cold and unfriendly, and Oliver doesn't dare ask to leave him switched on. He is put on standby, his final thoughts of missing Evie, worrying about Josie, and what nightmares await him in his sleep.

Chapter 13

It's Saturday morning and Harriet sits at the table with Theo and Beatrice. Usually on a Saturday, Monty prepares his 'legendary weekend brunch.' The quotes Monty adds himself, and mock scowls at anyone who calls it anything other than legendary. This morning, though, he's nowhere.

'Where's Monty?' Harriet asks Theo. 'He never leaves us to fend for ourselves for weekend breakfast.'

Theo gets some crockery out of the cupboard and gently shoos Beatrice away when she tries to help. 'He said he had to go out to meet some people.'

Harriet gets some juice from the fridge and pours out two glasses, hovering over a third. 'Is he coming back for breakfast?'

'Look,' Theo snaps. 'We can make our own damned breakfast without Monty for one day.'

Harriet steps back and raises her eyebrows, inspecting her friend. 'Okay, what's wrong?'

'Nothing,' he says, though his eyes flit to Beatrice.

'Beatrice,' Harriet says, 'do you mind getting my class notes from my bag?'

'Of course,' Beatrice says and gets up straight away.

'Right,' Harriet says in a loud whisper to Theo as soon as Beatrice is out of the room. 'Spill.'

Theo sniffs and gives a one shoulder shrug. 'He's up to something. He said as much, but he won't say what. Said he doesn't want me involved. The lack of justice, those people on the streets. He says he wants to help but won't say what he's doing. He's being so cagey. Those people he's meeting with, they're trouble. I'm worried about what he's going to do.'

'Here they are,' Beatrice says, a couple of folders in her hands.

Harriet takes them and casts her eyes over them for a second. 'Oh, there's one missing. Could you look again?'

Beatrice nods, then leaves the room. Harriet and Theo watch for the moment she's out of earshot.

'Maybe he's just going to the council or something?' she says.

Theo snorts a laugh at that.

'Well, he might,' Harriet continues. 'They did promise us reliable electricity down here, but the damned councils have done nothing to fix it. There's plenty of electricity across the grid. They just horde it up there for their damned Hel-Es and to waste.' Anthony used to fly everywhere by Hel-E. Even when she was used to her high-up lifestyle, that extravagance used to bother her.

'Yeah, I know that. Monty knows that. Those bloody Flesh Fraternity arseholes out there don't want to piss off the dicks at the top. Electricity is power, and up there they have it all. You've seen it on the walkways, heard how people are talking. All those lot out there, they're actually believing it.' Theo shakes his head.

'I don't know what he's planning. If he pisses off the people with all the power, what will they do?'

'Sorry, Ms Chapel. I can't find another,' Beatrice says as she returns empty-handed.

'Oh, silly me, it's here. And Beatrice, outside of school, please call me Harriet.'

They all sit back at the table and Harriet thumbs through her notes, but her eyes are on Theo. His face is twisted with worry, body tense, dark circles under his eyes. Monty's not that reckless. Surely, he won't do anything too stupid.

The lights flicker and cut for a second. That's the third time this morning. The lower levels get most of their electricity from the incinerators at the landfill, but it seems however much they burn and however much they limit their use, there's still not enough.

Harriet grits her teeth, shaking the image of Monty in trouble out of her mind. There's no sense in being rash. It won't change anything. When the lower levels complain, they are advised to be more efficient. Efficiency is a word that gets thrown around a lot. Funny, limiting waste and being efficient only applies to those on the lower levels. The crashing of rubbish down to ground level still adds the percussion to their days down here. The low level and below ground scavengers are efficient, eking out whatever can be salvaged from the ruins chucked down from the top, whereas those on the top levels wouldn't know moderation if it was explained in the stars.

Harriet idly flicks through the paperwork Beatrice brought over, then jolts upright. 'I didn't check the post this morning!'

She grabs the keys, then runs out of the apartment and down the stairs towards their post box. It's empty. She slumps, her neck bending forwards, and she turns to walk back up the stairs. Disappointment never gets old. Every time she raises her hopes and every time there's no letter, it's like a fresh blow. There's no getting used to that bruise.

She pauses when the front door opens, a whoosh of cold air coming in and she peeks over her shoulder. It's not a neighbour. Someone is approaching the letter box.

She jumps back down the stairs again. 'Excuse me, is that for 508?'

'Yes. Just forwarding it on,' he says. 'You Harriet Chapel?'

'Yes!' Her eyes light up when he hands her the envelope. She snatches it off him. On the envelope, it says her name. No postmark, delivered by hand.

'Literally just arrived when I was on my way out.'

'Did you see who delivered it?'

'Nice lady, frail-looking, reddish blonde hair—'

Harriet doesn't wait for any more descriptions. She shouts a thank you over her shoulder as she bolts out the door. Someone is hand-delivering Oliver's letters, which means someone has spoken to Oliver recently. *Reddish blonde hair*. It must be her. That's too much of a coincidence otherwise. She races to the adjacent building where she used to live and stares out onto the street.

There's no rush hour on a weekend and as she glances over the patchy crowd, she sees that coppery blonde hair walking away from her building, hair she once snuggled into and had such affection for.

She runs, barging past the odd pedestrian to catch her up and when she is just behind, puts her hand on her shoulder and pulls. The woman stops, then spins around and they both freeze.

Harriet stands, her mouth hanging open. She was sure it would be her but now she's here, standing so close, it's like all the oxygen has been sucked from the air. She's looking into the eyes of the woman she planned a future with. The woman who tricked Harriet into handing Oliver back to TRI.

'Josie.'

Chapter 14

She barely resembles the same Josie from three years ago. There are glimpses of her there, but she is far more frail, her complexion bloodless and shrunken, sucked in at her cheeks. Her untamed hair is a mess, so thin that through her roots Harriet can make out the outline of her skull.

When Harriet knew Josie, when they formed their friendship and more, those weeks were hard, emotionally and physically. Josie appears like she's only spiralled since then.

'Harriet, I—' She coughs, loses balance, and Harriet catches her.

Harriet puts her arm around Josie's torso, and almost recoils as she's so skeletal, her bones nudging into Harriet's waist. She leads her to a bench and Josie sits, plonking herself down as if her legs would snap if she stayed standing a moment longer. Even under her thick woollen coat, Josie looks withered.

Harriet tries not to stare. She recalls Josie from before, warm and determined, a love for her son so much like Harriet's. She was always petite, but she had a sturdiness about her, a spark. Now she's like dried bark, shrivelled and desiccated. The years tell a story Harriet both longs to hear and doesn't want to know.

Josie catches her breath, her rounded back heaving as if her lungs are a balloon slowly leaking. Her gaze doesn't leave the ground, her neck bowed like a spindly tree branch. A sapling never given the chance to grow.

'You've been delivering Oliver's letters?' Harriet asks.

That willowy neck lifts Josie's head a moment, then releases in a defeated nod. 'I put the boys to bed and turn them back on. They don't keep regular hours. Sometimes their bedtime is middle of the day, sometimes morning. It's a few hours' work and the only way I could still see Thomas.'

Harriet wrings her hands out on her lap, one soft one clenched, reflecting how she feels. A juxtaposition of angry and concerned, curious and jealous. This woman took so much from her, but she felt so much for her once, something that was leading to love. They were to have a future together. Now it's clear, even without her betrayal, that future would have been brief. Harriet doesn't need to ask what's wrong with her. She's seen the below-ground sickness enough times. It niggles for years: a niggling tiredness, a slight cough, an insatiable itch, headaches. Then it all coalesces, curdles and spits out some thin and watery existence of a life. Something unsustainable. It's a shitty way to go, especially for those who beat the odds and survived their early years down there. However much Josie wronged Harriet, she doesn't deserve that.

'He's a good boy, your Oliver,' Josie says, a rasping voice. 'He and Thomas are best friends.'

Harriet's hand goes to her chest, that ripping sensation tearing through her.

'I . . . I'm so sorry for what I did,' Josie says. 'I live with that guilt every day. But what was I to do? They offered me a chance to keep my Thomas. I never expected to feel the way I felt about you. He's my son. I had to take any chance they gave—'

'It's okay,' Harriet says, shocking herself at how much she means this. For so long, she hated Josie, was so angry at her betrayal. But she would have done the same thing. Even for one visit, she's sure she'd betray everyone she loves to hold her son one more time. She inspects Josie again. It's impossible to hate something so frail. Impossible to be angry and wish for revenge when shitty luck is dishing out punishment in spades. Josie has been looking out for Oliver, and for that, Harriet's gratitude bests any hate. 'It really is okay. You're a mother, I understand. I'm not angry.' And she's not, not anymore. Her anger has morphed to pity. How can she be angry with someone so weak? That's the sort of thing Anthony would do. She takes Josie's hands and turns to face her, her eyes boring into the top of Josie's head as her gaze remains low. 'I forgive you.'

Josie looks up, her pale face reddens, and tears glaze. 'You have no idea how much that means to me. You have to know I never took a penny of reward money from that man. I hoped I'd see you again, before . . . well . . . but I was too ashamed. Too afraid.'

Before. Harriet's breath catches at Josie's candour. She bites her bottom lip.

'You know the below-ground sickness when you see it. I'm not going to last much longer.'

Harriet's hold on Josie's hands gets tighter. Sinewy tendons underneath, her once pink skin now purplish. Her ragged breaths have the sweet odour of early decay. That's how it works with the sickness. Being born below ground, buried alive from birth, means the body decomposes before death. Souls are little more than compost.

'I said goodbye to my Thomas. I won't go back. I don't want him to see me get sicker.' She says this without a breath and, for a moment, she has all the resolve in her tone she used to have, that resolve that made Harriet feel safe. 'And thanks to your Oliver, I know he'll do just fine. Those boys really have each other's backs.'

'Oh, Josie,' Harriet pulls her in for a hug and the two of them sit and cry on one another for a few moments. Crying is exhausting. Harriet does it so much she's like a wrung-out dishcloth. Tears are healing though, like her bitterness leaks out with them. Josie's deeds before this moment don't matter. A mother saying forever goodbye to her son is something Harriet can't help but feel for. It's a pain so unique. A hollowness that can never be filled. 'Where are you staying?'

'That old storeroom—'

'No. Absolutely not.' Harriet pulls away and inspects Josie again. Living in a squat, alone, while sick. No, that's unthinkable. 'You can stay with me. I insist. You've kept me in touch with my son. It's the least I can do.'

Josie blinks, though the misty sheen doesn't clear. There are no tears. She's too dried out for that. That hazy film will rob her of her sight soon, as Harriet has seen so many times before. When it's even impossible to cry real tears are there any emotions left but emptiness?

Harriet supports Josie, then leads her back to her building, taking most of her slight weight as they alight the stairs. Beatrice spends her standby time in the third bedroom, surrounded by the clutter of Monty's work. The bedroom is the largest but the most jam-packed. Harriet justifies Beatrice can spend her standby time on a chair in the corner and free up the bed for Josie. They walk into the apartment and hobble through to the bedroom and she brushes some dust off the blankets, then lies Josie down on the bed. After, she brings her some tea and leaves her to sleep.

Theo recognises Josie straight away, and Harriet doesn't need to say more. They all know the below-ground sickness. The crap that leaks through the walls from the landfill above poisons them all in some way eventually. In Reading town's below ground, Harriet and Theo were lucky. The walls there aren't that porous. Other places aren't so lucky and the poisons drip down and infect everything. Harriet doesn't know where Josie is from or how long she lived below. It could be Reading or somewhere worse. There's no cure, as it's not one single disease. It's a group of conditions resulting from a whole spectrum of poisons that cause weakness and muscle wastage, always followed by organ failure. Harriet knows that pain relief is the best they can do for her. It's a waiting game now.

Harriet tiptoes back to the kitchen and sits at the table over a steaming pot of tea. Theo doesn't say anything for a while, just stares at the table.

'I'll look after her overnight while you're sleeping,' Beatrice says. 'I don't need to be on standby. If you let me know the best remedies, I'll help in any way I can.'

'That's so nice of you, Beatrice. Thank you. And Theo, sorry, but I couldn't leave her. She's been squatting in a storeroom.'

'You did the right thing,' Theo says.

'I need to tell Monty, though. He works in there.'

'During the day, Josie can rest in another room to stay out of his way. Monty will be fine. His sister died of the sickness. He nursed her right up until the end. We all know the deal with this thing. It won't be for long—' He clamps his mouth shut rather than finish. Saying she hasn't got long is stating the obvious.

A chill wraps itself around Harriet's bones. She sips her tea, but her icy insides don't thaw. Josie's illness likely awaits all of them at some point. No one born below ground lives to a ripe old age. Even escaping life below isn't an antidote for the sickness and in each new generation, the sickness kicks in younger. Theo's parents are in their sixties and probably the oldest below grounders ever. They're lucky, they always say. All below grounders attribute so much to luck.

Harriet remembers the letter, and for a fleeting moment she wonders if she dropped it, but finds it shoved in her pocket and takes it out.

'From Oliver?' Theo asks.

Harriet nods, gazes upon the spidery handwriting that says her name, then opens it.

Dear Mum.

I hope that you are okay and looking after yourself.

There have been a lot of changes here recently. Some of the teens have left to go on work experience. I hoped, really hoped it would be me and I would have a chance to see you. I think I hoped a little bit too much. But it turned out to be only girls. Even the second lot was just girls. They do different lessons to us so I suppose their work experience was more urgent.

So all the girls have gone now and it's only boys. I miss my friend Evie, but I suppose she'll be back soon.

Only two years left here now. How quickly that time has gone! It won't be long before I'll have my fully grown body and I can hopefully see you again. I wonder if you'll recognise me.

I really hope you are well. I keep worrying about you a lot. I guess that's what sons do. But I trust that you are keeping your promise and look forward to seeing you soon.

I love you, Mum.

Your son,

Oliver.

Harriet reads it in her head, blinks away fresh tears, then lays the letter on the table for the others to see. The letter reads much the same as the last one, but in between the lines, she senses a sadness there. There's none of the gossip or teenage joy he should be experiencing if he was away at a proper school. There's nothing about what he's learning. He's written to her again to tell her nothing new, which can only mean he really misses her.

Theo rubs her back. 'He's doing great. That's what I've read here. He misses you, of course, but he's getting on with things. And that means also the news about the explosion not destroying them is true, right? This is really good.'

Harriet nods, unable to form words, unable to explain her mother's instinct. She'd sound like some crazy, overbearing person if she did. In black and white it says he's doing okay. It's the grey that concerns her.

'You really care for this MechaniTeen?' Beatrice asks.

'Very much. He was my son.'

'I think some MechaniKid parents aren't as caring as you. He was a lucky boy.'

'This is actually what I want to talk to you about, Beatrice.' Harriet shuffles around to face her. Beatrice's forlorn face is without the enthusiasm she first had when Harriet met her. Her posture is defensive. Already she's built up a wall. Harriet needs to get past that. It's the only way to help her. She can't bear the thought of Beatrice returning to the Institute after work experience with such an awful view of the world. Harriet's been thinking a lot about how to protect the bots, and while she doesn't have much of a plan yet, she knows it all starts with speaking up. 'The way the police treated you after that assault, the way so many parents treat their MechaniKids, it's not fair. I think there should be some sort of rights for you and your fellow kids and teens.'

'Rights?' A crease lines Beatrice's brow and she looks up for a moment, as if searching her mind. 'I don't know what that means.'

'It's like rules,' Harriet says. 'To stop you from being mis-treated, to make sure you and all the bots are safe.'

'Why would they make these rules? People think we don't matter.'

'Oh, Beatrice.' Harriet wants to take her hands but resists. Beatrice's hands are on her lap and Harriet doesn't want to force her to be consoled. 'Is that what they told you at the Institute?'

'No, not really. But they liked to remind us we are not human, that our place is to protect and look after humans, whatever the cost to us. And there are those people speaking in the streets. They say we don't matter. That little boy . . .' Her voice trails off for a moment and she looks down again, then gives a one-armed shrug. 'I guess it just is how it is. My parents never told me I didn't matter. I think I believed I did, on some level. I need a bit of time to get used to the fact that I don't matter, that's all.'

'Don't you listen to those speakers,' Theo says. 'Most people know they're talking crap. They're just power-mad and hateful. It wasn't that long ago that Monty and me were the subject of hate. No one buys into the gay bashing anymore, so they've decided on a fresh vendetta. This isn't about you and bots. It's not about the Devil, or workers' rights. Some people just need something to hate, and bots are their latest target.'

'That's right,' Harriet says. 'If their message was about protecting people who matter, they'd be shouting their message at the top levels, using their voice to try to stop them poisoning the people below ground and using up all the electricity. You matter. Only a few people don't see that yet.'

Beatrice gives them a small smile, though with her downcast gaze she still seems unconvinced. Harriet's eyebrows draw in as she looks at Beatrice, a heaviness pressing on her chest. How can someone so young feel like they don't matter? Beatrice has so much to offer, yet TRI and this bitter world make her feel unworthy. Harriet needs to show her, somehow, that there are people who care.

Monty appears in the doorway then. His bruised face is grubby, like his clothes. He doesn't say anything.

'Hey,' Theo jumps up to give him a hug, then pulls away. 'Where have you been?'

'Just out. I'm going to have a shower.'

Monty walks to the bathroom and Harriet watches Theo, his lips pressed together, and he takes a huffing breath. Harriet can't worry about Monty right now. He's a grown-up. He can take care of himself.

It's the children she worries about. The children who have no voice. She takes the letter and goes to her room, holding it with the other letter, and the one photo she has of Oliver. She'll be damned if her son will ever feel like he doesn't matter.

Chapter 15

Harriet reads the letter at least a hundred times over the weekend. Josie drifts in and out of sleep, most of her time spent in some hazy half-awake state, a vacancy about her Harriet's company can't penetrate. In her moments of lucidity, Harriet sits at her bedside with her and reads her the letter, and thanks her for raising Thomas so well to be such a good friend to Oliver.

'He's just as gorgeous,' Josie says. 'Same blue eyes, same messy hair, that cheeky grin. You'd recognise him instantly.'

Harriet's eyes glaze as she pictures him. Sometimes her mental images of him are so vivid she's sure she could reach out and touch him. 'Oh, I have wondered if he looks similar. I'd hoped he would.'

'Their sizes are different. You know, as kids, they were all the same. Now some of the teens are bigger. Oliver and Thomas are obviously much bigger than they were as kids, but not as bulky as some of them.'

Josie tells Harriet stories of the bigger teens being mean and Oliver and Thomas looking out for each other. Harriet could burst with pride. Oliver has always been a protector. After witnessing the abuse her ex-husband rained upon her, he has come out of that not with a desire to hurt but a desire to protect. She couldn't be prouder.

'My job will be vacant. It doesn't pay much, and the hours are minimal, but they will often fit around your school hours. As I said, they're not regular length days for the teens, so sometimes the timings are weird, but if you can't make a shift you just have to let them know. I can't imagine they'll have filled it yet. My guess is the other staff will be taking over and hating it as it'll add time to their day.'

Harriet gulps some tea, too hot but she doesn't notice the burn as Josie's words turn over in her head. 'I could see Oliver.'

'Yes. Not for long, it is only minutes, but . . .' her voice drifts off and she grimaces. 'They'll know you now, from that video where you told that guy to piss off. And they'll know your name from when you adopted him.'

Harriet's shoulders slump. 'Shit. You're right. They'll never give me the job after I ran away with Oliver.'

'Come on, Movie Star,' Josie says with a smirk, a hint of her old self coming through. 'This just calls for a little role play. And this is the lower levels. There are creatives and costume designers everywhere.'

Harriet's eyebrows lift. 'Really?' She chews the inside of her cheek for a minute. A short walk from their place are shops that sell such things. She used them frequently years ago but has barely noticed them lately. 'I guess you're right. My acting days were years ago, though. And I'd still need ID.'

'That's the easiest thing to sort. I know someone below—'

'Below ground? Oh, God—'

'Relax. You can just email him. It's that easy. He'll send you an ID app.'

Harriet laughs. 'How is it that easy?' Her smile remains. She stares at the blank wall, but her mind's eye sees her son. In her arms she can imagine his hug. 'Okay . . . okay I can do this!'

'I'll give them a ring and tell them I know someone to take my place. They trust me, I've worked there for three years. This'll be fine.'

Josie sits up a little straighter, coughs for a while, then has a sip of tea. She's wearing a thick oversized jumper, has two duvets piled on top of her, yet still she shivers. Her bony hand takes out her phone, and she dials, pressing on the phone with cracked and yellowing fingers. Despite her frailty, she looks at Harriet then, and there's a twinkle in her eye as she speaks down the phone and explains to TRI.

As Harriet listens to Josie now, arranging for her to see her son, she remembers why she was so drawn to her. She had so much spirit Harriet always lacked. All fight, whereas Harriet was all flight. For a decade, Harriet put up with Anthony's beatings. When she left him, she didn't pine at all. She only knew Josie for a few weeks, was in her arms for mere days, yet she yearned for more. Length of time doesn't matter as much as depth of feelings. She knew Anthony for years, yet yearned for less. When there's love, any kind of love—Oliver, Freddie, Tipher, Josie—no amount of time is enough. Josie's betrayal cut her deeper than Anthony's violence ever did. Perhaps it's because she found such kin in Josie, because she saw a future for the two of them with their children. It's called falling in love for a reason. Every fall ends with a bump.

'The name of the applicant?' Josie says to the company on the phone, and her eyes widen and she looks at Harriet and thinks of an answer. 'Alyssa Wade.'

Josie utters a few more words, then hangs up.

Harriet hasn't taken a breath for the entire phone call. She dares one now and asks, 'They said it's okay?'

'Yep. They'll email me an application to give to you.'

That tightness Harriet always seems to have across her chest loosens, breathing deeper than she's been able to in ages. 'And who is Alyssa Wade?'

'That's your new role, Ms Movie Star,' she says with a wink. 'It'll be your new ID. She's someone I knew who will definitely not flag up on any system as a criminal.'

'How can you be sure?'

'She died years ago.'

Harriet's posture sags. 'Oh. Sorry.'

'It's fine. Her death was never registered. I always knew there was a reason why I never registered it.'

'You lost someone. That's awful.'

'Haven't we all,' Josie says and for a moment has a faraway gaze again. Harriet wonders if she's about to drift off, but she blinks and is back in the room. 'They said if your application checks out, you can start pretty much straight away.'

Harriet stands up and rolls her shoulders back. 'I guess I need to get started then and figure out a costume for Alyssa Wade.'

'You've got this.'

'Can I get you anything? More tea?'

Josie waves a weak arm at her, shaking her head. 'You go. I need some sleep. Good luck.'

Harriet walks into town, almost bumping into people as she looks at her phone, watching that awful video again and again. From that angle, the side of her face is visible, her messy brownish hair in loose and frizzy curls. A prosthetic nose and a wig should do it. Both should be easy to come by; it's the top-quality stuff she'll need, though. She can't rely on filters or camera trickery to add to the illusion. This has to be perfect.

She walks to the costume shops, finds a dark blonde wig, the exact colour of Oliver's MechaniKid hair. A wave, a few streaks of grey. She's not going for the blonde bombshell look. Alyssa Wade is someone poor enough to need a few hours of work.

The prosthetic is harder to get right, but after a few try-ons and some lessons in facial glue, she finds one that stretches from her nose across her cheeks, adding a hook to her nose and some rosacea on either side. A dark coloured woollen blouse and a shabby blazer to go on top is exactly the sort of thing Alyssa Wade would wear. As she walks home, she stoops a little more, like she still lives below. She chats to herself. Alyssa Wade's voice is more breathy, as if every step is a workout.

When she gets home, she tries it all on together just as Theo and Beatrice arrive back. Josie introduces her as Alyssa Wade, and they greet her as a new person.

Harriet and Josie laugh, then explain. Harriet peels away her fake nose, removes her wig, and Theo and Beatrice's jaws hang open as they step back in surprise.

'No way!' Theo says. 'I was totally fooled!'

'I don't really understand what just happened,' Beatrice says, 'but that was cool.'

Harriet looks at Josie, who gives her a thumbs up, and Harriet can't help but smile.

'I'm going to see him,' she says. 'After all this time, I'm going to see my Oliver.'

Chapter 16

After emailing her application, Harriet—no, Alyssa—is invited to TRI for an ID check. Extra security check, they call it, in light of the recent attempt to blow up their stock. They call the teens 'stock' in the email, as impersonal as ever.

Alyssa doesn't worry about such terms. Alyssa just wants a job.

Dressed in her hooked nose, her rosacea as red as ever, and after making a poor attempt to tame her dark blonde hair, Alyssa, armed with her ID, makes her way to the TRI offices the next day. She walks exactly as Alyssa would walk, a slight wheeze to her breaths, smiling Alyssa's smile.

Harriet remembers going to TRI with Oliver so many times. He flew through all the tests that show he has empathy, all confirming he was indistinguishable from a human.

Alyssa, though, has never been before. She is excited and nervous about meeting a prospective employer. Alyssa works in bars, like Harriet did, and is after a job that fits in a little bit better with her husband's hours.

She passes three Flesh Fraternity speakers on the streets, condemning the bots, people cheering along, referring to bots as beasts, calling for them to be withdrawn. Judgement day is coming, and the end is nigh! Alyssa pays them little regard. She has no issue with bots, is quite ambivalent towards them. She thinks these Flesh Fraternity weirdos take up too much space.

They never told her a time. Just pop your ID into reception, they said. Alyssa isn't in a hurry, so she walks all the way, just over an hour. Alyssa likes to walk. It's good exercise and it saves her going to the gym. It also saves her money on the AutoTaxi. Alyssa lives below ground. She hasn't the money to spare.

When Alyssa arrives at TRI, her heart races, her face heats, though under the layers of prosthetic she thinks at least that won't show too much. It's just nerves, she tells herself, and the closeness of the air from the walk. In the reception, when she stills, her body temperature heats and she takes off the blazer, fidgeting in the tatty woollen blouse as it itches and irritates. There's no dress code for the job, but she hopes she looks smart enough.

The receptionist takes her phone and scans her ID QR code. An image pings up on her screen and she compares it to Alyssa's face, then says that all seems in order and they'll be in touch. They're checking her criminal record, she says, and that's it. Alyssa thanks her and walks away with her stooped posture, a slight cough as she exits the building.

Harriet walks away, upright now, her breaths less laboured as Alyssa's ailments have left her. The woman at reception didn't recognise her as anyone except Alyssa Wade. There's a spring in her step, some excited glee as she knows the disguise worked. She'll get a phone call soon and then she can see her Oliver.

It occurs to her as she walks home Oliver might not recognise her. She imagines peeling away a little of the prosthetic, lifting the wig and telling her son: It's me, darling! It's Mum. And he would look at her, disbelieving for a moment, before wrapping his arms around her in a hug. She'd try to lift him but he's got so big, too heavy to lift now, yet he'd hug her tightly, say how happy he is to see her, then tell her he loves her.

So lost in her daydream, Harriet doesn't see the billboard in front of her and she walks right into it. She curses, rubs her forehead, ignoring the few sniggers from other pedestrians, the heckle of 'Look where you're going, love!'

She steps away, not daydreaming anymore. As she goes to move on, she looks up at the billboard and does a double-take. These billboards are next to every park, on every level, constantly ramming their message into people's brains. Its bright display is where anyone can buy some advertising space. And anyone is about right. She shakes her head a little, blinks a few times as if to clear the billboard because surely she can't be reading right.

She steps a few paces back to take in the entire view.

The Flesh Fraternity's word is divine! Fear the Devil! Ban the bots! The Flesh Fraternity will do even more than pray for a better world!

Harriet rolls her eyes while she walks away. As if the world isn't crazy enough already.

Chapter 17

Fresh from her performance as Alyssa, Harriet is buzzing. She's alive again, her inner performer reinvigorated. She didn't get stage fright at TRI. She was the lead role, played her part and so now, she knows, it's time for action. It's time for her to be in the spotlight again.

Sunday night, she opens up *Get Level* social media and trawls news sites. As she reads, her eyes bulge, and her stomach drops. The attack Beatrice suffered is not unique. Far from it. Across all levels, abusers have been pulled off young MechaniTeen girls who were simply trying to go about their work experience.

And it's not just teens.

Paedophilia isn't branded as such when assaults are on MechaniKids. It's just a machine, innocent fun, better than doing it to a real kid, the reports say. Joshua's end was better than what some of these kids are going through. There are new sites dedicated to it, and according to them it's harmless fun.

Harriet tastes bile, her chest hollows. It seems to some that these bots, who are almost indistinguishable from humans, are an outlet for urges.

'Can you believe this?' she says to Monty.

Monty's stirring a pot on the stove, and he tuts and shakes his head. The swelling around his nose has eased, the bruising not so much. He polishes a spoon on a tea towel before glancing at his reflection, then scoops up some sauce and holds it out for her to taste. Despite the knot of anger in her stomach, she obliges, and it's delicious.

'Search for anything on social media and you'll find someone to back that up,' Monty says. 'Just look up the stuff that doesn't piss you off instead.'

'That's no way to gauge public opinion.'

'It's how to stay sane, though.'

She narrows her eyes and keeps scrolling. Monty's hardly one to talk about staying sane. He still hasn't mentioned what he was up to, and Theo's given up asking. At least he seems back to his old self now.

Just looking at the kind of posts that please her is not the way to fight for bot rights. Social media is a pit that can be impossible to crawl out of. Each post is laced with hate. She doesn't even notice when Theo comes in the kitchen and Monty serves up.

There's a hand on her shoulder. She tears herself away from her phone and looks at Monty.

'You're spiralling, babe.'

Her face heats from shame, and Monty runs the back of his hand over her cheek, then pulls her hair up, piling it on her head like she was getting ready for the studio again, and he smiles. 'Harriet Chapel, period drama beauty. She's still in there.'

Harriet rolls her eyes, but Monty doesn't let go, his gaze intensifying.

'If you want to win this fight, shout louder. Don't let those arseholes drown you out. Come on! You're Harriet fucking Chapel! Be Harriet Chapel the movie star. People will listen to you. The bots need protecting, need rights, and you can make it happen.'

She's back in the West End. She can hear the brass band, feel the heat of the stage lights, so bright the audience is blackened out. It's the most lonely feeling, stage fright, the jitters, afraid of people watching, yet there's no one you can see in the glare. But Harriet can't afford to be afraid any longer.

Monty smooths her hair back down. 'It's now or never. You've hardly got youth on your side.'

She gives him a playful punch on his arm.

'He's right,' Theo says. 'Not about the youth thing,' he winks, 'but about people listening to you. They will. I'm sure.'

Supporters on social media don't necessarily mean supporters in real life. Keyboards are a shield and a weapon. But they're right. Some will listen. She smiles at her friends. 'Thanks, guys.'

Her dinner's going cold so she eats, picturing herself on some stage, shouting her views, convincing crowds of people to love the bots. If she imagines it enough, perhaps it'll make her brave, like muscle memory.

Harriet knows she's not going to win any debate by proclaiming the bots are human, that they deserve to be loved. But she can play a card, protecting the bots by shaming the perverted behaviours and how that may affect humans.

After dinner, she watches Beatrice tend to Josie, make her tea, and fetch her pills. She smiles at her, telling her stories about the children at school to make her laugh. 'Laughter is the best medicine,' Beatrice says, as that's what they taught her in the Institute. She learned how to make children happy and she devotes herself entirely to this. She stays with Josie all night. Whenever she isn't at school, Beatrice is ready to help in any way she can. She dusts off a new duvet Theo found, fluffs her pillows, doing whatever she can to keep Josie comfortable, and Monty and Theo spend the afternoon redirecting some heating into her room. When Josie has the strength, she tells stories of Oliver and Thomas at the Institute, about them standing up to bullies, the girls they talk to.

An onlooker would not be able to discern who is human or not out of those in attendance and being spoken about. Such acts of benevolence and kindness are shared among both human and bots. Surely, if to be human is to be humane, then it's a state of being not determined at creation.

There's a tug, a pull in Harriet that guides her hands over her laptop, typing for her, instinct making her next move, fingers gliding over the keys as naturally as breathing.

Complacency was defensible before when she hid under a blanket of excuses: trauma, cowardice, powerlessness. But complacency is the route to corruption.

No more. It's time she did something.

Mechani-Rights, she titles her page, inviting scores of people to join. Not merely using her initials this time. That video of her telling the protestors to piss off is everywhere anyway. She's no need to hide. Own it.

There will be ridicule. There will be people like Anthony who think she is defending a vacuum cleaner, a microwave, a laptop with eyelashes. But she knows, in her bones, these bots are not simply machines. They can feel and love and deserve to be happy.

Harriet doesn't pay much attention to fashion these days, but according to *Get Level* there's a latest craze among youngsters to wear clothes that expose their midriff and a little below, not for the look but as a safety choice, to show they don't have a charging socket. To stop them being assaulted. Evil humans are the ones assaulting, yet they proclaim their right to this planet over the bots. Harriet finds pictures and articles and posts them on her page.

Before she goes to bed that evening, she has almost a thousand followers all supporting her cause. Every charity and cause needs a celebrity face supporting it. Harriet was barely famous and only for about five minutes, but some will remember her. Some will recognise her. That might help add some weight. She adds an old headshot to the page from her much younger days, complete with her once dazzling smile.

She rolls her hair in curlers and lays out some make-up for the morning. If she's going to shoehorn herself back into the public eye, it'll help to look the part. Being attractive gains more support than someone who's let themselves go. As much as it pains her to admit it, for women, that's the truth.

The rollers dig into her scalp as she tries to sleep. She tosses and turns for ages before she nods off. On her mind is her cause, her determination. The rollers don't matter. A bit of discomfort is the least she can do.

It's showtime.

Chapter 18

Josie hasn't been back to the Institute. Thomas and Oliver expect to see her, but she doesn't come. They stand at their charging points and don't say much, but Oliver can tell from Thomas's face he's worried and misses his mum. When they wake in the morning, Oliver watches as Thomas is switched back on and his eyes open wide immediately, then close slowly when he sees someone besides his mum. Another staff member, grumpy and not as welcoming, doesn't even tell him to enjoy his day. Josie is always so gentle, so caring. Oliver misses his own mum but with Josie around sometimes, he felt still connected to his old life somehow.

Thomas worries but he never complains. Oliver wonders if he doesn't want to say he's worried about Josie because Oliver can never see his own mum, but Oliver doesn't begrudge him missing Josie. At least Oliver's mum said goodbye, and he knew he wasn't going to see her. The lack of knowing is worse. Josie has missed the odd standby before, but never more than one in a row.

One of the other staff puts them on standby again tonight. He does this roughly, manhandling them to get to their standby button, and there's no chance Oliver can ask him to leave him on.

Oliver's nightmares come back when he's on standby, only now they're worse, as if making up for lost time. He dreams of something bad happening to Josie, and Evie, and his mum. He dreams of the world outside turning to ruin like in the film they have to keep watching. When he wakes, the visions of the night stay with him, leaving him with a sense of his own body being crushed. He can still hear screams in his mind. His body is heavy with helplessness.

This morning, Oliver asks Thomas, 'Where do you think she is?'

'I don't know. She seemed so strange last time we saw her. She was really upset.'

Oliver misses Josie but also wants to ask her questions. To see if she knows about why they're trying to make them less empathetic, how many more times they're going to have to watch that horrible video.

It's still strange without the girls. Evie was always so sweet and nice. He wonders when they'll be back. Perhaps, he reconciles, that's where Josie is. She's looking after Evie and the other girls. That's a pleasant thought, that they're together.

'How clueless are you!' George shouts in his loud and unkind voice. 'You really don't know what the girls get up to?'

Oliver looks at the ground, lifts his shoulders, and shakes his head.

'Looking after men, of course,' George says with a chuckle. 'Human men. Come on. Don't pretend like you've never wondered what it would be like.'

Oliver has some idea what human couples get up to. His mother taught him some basics, and he read a lot of books about mammals. But what does that have to do with Evie and Mia? They're not human. And Evie doesn't want to do that. They can't make her. Can they?

His mind goes to Anthony. Bad men try to make women do whatever they want.

They don't watch the video today, though he's sure they'll have to tomorrow as the staff say as much. Oliver can't face it again. Nor can Thomas. Some of the other boys may find it easy to watch such horrible things but Oliver already imagines his nightmares. He has too much to worry about. Every night, his thoughts go to dark places and he envisions all kinds of horrors happening in the real world. Josie in trouble, the world falling down, Evie forced to do unmentionable things. He can't. He just can't wait in here while people he cares about might be in trouble. And he can't watch that video again.

Before they are put on standby later, Oliver leans over to Thomas and whispers quietly enough for no one else to hear, 'Let's get out of here. Let's go find our mums.'

Chapter 19

Harriet got out of the habit of checking her phone as soon as she wakes up years ago, when she first moved in with Anthony and walked away from her old life. She had no friends or work to think about. Others' opinion of her no longer mattered.

But today, as soon as she stretches the tiredness out of her arms, she reaches for that little device and logs on to *Get Level*.

She should have braced herself. She assumed she'd be waking up to crickets, but instead, her feed is full. She scrolls, her eyes taking on each comment more than once at first, then reading quicker and skimming, hungry to get to the next one, elation and despair smacking her again and again.

> **@2bridges** *It's good the humans take it out on the bots rather than the children.*

> **@Biscuits4eva** *Since the teens have been out, sexual assaults have much reduced.*

SmellyAlleySteve *They're abusing the teens instead.*

@JunctionJude *Good. Rather that than the children.*

@Afterdark *Kids are being beaten.*

@Milestoner *Rather that than the children.*

@SmellyAlleySteve *What type of person will beat or assault something that looks and acts just like a human.*

@JunctionJude *It's not a crime. Embrace the positives.*

Every comment either makes her chest swell or her gut cave in. Responses ping-pong from support to ridicule, hate to love, but as she reads on and on and on, the magnitude of what she's started kicks in.

News sites as well as social media are reporting the story. Again, with arguments both for and against. Some say, like the Flesh Fraternity, that bots shouldn't exist at all, and more voices like Harriet's who say they need protecting. Then there are the ones who claim they're the middle ground, who say bots need to exist and be subjected to whatever humans wish. But for every ounce of hate Harriet finds, every headline and viral post, lurking in the background is a counterbalance of love and just plain common sense.

Memes of her old movies, both positive and negative, are on every corner of the social. She's in her twenties in period dramas, an action movie, that terrible advert for furniture she did once. Pictures she hasn't seen in years where she was polished, pretty, dewy-skinned and sparkly-eyed. Thinner, by a long way, a suggestive smile that gave her the girl-next-door vibe the casting directors so often mentioned.

After years of running away from fame, Harriet is now right back in it.

She takes a lot longer than usual to get ready for work. Teaching ten-year-olds doesn't normally require any kind of glamour, but now she has to look the part of actor and campaign leader. As she rummages in her wardrobe—a brief task since she doesn't own much—she imagines it as a role, and that takes the nerves away. Her insides buzz like they're laughing at her, mocking her unease. Anthony's breath is hot on her neck, and she swats at that feeling like a bug.

This isn't a role. She's to play the part of Harriet Chapel. Her authentic self. Why does pretending otherwise make that buzzing calm down, as if pretending she's playing someone else is subterfuge for her anxieties?

She steels herself. In the mirror, her eyes bore into her own. *I am Harriet Chapel. I was born for this.*

She's a fair bit heavier than she was when she was in the movies. Her thickened waist can't be concealed, and there's only so much makeup can do to hide the pudge around her face and the dark circles. When she was with Anthony, she wanted to pile weight on so he'd find her less attractive, but never managed to gain much. Since reaching the other side of forty, it's like she absorbs calories through osmosis. Or perhaps it's three years of Monty's cooking.

After some outfit changes, she holds her head up high and decides to embrace it. Her leftover tummy is her memory of her baby Freddie. She's cherished it since and she should not have to hide it away. She looks in the mirror and doesn't see the radiant-faced beauty of her youth. She sees maturity. A life lived. Fuck doe-eyed innocence and pin-up good looks. She is a real woman tackling real issues.

She does, though, decide to skip breakfast to avoid any bloat, ignoring the hypocrisy of her rumbling stomach.

'You look nice,' Beatrice says as she waits by the front door.

'Thank you, Beatrice. So do you.'

'Someone special coming into the school today?' Theo asks.

She rolls her eyes at him, and after a dash into Josie's room to say goodbye for the day, the three of them leave for work.

***

When the children arrive at school, they don't notice Harriet has put in any effort. The parents do, though. Her first class of the day is her favourite ten-year-olds, though she says that all the classes are her favourites.

'I knew I recognised you from somewhere,' Pavi's father says as he drops him off. 'My wife made me watch those period romance dramas years ago. That scene with you and the stable boy—'

'Thank you,' Harriet interrupts before he has time to remind her of her intimate scenes. She never showed any significant flesh, thank God, and she's not ashamed of her old jobs, but a class full of children within earshot is not the place to discuss it. 'I'm glad you and your wife enjoyed my movies. Those were exciting times.'

'Yeah, but just because you were in the movies, doesn't mean robots deserve rights. They're useful, but I'm not going to treat one the same as I do my own child. That's weird.'

Harriet expected this. She sucks at improv, so she's practised her lines. 'The campaign doesn't stress that. It only says they shouldn't be abused.'

It knots her stomach to admit that. If it were up to Harriet, they would be treated as real children, but she's a realist, and ruling out violence and rape is a small and significant step.

'Pssst,' he hisses. 'Whatever.'

Harriet smiles away his dismissal, that dazzling smile that won her awards years ago. She can smile away any verbal altercation, make any abuser seem small with that smile. She takes a breath before turning her attention back towards her class. The children are in their usual chaotic mood, running rampant through the classroom until she manages to calm them.

'Now children, today we are going to practise—'

'Ouch!' One child sitting at the back of the class says.

Harriet walks over to find Caleb pulling Lexi's hair.

'Don't say ow, stupid,' Caleb says. 'Bots can't feel pain.' He then kicks Finlay.

'Will you stop that right now!' Harriet shouts at Caleb. 'You should never pull someone's hair. And stop kicking Finlay!'

Caleb lets go and stops kicking, folding his arms as he sulks. 'She wanted to borrow my pen.'

'Well, either let her or tell her no. You don't have to pull her hair.'

'You let Lily borrow it,' Lexi says.

'Lily can, but you can't,' he says, scrunching his nose, then faces Harriet again. 'I'm not lending my pen to one of her.' He kicks and hits Finlay again, then grabs his arm and yanks it, like he's trying to pull it off until Harriet shouts at him again to stop.

'What? You said I can't pull the machine's hair, so I'll kick him instead.'

Finlay isn't even a MechaniKid. Harriet pulls him away. She's going to have to write a report on this.

'It's fine to kick. Mum says it is. And I think Finlay is a MechaniKid. I'll prove it.' He reaches for Finlay's arm again.

Poor Finlay is such a quiet boy, and he cries to himself without fighting back.

Harriet pulls Finlay away and creates some distance between Caleb and the other children as his words repeat in Harriet's mind. Her jaw drops, unable to hide her shock. 'You have a MechaniKid at home.'

'Yeah. And mummy kicks it all the time. It doesn't matter.' He steps towards Lexi and kicks her again, before Harriet has had a chance to shield her. 'They only pretend to feel pain. Like the toaster can't burn itself. I think Finlay is definitely a bot, too.'

'No!' Harriet stands in between them. 'Lexi and the MechaniKids are here to learn about human behaviour. What do you think you are teaching her? When she is fully grown and has a job, how do you think she will behave if this is what she's learned?'

Caleb scoffs and stamps his feet as Harriet tells him to go and sit alone in the corner.

She exhales, stretches her neck out and tries to shake the tension from her arms. A little animosity is normal day-to-day, but it's not even ten on a Monday morning and she feels as though she's had a week's worth already.

Mummy kicks it all the time swirls around and around in Harriet's head, and she steadies herself grabbing onto one of the chairs. When she snaps back to the here and now, her gaze goes momentarily to Beatrice, who's standing in the corner, her hands clasped in front of her, her eyes to the floor. Beatrice, who doesn't think she matters, yet helps others so much. Attitudes are so broken, slowly becoming embittered by piecemeal actions and deprivations.

She considers calling Caleb's parents and explaining how their behaviour is affecting their son's, but thinks better of it.

Speaking to one parent is inefficient. There are more effective ways to use her time.

And a much more effective way presents itself that afternoon. She receives an urgent invitation that will address the issue to the entire country, and it has her bolting out the door as soon as school finishes, shouting to Theo to take Beatrice home.

She's prepared for the spotlight and now is her chance.

Chapter 20

Studio 99 is, as the name states, on level 99. It's been years since Harriet breathed the air up here, since she felt the sun on her skin, since she saw the cyan blue of the sky. Bubbly clouds like headless sheep drift above, Hel-Es whirr from building top to building top. The sun, intense and orange, heats her body and glints off the top floor windows. She squints. She didn't think to bring sunglasses. She'd forgotten all about the need for them. Up here, there's no view of the underside of the level above, no constant sound of rubbish raining down from the other side of the walkway fences, no chill from the constant shade.

This is where she first loved Oliver.

The news studio is a little further east than Anthony's penthouse, if indeed he still lives there. She pulls her sleeves back and lets her skin bake in the sunshine. She rarely showed any skin at all when she lived high up, always concerned about revealing her bruises. Now, such a sensation is like a spa and she bathes in it. It's the most comfortable she's been in years.

There's at least no chance of her bumping into Anthony. He never walks anywhere, always preferring to take the lift up to the roof and taking a Hel-E for his commute. Walking is an activity for bottom dwellers, or so he liked to remind her when she'd take Oliver to a park or walk to a shop. Those born and raised so high up take their view of the sky for granted. Harriet savoured it every day.

So Harriet walks the few miles from the lift to the studio on 99. She breathes in the silence. Life up here wasn't worth staying with Anthony for. She knows this. But wealth is seductive and binding. With every step, she feels those shackles digging into her ankles, pulling her back to this life.

She promised Oliver she'd never go back to Anthony. And a mother keeps her promises. He'll never ruin her life again.

She fights niggling nostalgia as she walks past parks where she once took Oliver, duck ponds he used to swoon over, flower boxes planted with real flowers that he delighted in, recalling his fascination with the insects that visit them. All such things used to bring her joy too, and she still smiles at the sight of them. The endorphins that nature delivers are inescapable, yet they also bring her emptiness and remorse. Loss strips away such enjoyment. So much of what she used to take pleasure in now has a bitter aftertaste.

She walks quickly, outrunning her sadness, shaking off that little tug on her arm that tries to pull her back to a bench where she could sit and wallow all day.

Wallowing is not why she's here. She's here to fix things for Oliver, not despair in missing him.

She keeps her hood up for most of the journey, a scarf pulled over the bottom part of her face even though the air is clean.

Her face being all over social media right now is a bind. The public posts are always hateful, the kind of stuff that Anthony used to say about Oliver. There's a volume to hostility that compassion cannot reach, like it has its own frequency. Such hate is ultrasonic.

The top-level walkway is free of Flesh Fraternity speakers at least. People aren't so prepared to make a spectacle of themselves up here. They are more tight-lipped and happier to conform. Why rock the boat when you're not the one who's going to drown? She doubts anyone up here has MechaniKids. Her situation with a wealthy and abusive partner was not unique, but she recalls the look of surprise on the TRI worker's face when he noted her address on 107. They don't need the incentives up here.

The entrance to the studio is nondescript, just a black doorway in the middle of a glass skyscraper, like every other building entrance at this level. She pointed it out to Oliver once on one of their walks. That's where TV shows are made, she said. He was so young at the time. He tilted his head and tried to make sense of it, though the concept was too abstract for him to understand.

Inside the entrance lobby, she winces at her echoing footsteps as she approaches the reception desk. She sounds too confident, too exposed, not the easily dismissed part of the furniture she usually is. She disregards that feeling, reminds herself that she is a performer, a thespian, and she deserves centre stage.

For such a minimalist space, the desk is obscene, gilded with gold leaf in some overly decorative pattern, with large silver trophies adorning the corners. The receptionist sits upright to be seen behind the furniture. A smile breaks through his designer stubble and he says hello, dazzling Harriet with the kind of Hollywood smile that reassures her this is definitely a place where cameras are in abundance.

'Harriet Chapel, I'm here to be interviewed for the evening news.'

He gestures to the mounted tablet for her to sign in, then she follows him down the corridor.

'You've got an hour,' he says. His voice is deeper than she expects, and she wonders if he makes it that way on purpose. 'I'll take you straight over to hair and makeup, and perhaps wardrobe.' He casts his eyes over the length of her. There's the subtlest wrinkling of his nose as he tries not hard enough to hide his distaste. And she thought she was looking quite decent today.

The smell of the hair and makeup room takes her back twenty years. Fruity chemically hairspray has her reliving movie after movie, the giggles and the excitement she used to feel while waiting for her scene, the flamboyant hairstyles, pinned with extensions of glossy curls that somehow stayed put, as if that hairspray is fairy dust. The hours in makeup just to look natural, the gossip and tantrums, the bitching and the affairs. Those were such heady days that for a while she thought would never end. Life was a whirlwind back then. She spun too fast and too young. Why did she never think to slow down, to savour more than just the sunshine? She was ravenous for life. Now, twenty years later, satiated and exhausted, she's purged, wanting nothing more than to linger in some gleeful encounter, to cherish the present moment, rather than seek the next.

The woman from wardrobe sizes her up and presents a blue dress with little white flowers, which she puts on and it fits well enough, though a little tight around her midriff, coupled with a cream blazer.

Hair and makeup work their magic, covering her greys, bouncing some life back into her hair. Where once she had curls, they have since succumbed to gravity, like everything, and usually hang with less life than a soggy dishtowel.

The makeup artist applies enough foundation and concealer to make every worry and sleepless night from the last decade hide away. Harriet admires herself in the mirror and sees more than just a hint of the actor she used to be. She looks at her reflection, the rosy cheeks, the smoky eye pencil they've applied. How long since she's been under such high wattage lights? In her eyes, she sees those lights reflected, adding a hint of sparkle.

Harriet, you've got this.

She asks for some warm water with honey and lemon. She always hated it but she swigs it, swishing it around her mouth before doing some vocal warm ups. She's a professional, after all.

'Harriet Chapel,' the runner appears at the door. 'You're on.'

In the studio, Harriet opts for the end of the sofa. It's long, easily room for more and for the first time it dawns on her, she might not be the only guest on the show. She practises her sitting position, a straight posture and crossing her ankles. The dress digs in around her waist more as she sits and shows her legs up to her knees. She runs through her lines in her head, not wanting to leave a thing to improv. She knows her arguments and tries to foresee every question.

A voice resounds, and her blood runs cold. The voice gets closer. *No. It can't be.*

His laugh. She'd know that anywhere. It sends every hair on her body standing on end. Her lunch claws up her throat and she swallows, her insides hollowing out and she strains to not roll into a ball.

What the hell is he doing here?

She doesn't look his way, doesn't greet him. She smells him when he's close, and the sofa dips when he sits.

The studio lights dim, a greyness encroaching on her vision. Despite a chill creeping over her, more sweat breaks out, the dress even tighter and her lungs can't inflate. She's dizzy, pins and needles tingling through her extremities.

Breathe, Harriet. Just breathe.

It's only a play, she tries to convince herself. She's on stage. This is stage fright, normal nerves. She just needs to relax.

If this were a play, right now she would shout at the director to cut, say she needs a drink, to call for makeup.

There's a glass of water in front of her but reaching over to grab it would mean angling herself towards him, to bend closer to him.

He grunts a breath next to her, and a shiver trembles through her whole body.

She tenses every muscle, keeping her posture upright. She squeezes her eyes shut for a moment and when she opens them the room is clear again, the glare is back, and she can inflate her lungs.

She is strong. Determined. Not a coward. She can do this.

She hears his tongue licking his lips, and she shakes off a chill. Her throat tightens, as if being compressed.

'Hello, Harriet.' His breath reaches her neck.

She doesn't say hello back. She lets her anger at his presence fill her. Her knuckles crack as she tightens her fists. He would have heard that, yet she fails to care. Let him see her rage, let him see her hatred for him. Her heartbeat pounds, preparing her for a fight.

If the show wants an argument, they've got one. She doesn't care why he's here. There's no way she can be civil to her ex-husband.

'Nice to see you, Harriet,' Anthony says when she hasn't answered.

Every muscle fibre in her body urges to get up and leave. She stiffens, holding her ground. Her stomach churns and her nostrils flare, fight and flight battling it out through her body. Why the hell is he here? Just to wind her up? She wants to run, to shower and scrub the thought of him off her. But if she leaves, no one will support the bots. She has to stay. A mother must defend her son.

She still doesn't respond, but turns her head a few degrees, then gives him a small nod. Even from that brief view, she can tell Anthony has struggled to look after himself without Harriet in his life. Not that he did a good job of that before. His blood pressure was borderline when they were together; now his temporal vein looks about to burst. He's gained a lot of weight. His complexion appears ruddy even through the makeup, and she can smell alcohol on his breath.

She resumes her position of facing the other way, forcing herself to keep her chin high and shoulders rolled back. A tingle of guilt threatens to take that strength away, and she grits her teeth and stretches her neck. Like her knuckles, it cracks, though her tension remains. Why should she feel guilty about leaving him? She never wished him harm, even when he was at his worst towards her. He's an adult, quite capable of screwing up his own life. But her guilt was present even when they were together. His drinking and abuse took off when their baby Freddie died. It was her fault, her below grounder body's fault. She's battled that inner turmoil for years.

She presses her lips together and swallows back that guilt. Freddie's death may explain his violence but it doesn't excuse it. This is what she's rationalised over the years, when she hates herself more than he could know, when she is so hollow she can't imagine ever feeling whole.

Now is not the time to show weakness. She has another son to think about. She won't let him see her sad and afraid. Because she's not, she tells herself over and over. *I am strong. I am in control. I am not afraid.*

She played a part in an action movie once. She had hours of combat training to shoot scenes where she stood up to gangsters, fought off criminals, even killed a few. The film was terrible, tanked as soon as it was released, but she loved the character she played. The sort of woman no one dared mess with. She closes her eyes for a second, remembering that role. She is Caitlin Hart. Master of men.

His hand goes to her knee. She flinches and he squeezes. A character slip. She needs to remember her character, how hard she was, how in control.

'Get your hand off me,' she snaps, with the same determined face Caitlin had.

'Is that any way to speak to your husband?'

'Ex-husband.'

The live audience take their seats, there's muffled chatter, scuffing footsteps, the sigh of the seat cushions. She can see them all now, watching her while whispering to the person sitting next to them. They're discussing who she used to be, how much she's changed, her cellulite and tired face. It's hot in the studio, and Harriet takes a big breath of molten air, a sweat breaking out across her hairline. Wet skin and a dry throat. Why can't that be the other way round for once?

Shelly Anderson takes her seat on the chair opposite the sofa. The once controversial interviewer with wonky glasses who now prefers to ask more predictable questions. Maybe this won't be too bad. Maybe this will be exactly like Harriet has rehearsed in her head.

Harriet takes a breath, and from Shelly's glance, she feels no warmth nor animosity. As she waits, facing Shelly Anderson, their countdown flashing in the corner of her vision, Harriet wishes she could bribe her or hug her or at least get a heads-up as to what she's likely to ask.

A runner approaches them. 'There's a twenty second delay. Try not to swear, as we'd rather not have to rely on bleeping out too much. Your main camera is camera two.'

He steps away before Harriet has even processed what he said.

There's no time for questions. Lights. Camera. Action.

'And we're live in three, two—' The studio director counts down and they're live.

Chapter 21

'Good evening, viewers at home,' Shelly says. 'Tonight we are discussing the hot topic of the moment. We're all familiar with MechaniKids nowadays, and now the first generation Mechan-iTeens are being released for their trials on work experience. No one can argue with the need for these bots, the gap in the workplace in future years is widely forecast to be significant. But the question is: should bots have the same rights as people? That is what we are here to debate. With us in the studio we have Anthony Miller, CEO of AM Investments, TRI's primary in-vestors, and Harriet Chapel, campaigner for Mechani-Rights.'

The camera faces the sofa. Harriet smiles, her chin high, the friendly yet authoritative face she practised on the way over.

'Anthony Miller,' Shelly says. There's a swoon in her voice. No doubt these two have had drinks together. Harriet sits on her hands to stop herself from making fists. 'Wonderful to have you on the show.'

'Great to be here,' Anthony says.

How typical they give him the opening words. He probably paid for them to work in his favour. Knowing him, he probably bought the bloody station just so he can be made some star of the show.

'AM Investments is certainly soaring high in the stock market,' Shelly says, her tone etched with awe. 'After the company's financial trouble a few years ago, this TRI collaboration has worked wonders . . .'

Their dialogue continues. Harriet bristles at their haughty laughs and flirty jibe bullshit, though after a bit of back and forth, her tension eases. Anthony is portraying himself to be exactly the kind of arse she knows he is, sticking to his predictable script. That calms her. She knows this man. She knows the sort of crap he's likely to spew.

'And Harriet Chapel,' Shelly finally turns to her. 'We all remember Harriet as the actor who once appeared in the movie *The Women of Easterly Hall* and *One Must Concede.* Or maybe not. It was a long time ago, and they weren't high grossing films.'

Harriet smiles away the dig, though a little tighter, a little more rigid.

'Your movie days are clearly long behind you, and now you're the face of the campaign for bot rights. Harriet, how do you justify that mentality?'

'This is about protecting humans. These MechaniKids and teens look exactly like humans. I witnessed a sexual assault on a teen, and the man did not know she was a bot, but as such, there is no crime. How long before he assaults someone else?' Harriet sits upright as she talks, and when the camera goes to her, she steels her expression. Not the Hollywood smile she's used so much before but a strong jaw, her brows slightly low, a tightness across her chest and biceps. She's strong, empathetic, someone who doesn't take any crap.

'I think it says people are enjoying themselves in a safe and harmless way.' Shelly turns to face the camera and after a lethargic second, bounces her eyebrows and winks. 'Is it really assault if it's a machine?' She angles herself to face Anthony before Harriet can respond. 'So, Anthony. AM Investments usually invests in developments, infrastructure and real estate. Why the change of tack here for the business? What is it that appeals about the bots? Or is it all just financial?'

Anthony's all smiles now, on his sales pitch. 'The gap in the workforce needs to be plugged. AM Investments are putting the needs of the population first, as always.'

'Then you would surely like your product looked after instead of being mistreated?' Harriet says, stealing the show back from him. She'll silence this man if it's the last thing she does. Only she'll do it the proper way, with common sense and decency. She looks towards the live audience, hoping to see their reactions, but they're blurred out by the lights. She listens for heckles of agreement or otherwise, but it's silent away from the stage.

'Machines are disposable, replaceable,' Anthony says. 'Damage is quantifiable with fines and costs. Nothing lasts forever. We expect breakages and replacements. We do not need to stop a machine getting bruised.'

Shelly nods, then faces Harriet again. 'So, surely, Harriet, your issue with the bots could be assumed to be revenge-seeking, because your ex-husband's investment and the very large order his company has submitted to TRI, is for PleasureBots, or MechaniSluts, as they are more commonly known.' A wry smile cuts through her face. Shelly Anderson gleams with pride.

Harriet's eyes bulge, her mouth opening and closing a few times while she takes it in. 'I had no idea. I had no idea such bots were being raised at all, let alone by Anthony. But . . .' she furrows her brow, then straightens her posture. No way is she going to cower from her ex-husband. The studio lights intensify, her back grows clammy against her dress, but she doesn't fidget. She stays rigid, assured, strong. 'But are you saying sex workers should be assaulted and subjected to violence? By allowing men to do that to MechaniBots, we are encouraging that behaviour. If they want to beat up something or rape, give them a blow-up doll. A MechaniBot is too lifelike, too human-like.'

'Let people have their kinks,' Anthony says with a smirk. 'It saves the humans.'

'We have no scientific evidence to back this up,' Harriet says. 'In fact, I have witnessed some children be violent towards each other, as the bot parents are towards the MechaniKid at home. Violence teaches violence.'

'Well, that sounds like an issue with the parents, not with the bot.'

Harriet's body temperature creeps up even more. No doubt her studio makeup is sliding off her face. Her bones feel hot, a fire in her belly. Great time to have a hot flush. She uses the heat, letting it ignite her. 'And you really think that if a man can force himself on a bot, and she is instructed to fight him off, to not comply, because he has an urge to rape, that will stop him from doing it to a human?'

'Absolutely.' Anthony says, oozing all the smugness she grew to hate. 'These bots are perfect to allow humans to safely take out their urges without harming anyone. Do what you want to it and it doesn't matter. You can take out all your physical desires with no harm whatsoever, whether that be sexual or violent.'

'Funny,' Harriet says. 'You still beat me black and blue when we had a MechaniKid in the house.'

Harriet slams her mouth shut. There's a sharp intake of breath from across the studio, a few seconds of silence which Harriet revels in. Yeah, Harriet sucks at improv, and revealing so much about her private life was definitely not meant to be on the cards. But she'll be the victim, if needed. She'll air all her dirty laundry in public if it makes her point, and if it ruins Anthony's reputation in the meantime, then that's a double win.

She'll do whatever it takes.

Fuck Anthony.

'Got proof, have you?' Anthony recoils his top lip, then faces Shelly. 'That'll be bleeped out or else I'll be suing you for slander.'

'Well,' Shelly says. 'This is all very heated and exciting. Perhaps we can find some common ground between you.'

'There are points I certainly agree with Anthony on,' Harriet says. She is not handing centre stage over to Shelly or Anthony. She's on a roll. His face turns towards her, raising an eyebrow and pulling his chin in. 'For example, there are jobs that are much more suited to bots than humans.'

'Exactly,' Anthony says. 'Bots will be plugging the gap. Those below grounders, those born in squalor, pollute their bodies too much. All those jobs they fill are going to be vacant in a few years' time. We rely on filth breeding, and they produce sickly babies who don't live because their bodies are in such a state. Now we don't need such scum anymore.' His eyes flit to her waist, to where she once carried their child, and his salesman's smile twitches up into a snarl.

There's a rhythmic *boom boom boom*, getting faster. In the wrathful fog of her mind, Harriet takes a moment to realise it's her heartbeat. *Boom boom boom.* The drumbeat getting louder as every muscle tenses. It's a marching beat, telling her to get on with it, to go into battle. To finish her enemy.

Remember your lines, Harriet.

How dare he bring up her child losses! He's off script, trying to get a reaction, to make her humiliate herself. He's cornered her, as always, throttling her more subtly this time. His eyes are on her, undressing her, peeling away her skin. She steadies her breath, ignores the heat flushing through her. She could kill him now. She'd like that, to feel his neck in her hands for once.

'So keep them in those jobs,' Harriet says, trying to sound level-headed but it comes out as if she is reading off the autocue.

'The dangerous ones that cause people to be riddled with toxins. Use bots for that, rather than create childlike bots with empathy.'

'Well,' Anthony says with an exaggerated sigh, as if she's boring him. 'That mindset is being phased out. Since my company is requiring so many, empathy isn't really needed.'

Harriet swallows. She knows her lines. She can do this. 'There are girls out there, human girls, having to expose their naked hips to prove they are not MechaniTeens, so not available to be raped.'

'Well, that sounds like the perfect solution,' Anthony says with a clap of his hands.

'And what of the girl who covers herself? In the harsh winters and she wants to wrap up warm. The girl who does not want her skin on show? Is she then a fine target?'

'She only has to say she's not a bot,' Anthony says. 'This poor victim can surely declare herself as human.'

'And if she can't? If someone has their arm pressed into her neck so she can barely breathe?' Images of Anthony doing this to her flash in her mind. It's the kind of images that would usually bring on a panic attack. But she can breathe well at the moment. No dizziness. Zero panic.

'Well, maybe we should make it a new and legal norm, for people to feel a girl's hip before he makes a move. If she cannot reveal herself for what she is, he should have the right to check himself. Just a squeeze on her right hip seems perfectly acceptable. Or cut her. A simple, painless cut reveals the bots for what they are. Bots don't bleed.'

Harriet's hands go to her cheeks and her watery eyes bulge. She takes a while to respond, disbelieving what she just heard. But it repeats in her head, over and over. A man as wealthy and influential as Anthony really just said that, to millions of people watching TV.

She takes her hands away from her mouth and shakes her head. 'Oh, Anthony. What have you done?'

Chapter 22

There's a knife in the kitchen. Long. Serrated blade. For cutting bread mostly. Monty bought it off a scavenger a year ago. Good knives are hard to find, he said. Good bread is even harder, thought Harriet, though she didn't say. Didn't want to burst his bubble.

There are other things knives are good for. A serrated edge cuts many things. She wishes it could sever ties to the past, she could cut away the part of her that knots when she's cornered. She wishes she could cut flesh with no repercussions. She knows whose flesh she'd cut, for he cut her enough. And he would bleed, unlike the bots he said should be harmed.

Perhaps she could channel this anger into creativity. Audition for a part in a thriller where her character cuts her husband to pieces. The training would be fun. Knife skills. Combat. She can smell the fake blood. Corn syrup. Anthony could watch her and know, when she's eyeballing the camera, when she's relishing in the innards being spilled, she's imagining they're his.

She used her movie accent on TV as she's always done. It disappears in her daily life now, but on camera, she's still playing dress-ups. They'll listen to her more intently with that accent.

Her points will be clearer. It's the kind of accent that can rally the troops. But in doing so, she's admitting those below ground carry no weight in their words. She's turning her back on them. Where does the cycle end if no one puts a stop to it?

She loads up *Get Level.* Perhaps there's some less literal cutting she can do there instead. She braces herself before reading the comments.

@SwanSong *Seems like a legit idea to me. Feel 'em then fuck 'em.*

@Biscuits4eva *I've got my penknife ready.*

@Milestoner *A needle would even do. A sewing needle, not a drugs one. I'm not an animal.*

@2bridges *They should just cut themselves. The bots don't scar. Just have a scar and that'll fix it.*

@SwanSong *No doubt TRI will make the bots with scars next.*

@VicsBack *You fancy a girl, just feel her hip. If she is or isn't, it's win win.*

> **@JunctionJude** *Cut them, then fuck them! My new motto!*

> **@AfterDark** *What about the innocents that will be harmed? Does no one care?*

> **@JunctionJude** *They can hurt themselves to prove it or show their skin. Simple.*

Harriet pockets her phone. She can't read anymore without wanting to scream. It seems now the scales are tipping in favour of those against the bots or at least willing to exploit them for their own means. Anthony must be delighted. There's little talk of blowing up his investment now. Instead, they want to merely damage and assault them. She sniffs back a tear. What sort of awful, unwelcoming world has Oliver got ahead of him?

Perhaps it's all bluffing, just stupid bravado and ego talking nonsense. Though she knows, for every ten people talking the talk, there's going to be one who really means it. And it's because of her pig of an ex-husband.

Most of the messages of love and support are private messages. Her own lack of anonymity hasn't yet inspired others into doing the same. Love for a bot is still secret, a modern taboo. Shame may fade, but it's impossible to erase completely, like a stain on the soul.

> *I miss my little boy.*

> *My daughter is as human as anyone.*

My little girl deserves to be protected.

Harriet replies to them all, saying she is with them, that she'll keep fighting.

Her reveal about Anthony didn't make the final edit, probably worries about litigation if such a wealthy man was publicly accused. It doesn't matter, that wasn't what's important. What's important is drawing attention to the perverted behaviours and Harriet has certainly done that.

No one in her household has asked about Harriet's TV appearance and she doesn't bring it up. They didn't watch it last night, all busy elsewhere. Centre stage in the real world doesn't mean centre stage at home. Beatrice and Theo walk with Harriet to school. Theo's still worrying about Monty. Beatrice is still withdrawn and untalkative, and Harriet does whatever she can to steer the conversation to happier topics but her responses lack any hint of joy.

Beatrice is quiet when Harriet asks questions about her. She looks at the ground when she walks, her hair falling in front of her face. A far cry from the excited and confident girl Harriet met when she first started.

The streets don't let Harriet forget her own worries. The usual speaker is louder than ever, multiple billboards now sporting their message. Their crowds are growing denser, more animated, the atmosphere thicker with an unwelcoming air.

'The benevolence of God is a last century ideal. Pandering to a forgiving God is the act of a coward! God is no threat! The threat is the Devil! The Devil is a bot.'

At least such crap will likely put off the religious people, not that there are many, for this isn't the word of any church. This isn't preaching about any God. Harriet isn't religious, but she's been to church several times, for an acting role, for a friend's wedding. Church for those people was comforting and uplifting. These speaker's altars are toxic. There's a poison in the air that isn't fixing anything. It's a poorly applied sticking plaster, an opioid for imaginary wounds. Some instant pain relief and brain fog that's going to make things a hell of a lot worse later. This kind of shit should come with a warning label.

Harriet gets her phone out to video them. She can release the video on her Mechani-Rights page and show what utter nonsense they're saying. As she presses the screen, a news headline flashes up: *Human Front blow up another warehouse.*

Harriet freezes. 'Theo—' She shows him her phone.

His jaw drops. 'Shit. What else does it say?'

'I . . . I don't know.'

'Did they miss?' Beatrice asks, her eyes glazed with fear.

'They'll update soon,' Harriet says, then gives Beatrice's arm a squeeze. She doesn't flinch or pull away. Harriet wonders if she'd like a hug and opens her arms to her, but Beatrice stands rigid and cold.

She looks at Beatrice, her childlike face on a young woman's body, the blue-black bruising still faintly visible around her neck, so reminiscent of bruises Anthony used to inflict on Harriet.

Harriet shivers as she thinks of Anthony. His purchase of bots for PleasureBots is no doubt to piss her off. She's the one being accused of a vendetta, but they have it the wrong way round. No way would she ever have been happy with Oliver being used in such a way, and Anthony knows this. He knows how to push her buttons. He can't thump her anymore, so he's finding other ways to hurt her.

They arrive at school and Beatrice plugs herself in. The lights flicker a little when she does, the electric draw significant. If she was charging overnight, there'd be no lights on or other electrical requirement to compete. But Harriet can't leave her overnight to be all alone, not after the attack. There are other MechaniTeens in the building who do charge overnight. Harriet knows she can't take them all, and if all of them needed to charge in the morning, then none of them would be able to. It would trick the electrics for sure.

Dexter's heavy footsteps and grunting breaths come down the corridor towards Harriet's classroom. 'Ms Chapel, I was just coming to see you. My office.'

Harriet follows. Dexter's tone is not a friendly one, but then, it never is. His office is equally unfriendly. She's never sent a naughty child to his office. No child is ever naughty enough to be subjected to Dexter. Why build a career working with children when he clearly hates them so much?

Dexter sits at his desk, scraping his chesterfield across the floor, with Harriet in a plastic chair opposite. The room is so clinical for a room in a school. Nothing in here seems remotely relevant to children. No pictures, no sports trophies. It's bare except for wall-mounted animal carcasses. The only evidence that Dexter works with children at all is the bookcase with volumes on discipline and the aroma of pine-scented disinfectant.

'What the hell was that on TV last night?'

Finally, someone is mentioning her appearance. Although, by the look on Dexter's face, he's less than impressed. 'The interview? Well, I thought—'

'I know you're a drama teacher, but that doesn't mean to say you should create drama.'

'We have MechaniKids in the school and teens on the faculty. We should be standing up for them.'

'The complaints I've had! My inbox is jam-packed with emails from outraged parents, worried their children are going to be treated as badly as machines.'

'That's not what I said.' She grips the armrests of the chair so tightly she could rip the things off. 'I said that bots should have some basic human rights.'

'*Human* rights is exactly my point.' His face goes such a deep shade of red, Harriet leans away in case he explodes. 'That is exactly the parents' point. You may have some vendetta against your ex-husband—'

'That is not what this is about!' She's shouting now but can't help it. If Dexter can explode, so can she. 'If you'd seen the show, you would know that none of what you are saying is what I said.'

'You have given me no choice. I can't have a member of staff on TV demeaning every child in this school. Your employment here is terminated immediately. Pack up your things. I want you out of here before the children and their livid parents arrive.'

'But . . . I have classes.'

'I am sure the children can cope. It's not like you teach anything important.'

Harriet's breaths shallow and she pushes herself up from the armrests, her hands taking a second to release their grip. She could punch that big red face. It wouldn't even hurt. It'd be like hitting a slice of watermelon. She turns and leaves the room before she can give Dexter the satisfaction of any reaction.

Theo is working on Delilah in the workshop. Her tiny little body rigged up to some computer. He almost drops his tools when she tells him.

She's determined not to cry, but the sting in her eyes threatens that intention. 'I'm gutted. I just can't believe it.'

'Dexter hates the arts. He's always looking for a reason to get rid of them.' He shakes his head and strokes her arm. 'I'm really sorry, Harriet. Want me to walk out too in solidarity?'

'No. God, no. I'm already worrying about the rent.'

'Don't. We'll be fine. We're paid up for this month and we'll figure something out.' He has his usual reassuring smile he wears so well.

'Please bring Beatrice home?'

'Sure. Look, though, quickly. Delilah's programming. You were right. She was wired differently to Oliver and the others. It's like they program the girls to be more . . . available.'

'Well, now we know. Is that all girls?'

'She's the only girl kid we've brought up so far. The rest have been boys.'

Harriet nods and chews the inside of her cheek for a moment. 'Can you look at a living MechaniTeen? Without harming her? If so, maybe you could have a little look at Beatrice?'

'I'm glad you said that, as I've already done it. A few days ago. Sorry, I was worried you'd be mad.'

Harriet's jaw tightens. She should be mad, but the apologetic look on his face makes being mad difficult. And she knows it's a sensible thing to do. She forces her tightness to loosen. 'And the results?'

'It seems her programming isn't like Delilah. She's like Oliver. So not all the girls are the same.'

'Well, hopefully if I get the job there I can do some digging. Maybe I can get some answers. Although with another explosion, Josie thinks they'll be taking their time with criminal record checks. Though I'm going to really need that job now.'

'Hey, you going to be okay? Want me to go punch him or something?'

Harriet chuckles. She can't wallow. Not here. 'Yeah. I'll be fine. And no, obviously not. It's probably good for me to be home and spend some time with Josie.'

Harriet leaves, pushing through the Flesh Fraternity fans as when she arrived, as if she needs reminding of all the craziness in the world. She stops a little way from the school and watches the children arrive, the kids too, some clearly cared for, some not so much. She shakes her head as she walks away, imagining the smug look on the likes of Polly's dad when they find out she's gone. She's a shamed parent again, just because she sticks up for those like her own child. Some may try to shame her, but she holds her head high. Somehow, she is going to make this world a safe place for her son.

Chapter 23

With Josie still not back, Oliver and Thomas make up their minds. After another day spent watching that video, Oliver feels like his chest is ripping in two. As much as he tries to tell the staff he has a headache, that he feels sick, they don't believe him. Bots don't get sick. Bots don't get headaches. Whatever ailment Oliver claims, he's reminded he's not real. They wave a metal bar in front of him like they're going to hit him until he sits down and stays quiet.

'Are you worried?' Oliver asks Thomas on their way back to the communal area.

'Yes. And with that damned movie we keep watching, I can't stop wondering what's going on out there.'

'Evie didn't want to go. Maybe the girls knew something that we don't. I think we should leave. Right now.'

'Where would we go?'

'To my uncle Theo's or the refuge. Maybe my mum is still there or that's where your mum's gone. I know some people below ground as well—Uncle Theo's family. They might help.'

Oliver has planned it all. They'll need to be fully charged, so they'd have to leave in the morning. He's been paying attention.

He knows where the exit is, and he knows that after someone comes to turn them back on, there's a lull before the staff takes them through to the workroom, and they are all expected to entertain themselves for a while. And then in the workroom, they don't do a headcount, not that Oliver's ever noticed.

'You sure you want to do this?' Oliver asks Thomas.

He nods without hesitation.

'Okay. First thing in the morning, when we're charged. They sometimes leave us for about half an hour after turning us back on. And then, when we're in the workroom, they might not notice for a while.'

'So we just walk out?'

'I've been watching. It's what the staff do. That door down the corridor is the way out.'

'What if they catch us?'

'They're torturing us already. How much worse could things be?'

Thomas nods again. He juts his chin out, lifts his head high. Oliver knows if he was sure his mum was in trouble, he'd do whatever it took to leave. He hopes Thomas is as determined.

Once they're out in the real world, they can find his mum and she can help them find Evie and Josie.

One more night, Oliver tells himself as the staff comes to put them on standby. One more night of nightmares, and then they'll be free of this place. One more night, and he can see his mum again.

Chapter 24

Monty's latest craft project is a set of three lampshades made of reclaimed wire. They're almost finished and stunning—as always. They're laid out in the corner of the kitchen where he left them. The entire apartment is made up of Theo and Monty's knick-knacks. They've done so much to make it feel like home.

She's suggested many times they might prefer her to move out, to which they always insist isn't true, saying they enjoy her company. They're too kind, but between their cooking, decorating and DIY skills, she wonders what she adds to the home-life. Theo fixed up a load of air purifiers for their apartment, whereas Harriet broke the kettle. They need her help with the rent most likely, and now she's not even sure she can do that.

The hate in the streets, the Flesh Fraternity and the Human Front on their mission to destroy all the bots, the attack on Beatrice, the anger from parents. It's all too much, and she wraps her arms around her waist. Harriet can't help feeling like the world is a pressure cooker, as if the underside of the level above is closing in, squeezing the goodness out. The anger and animosity simmers just below boiling point. A volcano about to erupt.

She flaps her blouse. It's cool in the apartment, yet her body temperature spikes. Probably a hot flush. They've been beginning, simply to remind her of her childlessness, as her final chance at that life sails away. She sweats at night mostly, when she fidgets and frets, lonely and worried. But now, what's causing it? Merely hormones in a soup of shame, embarrassment, nerves? *Shamed Parents* was coined not because they felt ashamed, but because others tried to make them feel that way. Loving a child who is different shouldn't be such a bad thing. Surely it's more shameful to love nothing or no one. Shame is to find bitterness where others find comfort.

She puts the kettle on, struggling for breath, her chest tightening as Anthony's voice circulates in her head.

Useless bitch! You're nothing without me.

Nausea grips her stomach, her eyes brim, and she holds onto the counter as she doubles over, willing herself to breathe.

You're weak. You're poison. You killed our son.

She squeezes her eyes shut, tears spilling over onto the floor. Her throat squashes as she senses the indents of his fingers.

'Hey.'

Harriet bolts upright at the greeting. The voice, gravelly and frail but still the sweetest sound. Behind her is Josie, her brows drawn in, face full of concern for Harriet. Poor stupid weak Harriet, when Josie is the one facing death.

'S . . . sorry,' Harriet says, her tone breaking with stifled tears. 'I just . . . I'm home and—'

Josie, thin and ailing, is next to Harriet in a split second. Her heavily-clothed arms wrap around her and Harriet cries into her neck. She's selfish to cry, to feel sorry for herself in front of Josie, but her embrace draws it out of her, letting her breathe again.

Harriet makes them tea, then sits at the table as she launches into the details.

'But you did nothing wrong!' Josie says with a cough.

Josie's eaten so little since she arrived. Despite the support she's showing Harriet, she's fading. The loss of appetite is a sign of the end stages of the below-ground-sickness. There'll be no convincing her to eat any more.

'The headteacher's a dick,' Harriet says. 'Literally thinks kids should learn maths and nothing else.'

'I'll bet the kids love your classes.'

It cuts deep because she knows it's true. The kids really will miss drama. That's what hurts the most, but she can't wallow for long so she pushes off the negative thoughts. She needs to be practical and pay rent. 'Now I need a job.'

'You could go freelance. An after-school drama club? I'll bet demand will be high now that the school won't be teaching drama anymore.'

'I could . . .' Harriet says, her mind drifting. Could she really? If so many parents are livid with her, then probably not. 'Hopefully I'll hear about the TRI job soon.' Harriet loads up her phone to check the news. 'They're saying the explosion missed again. Another old storeroom, no stock.'

Josie hasn't sat down yet. She paces, claiming it's less painful that way, though she winces with every step, lifting her spindly legs as if they're tree trunks.

'I'll call the doctor,' Harriet says. 'They do home visits for pain relief. I read about it.'

'I already called. I'm on their list. They said it might be a couple of days.'

Harriet's jaw drops. 'A couple of days? I'll chase them, tell them it's urgent.'

Josie sits then, close to Harriet, resting her hand on her arm. 'You're doing your best to make the world a better place for our boys. That's all I want you to think about.'

Harriet smiles at her, and the part of her arm in contact with Josie tingles. Harriet was once—no, many times—told she was distant, that she didn't love enough. But that was never true. She loves too much. She simply found it hard to demonstrate. Until Oliver. A child does that to a mother. It brings out the best in them.

Harriet's face heats and she looks away, her heart picking up its pace. She looks again at Josie, the woman she cared about so much. She's a waif of smoke, just as intoxicating, and so thin she could be see-through. Is it wrong for old feelings to reignite when Josie's in such poor health? There's a kinship there Harriet's so drawn to. In another life, they could have been close forever. Their relationship deserved so much more of a chance. If Harriet hadn't been so angry, if she'd just said she understood, perhaps they wouldn't have lost those three years. Josie's been looking after Harriet's son. She's family. She should always have been.

***

Harriet spends too much time pacing, biting her nails, terrified and anxious as she still hasn't heard from TRI about the job. She chases the doctor for Josie and that frustrating phone call makes her even more impatient. Josie tells her to relax, and she tries. Josie has far more to worry about; she just handles it better. They talk about their boys, reminisce about those early years.

When Theo gets home from work, his face is grave, pale. Beatrice is much the same.

'It's bad,' he says. 'The way the children are with the bots. They were kicking them, touching them. They're children, for fuck's sake. Where do they even learn that? Two children cut themselves to prove they're not bots, even though everyone knows they're not. It's like a bloody fashion craze. Several of the older kids had knives taken off them, not before they cut others, though. One of them cut a bot and he was told off a bit, but that was all. The child who cut another human was in detention. Beatrice . . .' his voice trails off.

Harriet turns to face Beatrice, her face is as forlorn as ever. 'Did something happen at school, Beatrice?'

She shrugs.

'Did someone hurt you?'

'No,' Beatrice says with a defeated sigh. Her glossy black hair hangs in a curtain over both sides of her face. 'You can't hurt a bot.'

'Hey,' Theo says softly. 'Show her.'

Beatrice shudders, then pulls back her sleeve. Blue-black lines slash through her wrist.

'They know she's a MechaniTeen, but they cut her anyway,' Theo says. He sits at the table, his face fuzzy with sleeplessness, and he runs his hand over his head. Harriet doesn't want to ask where Monty is. She's not seen him all day.

Harriet puts her face in her hands and cries silent tears. This is her fault. If she hadn't done that interview, if she hadn't riled Anthony, he wouldn't have said that.

'I know what you're thinking and don't,' Theo says, as sternly as she's ever heard him. 'This is not your fault.'

She lifts her face and looks at him, then over to Beatrice. Poor, beautiful Beatrice. What must the children's home lives be like for them to think such behaviour is okay?

'I spent all afternoon repairing bots,' Theo says, taking a couple of beers out of the fridge, passing one to Harriet. 'I've not got enough parts for this. The children without knives were punching the kids, pulling at their limbs. It was brutal. I can't believe it's this bad.'

'I can,' Harriet says. 'Someone as wealthy and powerful as Anthony tells people on TV it's fine to abuse them and everyone thinks it's okay. Money talks. People do what the richest say.'

'I called some parents. I had to hide away the tools in the workshop, as children were fishing for them to hurt each other. The two parents I called just said, what did I expect? Bots are allowed in the school so we should expect this behaviour.'

Harriet pushes her beer away, her stomach too twisted to want anything. 'Beatrice, I'm so sorry. This isn't fair. This isn't what it is meant to be like for you. I'm going to keep trying to make things better for you. Lots of us are.'

'Thank you. It was quite awful today. I didn't know humans are meant to be like that.'

'They're not. Really, they're not.'

She wishes she could offer Beatrice something to comfort her. With humans, a hot bath or some comfort food can help. For Oliver, it was always a hug. All Harriet can do is praise her, tell her what a good job she's doing, and try to reassure. It seems paltry, but it's all she's got.

Harriet's phone pings and she looks at her email, giving a little yelp. She reads the email several times before she believes it. Her heart leaps to her throat as she reads again and again, allowing reality to sink in. 'It's TRI. I can start tonight. I can see Oliver this evening.'

Chapter 25

As Harriet gets ready, she fidgets and frets. Every bit of excitement is trampled by her worries. Whenever she closes her eyes, she sees Delilah, Joshua, little bodies torn apart for no reason. She worries for her own son. How do any mothers cope in a world so brutal, so fraught with threats, where violence is more common than hugs? She's glad Oliver is at the Institute. The bombings have missed, but even with her worries about another she feels he's probably still safer there. And she'll get to see him soon.

She dresses in the same outfit she wore when she went for her ID check. It's the only outfit Alyssa owns. Josie tells her it's overkill since they really don't care about any dress code and no one will suspect her anyway, but Harriet needs to be in character. She can't risk anything going wrong.

Monty arrives home and seems like the Monty Harriet knew from her audition days who would help her get ready for hours before and rehearse her lines. He leaps into action, helping her apply her face prosthetics and the wig. It itches, but she can bear it. She had to wear wigs in West End shows before. The hot stage lights coupled with dancing made it feel like she had nits. She coped with that for the measly paycheque and shitty reviews. She can cope with a lot worse to see her son.

When she's ready, they both stand in front of the mirror. Harriet looking exactly like she should as Alyssa Wade. Monty, a tad dishevelled with three-day-old stubble, but otherwise clean, smiling, dressed neatly, the bruising around his nose has faded to an almost imperceptible yellow.

He grins and his arm drapes over her shoulders. 'You've got this, babe.'

Josie stands to say goodbye, pushing herself up by her arms that look like they could snap. Her clothing must weigh the same as her body. She sniffs and wipes a tear away with a tissue. 'Tell Thomas I love him and say sorry for me. Tell him . . . I don't know. I don't want him to know I'm sick. I don't want him worrying. Just tell him sorry and I wish I could be there. He probably won't ask questions. He's so polite.'

Harriet pulls her in for a hug. She's even thinner, if that was possible, and her ribcage digs into Harriet's chest.

Monty and Theo walk Harriet to the door and wave her goodbye.

'Give that little dude a hug from me too!' Monty calls after her and gives Theo a peck on the cheek.

Harriet waves back and walks away, as if on air, so excited she could run all the way but even that would be too slow. She takes a lift up to level 6 to take a taxi. No chance is she wasting time walking. She'll be early, but that's fine with her. The taxi drops her right outside and after a couple of steps, she remembers to be in character and adjusts her walk to a slight shuffle.

She uses an ID code on her email to let herself into the building. One door opens, and she's stuck behind another with another scanner. Laser lights inspect her all the way down. A new addition, the email said, in light of the latest threat. Then, the second door opens, and she follows the directions they sent her. A staff member will show her what to do for her first shift. After that, she's on her own.

She's almost dizzy as she walks down the corridors, the butterflies in her stomach fluttering into a frenzy. She doesn't see the plain walls around her. She sees Oliver, his cheek dimples, his sweet smile and blue eyes. Her hands are probably clammy but she doesn't notice as she rubs her fingers in her palms, imagining his soft skin, his mess of hair.

The lift that takes her down to the Teen Institute is unmarked, as the instructions tell her to expect, and after typing in the next code on her list, she takes it down to below ground. When she steps out, she's in a wide section of tunnel and the door shuts behind her. To her left, the tunnel leads elsewhere. To her right is a metal door with a code panel and intercom. Adjacent to that is a second code panel that the instructions say she uses to call the lift back down when her shift is finished. The lift whirrs as it makes its way back up, but where she stepped out is now barely visible against the dark and muddy background.

It's damp and cold as always below ground, the smell of wet clay. Only a few seconds below and she can feel her pores clogging with muck. In the ground are footprints, two sets making their way to the black tunnel to the left. Some staff here must live below ground.

She taps the penultimate code into the panel, not wanting to spend any more time in the tunnel than she needs to, Josie's sickness vivid in her mind. From nowhere, a green laser cuts through the dark. A second scanner. Once again, she is inspected before the door buzzes, then it clicks as it opens, and she steps inside.

The Institute hums with air purifiers and fans. Plenty of sections of the walls are uncovered, the bare clay visible and dripping in places. Dehumidifiers add to the din and she has to cover her ears when she first steps in. A few paces away and it's bearable. The floor, at least, is solid and a metal walkway clangs beneath her feet as she walks along towards where the map says the communal area is. When she arrives, it's deserted and so she retraces her steps and walks back the other way. There's a noise up ahead, like gunshots and banging, a few screams. Lights flash down the corridor and it seems it's movie night for the MechaniTeens. She tiptoes as she makes the last few steps, then hovers in the doorway and watches.

The teens are all sitting in rows watching the film and her eyes scan the tops of their heads for one that could be Oliver. They're grubby mostly, torn clothes and muddy skin. All boys, by the looks of it. It's a struggle to stay in character as her hand goes to her chest when her heart feels like it's going to burst. Oliver is within touching distance!

Some of the teens are restless, flinching at the film, whereas others are engrossed. Harriet casts her eyes towards the projector and a sharp intake of breath threatens to reveal her. Her hands go to her mouth and she steps back around the door, pressing her back into the area of wall that's covered. The film is awful. People suffering, buried, dying, children hurt. It doesn't look like any movie she's ever seen. It looks like footage from tunnels collapsing, from cities above ground burying those below. And it all looks so real. Oliver would hate that! She yearns to run to him, to hug him and tell him not to look, but she must stay in character.

'Can I help you?' The staff member makes her jump and, for the briefest second, she forgets her fake name.

'Sorry . . . I . . . I'm Alyssa Wade. It's my first day. I'm here to put the MechaniTeens on standby.'

The man steps back, his hips swaying as he does. Harriet has seen such a posture before, the waddling steps of people who spend too much time below ground. The pallor of his skin confirms this. He smiles revealing yellow teeth, and lifts a skinny arm up and checks his watch. 'You're early. That's great, actually. I can show you round, then leave you to it. Follow me.'

She follows him back to the communal area where she already visited, and he keeps talking the whole way.

'It's only boys here at the moment. They shouldn't be any trouble. There's the odd fight if they've had a tough manual labour day, but this evening they'll just be tired. Nearly two days their batteries last for, though the film drains them quicker than their other work. They've been watching that film for over thirty hours. They'll be pleased to go on standby.'

They enter the communal area. Along the wall are charging cables, the dusty outlines of footprints next to them.

'So, they all line up around here. They have their favourite spots. There will be gaps, as the girls have gone on work experience. They often plug themselves in. I swear some of them get high on that! Then all you have to do is put them on standby. It's fiddly. You take this—' he picks up a little metal rod '—and just above their charging port you stick that in and their head flops down and presto. They stay standing, though. If you can't find the rod, there's more in the office down the hall. Then, when you've turned them all on standby, hang around for maybe an hour, just to check there are no issues with electricity. Then come back eight hours later and do the same again to turn them all back on. Check for any that haven't charged properly and when the morning staff arrive, you're free to go.'

'That's it? I don't have to talk to them or anything?'

'You can if you like. They're just robots, though. Not sure what you'll have to talk to them about.'

'They don't need cleaning, or do they read books or anything?'

He shrugs. 'They're just robots. They do seem human, weirdly so, but they don't need any more looking after. But do what you want, I guess. And if you don't mind, since you're here, you can start right away. That film finishes in about an hour. Some of them get a bit upset about it. The empathetic ones. Boss is trying to harden them up. There's no need for the empaths anymore, so we're training it out of them. If any seem upset, just tell them to toughen up and it'll get easier. They'll all make their way to the communal area when it's done. Put the projector away, it goes in the office. Don't worry about being too tidy. It's best to give the bots twenty minutes or so to unwind a bit. Then put them on standby, which takes about half an hour. Do a general check of the area. Oh, and I should show you the generator, just in case.'

He spends the next twenty minutes hurriedly showing Harriet the backup generator, the fuse box, how to spot if there's an issue with the dehumidifier, the readings of what should be normal for the air quality. There's a folder in the office, he says, that has it all written down and the protocol, along with emergency contacts. The whole time he keeps checking his watch.

'Sorry to rush through it all, but I'm always in a hurry to leave. Got a newborn at home and my wife isn't well. Anyway, leaving a bit earlier today is a huge help.'

'It's fine, really. I'm here, so might as well begin.'

'Great. So, I'll be off. The new alarm will go off if anyone tries to get in or it detects explosives in the area, so don't worry about all that stuff on the news. It's safe here. No one besides the staff knows how to find this place. They're just idiots blowing up old warehouses with nothing in them. Thanks so much.' He checks his watch again. 'Half an hour till the film ends. I really appreciate it.'

He pushes the door open. No exit code or laser scanners for the way out, Harriet notes, and when it's closed, her body fizzes with excitement. She relaxes her posture, happy to be Harriet Chapel now, then races back through to the video room. The teens don't turn her way. She continues to watch them from behind, patrolling the back of the room and trying to guess which one is Oliver.

The film goes from horrific to terrifying. The fear in some of the boys is so clear and she sees many of them look away and cover their eyes, some of the others tell them off for that. One of those looking away must be Oliver. There's no way he'd be happy watching such a horrible film. They're trying to get rid of their empathy, like Anthony said. Such a thought chills her bones, and she wraps her arms around her chest. Her sweet-natured boy. How awful to try to toughen him up. Even Harriet, who is quite hardy to the cruel world, winces at the movie, the gore and fear twisting her stomach.

Half an hour crawls along. Harriet rocks on the balls of her feet, chews the inside of her cheek and counts the seconds. When the projector screen goes white, she runs to the light switch and turns it on, forgetting all about Alyssa's walk. Half of the boys appear shell-shocked with red-rimmed eyes and furrowed brows. The other half smirk, fold their arms, and are way too comfortable given what they've just seen. Harriet shivers.

'Now boys, I'm Alyssa, and I'll be putting you on standby to replace Josie. Please make your way to the communal area.'

The boys all stand and make their way there. There are utterings of banter, a few shoves, but they go where they're supposed to. There's about a hundred of them, and it's hard for her to see over their heads to find Oliver. Josie said Harriet would recognise him straight away, that he still resembles her little boy. She listens to their voices, all so much more mature than Oliver's little boy voice. None sound familiar.

Harriet packs away hurriedly, then waits in the office. From behind a glass wall, she watches the boys interact. Some are loud and bolshy, some are quiet, some are really timid. She wonders what it was like with the girls here. She can imagine Oliver having girls as friends. As a kid, Oliver was never concerned about which gender of child he played with, only that he enjoyed their company.

They all move to their preferred spot, and she watches them for twenty minutes. None of them definitely seem like Oliver, but she has a shortlist. She inwardly kicks herself. A mother should be able to spot her child easily. Josie says he's still blonde-haired and blue-eyed, and Thomas red-haired, freckles dusting his nose. She has a few possibilities for both of them, but none of those are standing together.

When they all seem quite settled, she walks out to the communal area. 'Okay, boys. Time to go on standby.'

Most of the boys are already in their positions by their chargers and are busy fumbling with the cables.

She's still not sure, and she silently curses her disguise. Oliver could be any of these boys and he won't know she's right here.

She steps around them all, then decides she has no choice but to ask. 'Where are Oliver and Thomas?'

Every boy looks side to side.

'That's weird,' one boy says. He has the blackest hair, slick and straight. 'Oliver and Thomas are usually right there.' He points to the far end.

'I haven't seen them all day,' another boy says.

Harriet freezes a moment, her stomach dropping several storeys. 'Okay . . . Well, so I can learn, all of you tell me your names as I put you on standby.'

They do. Each boy is incredibly polite, bidding her goodnight as she presses their standby button. Josie was right about the different sizes. Some are taller than Harriet and as broad as many full-grown men. Others are more svelte and appear younger. When every boy is sleeping, not one boy has said the name Oliver, nor do any of them seem like her son.

She wonders for a second if she's at the wrong Institute. Maybe there are more. How many MechaniKids were released in the first wave is a mystery to all but the top staff at TRI. But no, the boys knew Oliver and Thomas. They noticed they're not here.

She looks side to side, her heart in her throat, her vision shimmering with an early migraine. Frantic now, she runs to the office, then back to the movie room, screaming their names. 'Oliver! Thomas!'

She leans against the wall, pressing her hand into her beating heart, her shuddering breath refusing to steady as she remembers the two sets of footprints walking down the tunnel.

The realisation makes her gasp, and she clutches at her stomach.

Josie hasn't been back. She never told them she's sick. They miss her and, of course, they'd go looking for her. Her little boy, always the protector, worrying about Josie.

Any pride she has for Oliver's actions is crushed by her dismay. Harriet's panic shakes through her, sweat collecting in every joint and hairline, her voice weak as she still calls Oliver's name.

Those footsteps. That's all she can think about.

The room spins as her chest caves in, her heart cramping with her loss. Again and again, her loss.

She's too late. Before she could get to him, her son has gone.

Chapter 26

It was easy enough for Oliver and Thomas to leave. There was no lock to exit as Oliver suspected from his time observing the staff. All the security seemed to be to stop people from trying to get in. Oliver supposed they never thought about the teens trying to leave. The staff assumed obedience. But Oliver wasn't raised that way. He wasn't raised to be bad, but he was raised to be curious, to question, to explore.

Perhaps bots like Oliver aren't what the company wants. They want soldiers, compliant enough to be mistaken for military. The staff have never treated Oliver and his peers like humans, so why would they assume they have any kind of human desires or curiosities? To the staff, they are merely machines.

'I think we must have been living below the TRI warehouse,' Oliver says when they first start walking. The few low wattage bulbs that light the space show the walls are brown and appear damp, the ground soft underfoot. 'Somewhere close to there. Which means we're somewhere below London. There will be steps somewhere to get us above ground. Or—'

'Or what?'

'I know some people who live below ground—Reading town. They maybe aren't that far away. I think if we get somewhere where people are, I should be able to find it, or we could ask.'

Sylvia and Casper, Theo's parents, were so kind before. They might be able to help them get to Oliver's mum.

Thomas has never been below ground before, so it's up to Oliver to lead the way.

They've been walking for hours and, for once, Oliver's glad they've been doing so much manual labour. His body is used to being on his feet. He keeps listening for footsteps approaching, expecting the staff to realise they're missing and come running. The pair of them are so quiet when they're working, so rarely draw any attention to themselves. If George or one of the more boisterous boys escaped, everyone would realise straight away. No one notices when someone quiet and non-troublesome runs away. He hopes, anyway.

Oliver keeps trying to remember what happened three years ago when they first arrived at the TRI warehouse and he got his teen body, but it's a blur. He was so shocked by his new limbs he didn't give much thought to where he was going. But he's sure he didn't go far.

'We can't charge below ground.' Thomas says.

'No.' Oliver hangs his head. 'But our batteries last quite a while, even longer if we take it easy, so we've got a while to worry about that. We can't think about too much at all. And Sylvia and Casper might know if my mum is okay. That movie we had to watch, I just keep thinking about them and the other people who live below ground.'

'Okay. If you think you can find them.' There's doubt in Thomas's voice.

They turn a few corners and are still in a quiet and featureless tunnel. Their footsteps squelch. There's no hustle and bustle of the busy street that he remembers. It seems a far cry from the bustling underground town that Oliver visited before. A sense of fear makes his limbs tremble. When he was here before, a tunnel collapsed. Perhaps there's no people living underground anymore? He shakes out his arms and keeps walking. Now is not the time for negativity. Surely if they keep walking, they'll find people eventually. Or maybe a lift.

Oliver looks around, still scanning the walls for a door or a sign. 'Or else the first staircase we find, we go up. Get a lift up and see where we are. We walked to the TRI building before from the refuge so we can find our way back.'

Thomas's hands are in front of him, not swinging at his sides like Oliver's. One hand squeezes the other like he's wringing out a wet cloth. 'I don't know,' Thomas says. 'I've never had to make decisions.'

Oliver slows for just a moment, then regains his pace. 'Me neither. But we're not kids anymore. We can do this. Let's just keep walking and see if I recognise anything, and go from there.'

'Okay,' Thomas says, and his hands drop to his sides.

They're in near darkness with only the odd sensor light flicking on. Oliver's doubt starts off as a niggle, but as time goes on, it starts to crush him. They should be in town by now. There should be some people, surely. Though they have no concept of time down here. They've no clock or watch, no window. All they can do is keep walking, keep hoping.

There's some commotion up ahead, and they pick up their pace. Oliver looks over his shoulders to check the noise isn't echoing from behind, and it isn't. People. They can hear people. Not shouting or screaming or anything awful, just background noise, chatter and movement.

The sensor lights become more frequent and up ahead, they're shining even brighter. As they get closer, in that light are silhouettes and shadows of movement. A town, that's all it can be. Oliver isn't sure exactly where, but a town means there's people. A town means there's a way out.

Chapter 27

Harriet leaves the Institute and stares at the footprints. Two sets, walking next to each other, away from the Institute to the dim tunnel beyond. She crouches down and touches them, not caring about any toxic contamination or dirt. They're his prints—she knows this in her bones. She presses her palm into the imprint, tracing the outline with her finger, just wanting to put her hands where her son has trod. He has big feet now, not the perfect and chubby little ones he had as a kid. He's grown so much.

Her heart rips to shreds and on her knees, she cries. Tears trace their way down her cheeks, dripping off her chin and onto the ground where her son walked just hours before. Her lungs heave in the dank air, the dim tunnel getting dimmer as all the hopes she had begin to fade.

The teens have been awake for over thirty hours. If Oliver left when they first got up, he could be anywhere by now. He walked straight past the lift entrance. Not surprising, as it's so hard to see, and he'd get nowhere without the code.

She wants to scream his name, to run after him, to hold him with her broken and crumpled body and be whole again. Again and again, she must experience loss. The world repeats its story as it spins, those painful waves battering her each time.

As she has so many times before, she picks herself up and stands. Hysteria is for those with nothing else to lose. She brushes the dirt off her knees and forces some rationality into her mind. He's a sensible boy. He's not a tiny boy anymore but a teen, mature and strong. She briefly contemplates following the footprints but if he's been walking for hours, she'll have no hope. In her tattered heart, she knows where he'll go. He'll be trying to find her somehow. He'll be on his way to his Uncle Theo's.

She bolts for the lift and rides it all the way up to 10, the top vehicle level where the fastest taxis are. They're always available, so few people can afford them. Harriet certainly can't but she can worry about that later. She rides the taxi all the way to the closest lift to home and takes the lift back down to 5, sprinting the couple of hundred metres through the park to her front door, collapsing into it and with panting breaths, calls out for her son.

'Oliver! Thomas!'

Josie, draped in a woollen shawl, drags herself out of her room, and Theo appears from the kitchen.

'Harriet?' Theo asks, concern knitting his brow.

Josie's eyes are wide, her mouth hanging open.

'They . . .' Harriet holds her chest and tries to catch her breath. 'They're not here?'

'Who?' Theo asks.

'The boys!' Her knees buckle, and she slides down the wall and sits on the floor. 'They've gone. Oh, Josie. They've gone.'

Josie steps closer, though Theo reaches Harriet first and he sits, putting his arm around her. She leans into him and her body convulses with tears.

'I was meant to see him today. My son. But he's gone.'

'You need to say more, Harriet,' Josie says, her voice a rasping whisper punctuated with coughs. 'Please explain.'

'I was there to put them on standby, but they weren't. I asked all the other boys—only boys there—and they said it was weird. They hadn't seen them all day. A hundred boys there and none of them are Oliver and Thomas. They've both gone. Footprints down the tunnel leading away, God knows where. They were Oliver's footsteps. I know it.' Harriet rests her forehead on her knees and sobs some more, then lifts her head slowly again to look up when she hears the sound Josie makes. It's breathy and crackly, but unmistakably a laugh. 'What?'

'They've gone. They've escaped.' Josie puts her hand to her stomach as she doubles over, coughing out her laugh. 'Clever boys. So resourceful. What little legends.'

'Gone! Escaped!' Harriet screams. How can Josie find this so funny? 'I was meant to see Oliver today!'

Josie stops laughing but her face still wears a smile. 'Those boys are like homing pigeons. They'll come home. Or some-where else they know.' Her hand goes to her heart. 'My boy, Thomas. He's looking for me.'

Harriet pulls her chin in, considering Josie's words. 'Really? Oliver has barely been anywhere and not in years. He won't know where anything is.'

'Josie's right,' Beatrice says. Harriet hadn't noticed her there, but she's standing in the hallway, quietly listening. 'I remember my way even to my old house from here. I would have made it the other n—' She clamps her mouth shut.

Harriet stands and slowly walks over to Beatrice. She's looking at the floor, a blush creeping up from her neck to her cheeks, her arms folded across her, her hands tugging at her sleeves.

'Beatrice,' Harriet says in a hushed tone. 'That night you were attacked—were you going to see your parents?'

Beatrice looks up at Harriet then, her mouth downturned, so much sadness in her eyes. 'Is it stupid that I miss them? I just wanted to visit. I know I'm a teen now so I'm meant to be fine without them.'

Harriet takes the final step towards her and pulls her in for a hug, her chin resting on her hair. She breathes her in. 'No, darling. It's not silly at all.'

Beatrice's arms reciprocate, wrapping around Harriet. It's the first hug Harriet has shared with Beatrice, and they stay like that for a while. A wall comes down as Harriet can tell when each of Beatrice's muscles relaxes, her embrace softening by the minute. For the hundredth time, Harriet wonders what crap they've been teaching them at the Institute. For Beatrice to feel shame that she missed her parents makes fresh tears come to Harriet. No wonder Oliver had to leave.

'She's right, Harriet,' Theo says. 'Oliver is a smart kid. I'll bet he's on his way right now. Not here, but our old place. Why don't we go let the new tenants know to look out for them?'

Of course, Oliver won't even know where to find them now. The old place is just across the walkway, a short walk but suddenly Harriet perceives that distance as miles and miles. She can't picture a grown-up or teenage Oliver making that walk. Her mind's eye sees her little boy, his tiny six-year-old legs walking a great distance. Parents usually have time to build up to their children growing up and utilising more freedom, but for Harriet, it's sudden, a sledgehammer of realisation. Oliver may look ten years older than when she last saw him, but he's still her little boy, unworldly and alone.

'I'll wait up,' Beatrice says. 'If Josie can manage without me tonight. I can spend the night looking out the window. From there I can see the other building, as long as the streetlights stay on.'

Josie waves her hand and walks to her room. 'Fine by me. I'm just going to sleep as much as I can. Wake me when they get here.'

Josie doesn't seem worried, and she knows the boys best, Harriet reconciles. If Josie can trust them, she should be able to.

Theo nods. 'That sounds like a plan, don't you think? I know it's hard, but you're just going to have to sleep on it. Trust him. He'll be here soon.'

'I do trust him,' Harriet says. 'It's the rest of the world I don't.'

In another time, maybe she wouldn't be so worried. If there was no animosity towards bots, if there wasn't the mantra of 'Bots don't bleed', and she hadn't seen little Joshua ripped apart and tied to the fence. How aware of that will Oliver be?

He's smart. Again and again, she tells herself this. He's not going to go around showing off his charging port.

Harriet checks her phone, the news and the socials. The anger towards bots isn't going away. If anything, it's escalating. She only wanted to make things safer, plead their case, but she hasn't had enough time. She vowed to make this world safer and more accepting for Oliver, yet he's out in the world too soon.

People are cutting bots, exposing them, and she's no idea what happens to the ones they discover. But what can she do? Her son and Thomas are out there alone in the world and all she can do is wait.

Chapter 28

Oliver and Thomas walk for hours through a town, then another, with just a brief quiet spell in between. Thomas asks if Oliver recognises this one yet, but he doesn't. So they listen. They hear town names that aren't Reading. Slough, Maidenhead, Wokingham. But after a while, they start hearing about Reading, that other people are headed there, that it's not far away.

The tunnels are now more like Oliver remembers. Crowds of people, some walking in straight lines, some zigzagging and bouncing off others, though fewer people than last time, the crowds less dense. The constant sound of scraping and drilling. Oliver remembers to look straight ahead or at the ground instead of at the people, and to not get too close to the walls. He tells Thomas this too, leaning in and talking quietly. Tapping into his memory from three years ago is a little tricky, and he can sense his battery working harder as he tries. He remembers what the doors look like that go to staircases, but they don't see any.

They mostly keep their heads down. In the Institute, they're average height, but here, they're taller. People walk with bent backs on skinny legs. Oliver and Thomas usually have good posture, but copying the others here, they have to bend to fit in. It wasn't an issue when he was last below ground. Oliver was little so he didn't realise. At least they're a bit grubby from their Institute work. That helps them to blend in.

Oliver steals glances to the sides now and then to try to see the doors, and he remembers the way the tunnels open out into wider areas. He's never been able to smell and thinks that here, that's not a bad thing. His mum used to moan about the smell and pulled her scarf over her mouth. Oliver and Thomas don't have scarves to do this with, so he makes the right face, scrunching his nose as if he can smell the horrible smells.

'Recognise this?' Thomas asks.

'No. I mean, it all looks the same. I thought there'd be some—' His voice trails off when he sees a plaque on the wall and he slows his pace. Some people behind bump into him and then have to walk around him, but Oliver needs to stop and read it. He grabs Thomas's wrist and they step to the edge of the people walking so they're not in the way.

There are a few of these plaques around; little dedications to the people who built the tunnels, but this one is a memorial to the eighty-nine people who died when the tunnel caved in three years ago.

'I was here for that!' Oliver says in a loud whisper. He looks around at the walls. There's scaffolding, wooden and metal struts supporting the walls and ceiling, along with several thick planks covering what used to be a doorway. 'We must be close. I think I know the way.'

They take a right at the next opening. The stream of people here is quieter still, just a few of the zigzagging ones still milling about. After another few minutes, he remembers the whole way as his mum was so poorly that day. She'd been buried and hit her head and Uncle Theo and some friendly strangers carried her all the way back to Theo's family's home. They wouldn't let Oliver help, even though he really wanted to. They didn't want him getting mucky. But he paid attention and watched as they carried her, making sure she was okay.

They arrive at what he's fairly sure is Theo's family home, and he taps on the door. It's a rough metal thing supported by rusty hinges and when he knocks, the whole thing wobbles.

There's no answer for some time, and Oliver starts to think he's got the wrong house, or they've moved. To be sure, he knocks again.

Footsteps scuff towards them, and a pale man opens the door. 'Hello? What do you want?'

Oliver recognises the man instantly. He looks a lot older and more frail, but it's definitely Uncle Theo's dad. 'Mr Casper?' Oliver says. 'Do you remember me? It's me, Oliver. Harriet's son.'

The old man rubs his eyes. They're red and cloudy, and he scrunches up his face, making his wrinkles even deeper. 'Harriet's son? Sorry, boy. My memory . . . hang on, I'll get my wife.' He plods away and Oliver and Thomas wait at the doorstep while Casper shouts down the hallway.

A woman's voice answers, though from what she's saying she can't hear him very well. Oliver and Thomas still stand in the doorway, shoulders rolled forwards and hands clasped in front of them. Oliver peers up briefly to see Thomas's face getting redder, and he bites his bottom lip.

Casper's footsteps are joined by another set, heavy breaths wheezing along.

'Oliver?'

Oliver looks up to see Sylvia, a lot more steady than Casper, her face a picture of shock.

'Well!' she says. 'As I live and breathe! How you've grown! Come in, come in.' She waves her arm to gesture them in and Casper stands to the side. 'And who's this?'

'My friend, Thomas,' Oliver says. 'I was worried you wouldn't remember me.'

'Let me just look at you a moment.'

Oliver cocks his head to the side, blinking a few times, trying to gauge her reaction as she stands in front of him. Her hands go to her cheeks and her eyes are glassy. She has bright white hair pulled back, and her face looks worn out, like it's deflated. They both appear a hundred years older than when Oliver last saw them, and he thinks for a second that maybe they've been in the Institute for much longer. It must be confusing for them. If it's been only three years, then Oliver appearing ten years older must seem really weird. Oliver stands still, tries not to fidget, and smiles.

'How time flies!' Sylvia says. 'What a handsome young man you are. They must be feeding you all the good stuff at that boarding school. Come through. This way, you remember.'

Oliver and Thomas follow Sylvia through, Casper some way behind, and they sit at a little kitchen table where Oliver learned to play Uno once. He remembers the space being bigger, how he had to stretch up to reach the cards on the table. He's forgotten what it was like to be that small. A couple of candles give them a little light and Sylvia lights two more.

Sylvia offers them some juice and biscuits which they refuse, but she places it all in front of them anyway. The crockery is all chipped and misshapen, like it's been remoulded from other old bits and bobs. The table and chairs are all a little wonky, some rolled-up paper under one of the table legs that Oliver has to take care not to kick out of place.

'So,' Sylvia says when she sits down, her knees creaking as she does. 'You boys in some sort of trouble?'

Oliver's eyes lock with Thomas's for a moment as he searches for his words. They are sort of in trouble, but he doesn't want to explain all of that. 'Oh. Erm . . . no.'

'I'm a nurse, dear,' Sylvia says, raising her eyebrows and pulling her chin in like she knows everything. Oliver thinks she probably does. 'I've seen all sorts. You don't turn up on doorsteps like mine unless you're in trouble. Especially not at this hour. You're lucky Casper here wanders at night. I never get any damned sleep with his confusion. But if it weren't for that,

I would have been tucked up in bed and you'd be waiting on my doorstep till morning.'

Oliver winces. 'I'm so sorry. Actually, I've no idea what time it is.'

'Near enough midnight. You boys not got watches or phones?'

'No. Well, yes, but we left them at school. They don't let us keep them with us.' Oliver talks slowly, making up his lie on the spot is hard. He's never had to lie before.

Sylvia looks at them with narrowed eyes and nods. Oliver can't tell if she believes him. 'So, come on. Spill it. I won't judge. You're as good as family. I just want to help.'

Oliver's chest lifts and sinks again as he finds some courage and the right words. Thomas is no help, his cheeks are bright red, and he looks nowhere but at his lap.

'We've run away,' Oliver says, 'but not because we're in trouble. The school . . .'

Sylvia nods, egging him on. 'Yes?'

'It wasn't for us. They made us learn things we didn't agree with.'

'Young liberals.' She tuts. 'Well, I guess it's good to have ideologies. So, what else?'

'They said we're too soft, that we need to be tougher. But that's just not who we are.'

Sylvia smiles and rubs Oliver's hand. 'You remind me so much of my Theo at your age. He was always a sweet young man. Still is. But running away from school is a daft thing to do. There are better ways to make changes.'

'One of our friends is out on work experience,' Oliver says. Perhaps a hint of the truth will make Sylvia understand. 'And she didn't want to go and we're worried about her. We think they might be making her do the sort of work that she really doesn't like. So we thought we'd try to find her. But really, we've no idea where she is. We just knew we couldn't stay there anymore.'

'Too caring for your own good,' Sylvia says, sitting back and folding her arms. Her gaze goes to Casper a moment who seems uninterested, his gaze far away and his mouth hangs agape. He looks more asleep than awake. 'What can I do to help?'

'Can you, maybe, call my mum or Uncle Theo? I really want to see her. I know I'm not supposed to miss my mum at my age, but I do.'

'You're never too old to want to see your mum,' Sylvia says with a smile.

'And maybe they can help find out where Evie has gone. And they might not send us back to school. We're worried also as Thomas's mum works at the school, and she hasn't been in for a while. No one will tell us where she is. We just have this feeling. She was friends with my mum, so she might know.'

Sylvia sips at some of her drink and ponders for a moment. 'Sounds like you boys have got a lot on your plate. It's tough being a teenager at the best of times. Why Harriet thought she'd send you to that school is beyond me. I know you're clever, but young men should be with their family. Don't you think so, Casper?'

'Yes, dear,' Casper says, though from his blank face Oliver doubts he's followed the conversation.

'Well . . .' Sylvia sips some more of her drink. It steams but doesn't look like normal tea. 'I'm not calling your mum at this time of night. She'd get all in a bother and come straight here and those lower levels at night are not safe. They go on about below ground like it's the worst place, but let me tell you, we may have issues with pollution and that, but the people aren't the rapists and muggers they are up there. Well, not all are. Anyway, I don't want your mum endangering herself. So, you boys can rest here for the night. Take Theo's room, and I'll call in the morning. How does that sound?'

Oliver smiles. 'Thank you. That sounds perfect.'

'Sorry to be so much trouble, Mrs Sylvia,' Thomas says. 'I really hope Harriet knows something about my mum.'

Sylvia takes Oliver's face in her hand. 'Such good manners, both you boys. Right, let me show you to your room for the night.' She pushes herself up with her hands, takes a couple of lit candles, passing one to Oliver, and walks down a short corridor, pulling back a plastic curtain.

Oliver remembers this room. Theo's bed is pushed up against the wall, a chest of drawers with a few puzzle games and books on top collecting dust.

'Sorry there's only the one bed,' Sylvia says. 'The other room is totally out of use at the moment and I can't see us fixing it up any time soon. I'm hoping Theo will come when he has a minute to spare. You boys okay to share? I might have an extra blanket somewhere.'

'We're fine, really, Sylvia. This is perfect. Thank you so much,' Oliver says.

'It's much nicer than we're used to at the school,' Thomas says.

Sylvia's eyes widen. 'Really? Well, I'll certainly be having words with your mum about that school. You think they'd at least give you a bed each. One candle enough, is it?'

'Yes. Thank you,' Oliver says. 'Really, this is perfect. We're so grateful.'

'Such polite boys. Well, goodnight. I'll come and wake you up in the morning. No doubt you teenagers would like to sleep in till midday, but I'll call your mum after breakfast. Well, I'll call Theo, not sure I've got your mum's number. And I've only got Theo's mobile number since he moved house, but that should do. How does that sound?'

'Thank you.'

They say goodnight and Oliver puts the candle on the table, and they both sit cross-legged on the floor.

'She's so nice,' Thomas says. 'But really doesn't know we're bots.'

'I can't believe I'm actually going to see my mum tomorrow!' Oliver can't stop himself from smiling. Any other problem or issue pales to nothing when that joy is erupting in his chest.

'We should find a stick, like the standby ones, and each go on standby for half the night to save battery. Just in case.'

'We should have grabbed a stick from the Institute.'

'Yeah. Should have thought of that. Let's try to find something.'

They stand and search through Theo's things. On his shelf are a couple of photos, obviously him and Harriet as children with another boy that Oliver recognises as Harriet's brother who died. She always said Oliver looked like him and she was right. He wishes he had a photo of his mum. How cruel of TRI to think they can just leave that part of their life behind and become teens and not miss their families. Oliver has been angry a lot over the years, but seeing that photo makes him really angry. He knows he's not a real boy, but why does that mean he has to suffer?

'This will work,' Thomas says as he holds up a little wooden stick. 'You want first or second?'

Oliver is so tense and wound up, he opts for first. He needs to calm down and going on standby seems like the best way, or else if he gets any more cross, he might use up his battery before he wakes up Thomas. He doesn't speak to Thomas about his anger. He never does. Thomas has seen Oliver angry. He's witnessed him fighting at the Institute, but Oliver never explains how it feels. Thomas is always so calm. He never seems angry about anything. It's up to Oliver to see the world for what it is so Thomas can carry on being happy. Oliver takes on enough hatred and bitterness for the both of them.

They sit back on the floor. It's so nice to sit when resting, and it again makes Oliver angry the Institute never even thought to give them that simple luxury. Before Thomas puts him on standby, his last thoughts are of TRI, and his hatred for them.

Chapter 29

Harriet barely sleeps. Every time she checks her watch, a mere half hour has passed. The night ticks away at a snail's pace as she frets, keeping one ear open for Beatrice to come, telling her Oliver's arrived.

There's no sunset or sunrise this low down, no pulling back the curtains to get that daily dose of circadian rhythm-inducing sunlight. The streetlights get a bit brighter, some gulls squark, the noise outside gets louder. That's the only indication the world is waking. When it gets to six a.m., she gives up trying to get a moment's sleep and gets dressed.

Beatrice updates Harriet as if she's somehow failed. Her cheeks colour scarlet and she looks at the floor. 'The streetlights were on all night as well, but I didn't see them. I'm sorry.'

Harriet reaches for her and squeezes her arm. Beatrice doesn't flinch. That wall has stayed down. 'Thank you for looking out for them. Please, don't apologise.'

'I'll keep looking until I have to leave for school.'

Theo and Monty are up already. They appear as unrested as Harriet.

'I'll be in all day,' Monty says. 'I'll speak to the new tenants as well. Between us, we'll know as soon as they get here.'

'There's no need to keep staring out the window,' Theo says. 'Look what I've fixed up. It's a camera, and it feeds directly to all of our phones. We sync it to each device and you can watch all the time. Between us, we'll know as soon as they're there.' He takes Harriet's phone and shows her how to access it.

Harriet's chest inflates, a warmth tingling through her. 'Were you up all night fixing that?'

Theo shrugs, as if what he's done is nothing at all. 'Just a couple of hours.'

'I offered to help. But apparently I never listen when he talks about electrical stuff,' Monty says with a lilt of joviality.

She pulls them in for a group hug before she starts crying again, before her knees give way, before she bursts with love.

***

Harriet leaves for her shift at the Institute. A part of her thinks maybe Oliver and Thomas have returned there, that perhaps they just went for a little adventure and now they're back and charging. That optimistic part is so often dormant, squashed under layers of suffocating reality. But all she has right now is hope.

Josie and Monty being home gives her a bit of confidence, though she checks the camera on her phone constantly. With the busyness of the morning it's hard to tell if any people are

Oliver, so she watches to see if any teenagers are hanging around and seeming lost or confused. The boys knowing their way seems unreal, but Beatrice insists, and right now, there's nothing more they can do.

Harriet's in her disguise, though ignores her character's walk for the journey. It's before school rush hour sadly, as she'd love to linger and get a glimpse of the children in her class. She can't afford to take a speedy taxi everyday so takes the lift up to 6 to get a lower-level taxi. They're a tenth of the cost, generally grubby and take three times as long. There's talk of putting a monorail in one day, since the train lines at ground level have been a thing of the past for so long. The landfill claimed those tracks decades ago. A monorail would transport many people at once, be a lot cheaper, they say. But since the AutoTaxi companies make so much money, why would they want those replaced?

It takes her twenty minutes in line to get a taxi, and she'd love to breathe a sigh of relief when she's on her way, but the air is like stale smoke and mould. For the entire journey, she taps her hands on the seat, impatience gnawing at her.

Fresh dreads present themselves in a constant spiral. Her latest worry is the possibility of TRI finding the boys and punishing them. That has her biting her fingernails even more. What kind of punishments do they dish out for teens? She imagines electric shocks and whips, buckets of water and white noise. She should have asked Beatrice, but then Harriet can't imagine Beatrice ever being punished. If such a thing happens, Harriet will have to stop them somehow, and wishes she brought a can of mace with her.

When she arrives at TRI, she races through the security procedures, still energised with her last essence of hope, and dashes to where the boys sleep. The communal area is quiet and still, the boys all peaceful on standby. She circles the room and inspects each one, counting heads. They're all just as they were last night. No two extra boys. Oliver isn't here. It was unlikely, but her body sags as she can't help her disappointment.

She gazes at the boys while they sleep. They're all dressed in the same brown and beige trousers and T-shirts, mucky with dirt stains and dust. Their skin too, collects dust in the creases, unwashed for a long time by the looks of it. Gravel clings to their hair, knotted and clumped. It seems a shame to let them fall into such a state. A rinse, a brush, and they'd all be as good as new.

Despite their unkempt appearance, they look so tranquil when on standby, even standing, though she thinks it would be a lot nicer if they had a chair or a bed. The room is too small for much furniture, but a stool each, a blanket, even just a cushion for the floor would fit.

She grabs the rod and encircles the room, turning each teen back on. Their faces look confused for a moment when they see her, obviously expecting Josie or a staff member they know, but after a few seconds, they remember her.

She hangs around as the boys start to pace, listening to their general chatter. Many greet her with smiles, say hello with their teenage voices, so much deeper than Oliver's kid voice, the odd husk and squeak.

She moves back to the office and watches them for a few minutes as they start chatting and interacting. They don't have the playful energy of kids. Some are so much more confident than others, loud and assertive. Harriet can imagine what it's like when the girls are here, all coquettish smiles and bragging, if she remembers teenage boys correctly.

Some of the boys stay closer to the wall, small groups, quietly talking. In those boys, she sees more of her Oliver. Not timid, just happy with a closer group of friends, keeping themselves to themselves.

Harriet's ears prick up when Oliver's name is mentioned, and she steps to the office doorway to listen.

'Wonder where Oliver and Thomas have gone?'

'Bet they've gone out on work experience. Lucky them!'

'No, I don't think so. The staff always read a list of names out and they haven't done that.'

'Probably shut them away somewhere to watch more of that film,' one teen laughs. 'Since they were so upset by it.' He puts his fists up to his eyes and makes a mock crying gesture.

'Oh, that would be awful. I hope not.'

'Well, you're as much of a wimp as them.'

Harriet listens, holding her breath. Just hearing her son's name makes her want to cry. He was here. Her son has walked these floors. These are his classmates. They all know her little boy.

She waits until the staff arrive to start the teens' daily activities. It's a different man from the one last night. He walks with heavy footsteps, huffing, looking like the kind of man who has been in a hundred bar fights and won most of them. He greets Harriet with little more than a gruff sound. Harriet doesn't hang around for pleasantries. Oliver isn't here, so she needs to get going. She grabs her coat and makes for the door, then freezes as she hears a teen speak to the man. Her shoulders slump and she looks at the ground, hoping for some hole to open up that she can dive into and hide.

'What do you mean, where have they gone?' the gruff staff says.

'They weren't here last night,' the teen says.

The man steps up to Harriet, and she turns slowly to face him. He's so close it's threatening. He's at least a foot taller and twice her width. Oliver must find him terrifying. 'You didn't report any teen missing?'

'It . . . It was my first shift,' Harriet says. 'I thought it was normal. All the ones from the TV room were put to bed.'

The man groans and clenches his fists. 'That bloody Keith was on the daytime shift yesterday. He should have known.'

He marches through to the office and picks up the phone. Harriet listens to him screaming at whoever he talks to as he reports the missing teens. High alert, escapee protocol, lock the doors, alert the others . . .

Harriet doesn't hang around to await any instructions. She leaves, runs for the lift and checks her phone as soon as she is back in a taxi. Nothing from Josie or Monty, but she texts, telling them what she just heard.

Her heart races as fear, adrenaline, and panic all fight for their own share of her heartbeat. It's confirmed. The boys have escaped. They're not on work experience. They haven't returned to the Institute.

As terrified as she is for the boys, a warmth fills her and she smiles just as Josie did. The cheeky little runaways. The daredevils.

Her boy is coming home.

Chapter 30

Oliver was on standby for three hours before Thomas woke him and they switched. There's a clock on the wall and it ticks every second, which seemed annoying at first when Oliver was sitting all alone, but actually, it's quite a good thing to focus on. With Thomas asleep, Oliver stares into the darkness, imagining his mother's face, her joy when she sees him, her hug, and knowing for sure that she's okay and not with Anthony. Worries creep in and niggle at him when he thinks of Josie, too. Her absence is unexplained, and all manner of reasons flit through his mind. He looks at Thomas and thinks how awful it would be for him if something bad has happened to his mum. She needs to be okay. Both their mums do.

Shuffling footsteps and the toilet flushing ring out, and Oliver assumes it must be about the right time to get up. He wakes Thomas and puts the stick in his pocket with his charging cable.

Sylvia pulls back the plastic sheet that covers the doorway. 'Morning, boys. Oh, look at that. You're up already! Did you get some sleep?'

'Yes, thank you,' Oliver says.

'Well, come and join us for breakfast, and then I'll go call your mum.'

Oliver's smile widens, and he jumps to standing and he and Thomas go back to sit at the kitchen table. It's still lit with candles as it was the night before. Oliver's quite accustomed to life below ground but he recalls how much his mum loved the sunshine. She grew up below, so that must be why. He hopes he'll get to see the sun and sky again.

Sylvia piles up food in front of them as Oliver and Thomas both protest.

'No, thank you, Sylvia,' Oliver says. 'We ate so much before we left and want to save our appetites for when Mum arrives. I can't wait to eat with her.'

'Suit yourselves. But I'll leave it there anyway, just in case you fancy a nibble.'

Casper isn't with them, and Oliver assumes he must be in bed. He's never seen anyone as old as Casper, and imagines he must need to sleep a lot.

Sylvia finishes her breakfast and they don't talk much. As she finishes, she sips her hot drink, the steam fogging up her glasses. She takes them off to clean on her sleeve. Without them, her eyes look much smaller.

'I'll have to go to the health centre to call. You boys don't mind staying here in case Casper wakes up?'

'No, not at all.'

'I doubt he will. I leave him for a few hours here and there when I know he's tired. I'd call from here, but we've got no electricity. Down here, we're all on stricter rations at the moment. The damned lot up there taking more than their fair share. Some new tech in the workforces needs it all. These bots, I think, sapping all the charge and for what? So lazy above grounders can work less? Excuse my rant, but these things make me mad. They buy up all this stuff with no thought as to how it affects us down here.' She shakes her head.

Oliver tilts his head, blinks a few times, trying to figure out if Sylvia is mad with him, or bots, or the situation in general. He isn't sure. His hands clench and he sits on them, noting Thomas doing the same. His whole body is tense, his skin reddening. He locks eyes with Thomas for just a second, suddenly aware of how inhuman they are. He never considered how much their kind might be draining the system down here.

Casper appears in the doorway then, so pale he's almost transparent.

'Oh, Casper,' Sylvia says and palms her forehead. 'You're supposed to be in bed.'

Casper doesn't answer, doesn't react at all, but sits at the table with a vacant expression. He looks so frail Oliver can't imagine him going anywhere.

'We can still watch him,' Oliver says. 'I can't imagine he's going to start running around the tunnels.'

'You're such a dear.' Sylvia pushes herself up and puts her cup and plate in the sink. 'Give me an hour. You boys help yourselves to whatever you need. I'll go call Theo and I'm sure he can let your mum know. Now, where'd I put his number?' She rifles through some paperwork on the side. 'I knew his old house number by heart but haven't been able to learn his new one yet. And mobile numbers are so long . . . Got it! Right. Sit tight boys. I'll be back soon.'

Sylvia leaves to use the phone and when she's gone, Thomas says to Oliver, not that quietly since it's clear Casper is deaf, 'I think we should go. They don't like our kind here. If they knew we're bots, we wouldn't be welcome. What if other people find out?'

'I agree. But we can't leave Casper. We said we'd look after him.'

Thomas looks at Casper, inspecting him for a moment. 'He's not going anywhere. I mean, like you said, he's hardly going to start running around the tunnels.'

'Let's just wait a while. Then he's left alone for less time.'

Thomas makes a huffing sound like he's frustrated, leans back and folds his arms. 'Forty-five minutes? Then we've got fifteen minutes to get the hell out of here.'

Oliver nods and sits back, counting the seconds away in his head. The plates of food are still on the table, so he boxes it all up and puts it in the cool box. The temperature difference is minute, but it seems that's what they rely on for a fridge. Then he paces, Thomas too, and Casper stares out at nothing.

'We should write a note,' Oliver says, and they search around the place for a piece of paper and a pen.

'How long do you think it's been?' Oliver asks.

'I think about forty-five minutes.'

'Casper,' Oliver shouts at the old man. 'Actually, we're just going to go straight to Mum's. So, we've left a note for Sylvia.'

'What?'

'We're going to my mum's.' He points up, to gesture above ground. 'Thank you for having us.'

Casper shakes his head and resumes staring at nowhere. They sit for a moment and Casper's chin dips down, before some dribble escapes his mouth and he starts snoring.

'I guess he's asleep,' Thomas says.

'Okay. Let's go.'

Once out in the tunnels, they pick up their pace, filing in with the quickest walkers. It's so much busier than it was when they arrived, the crowds so dense they can't weave through. They're not keeping their heads down now. They're in a hurry, rushing to find a door and get above ground as quickly as possible. The people down here have so little. The lights are dim, there are no electrical devices, and guilt claws at Oliver's insides when he thinks he and the fellow bots are using up so much electricity there's not enough left for these people. He shakes that thought away. He didn't ask to be built. This, again, is TRI's doing. That's where the anger should be.

They walk for just a couple of minutes before Oliver spots a door. He grabs Thomas's wrist and they push through the people towards it. Once they're on the other side, they're immediately greeted with a staircase. They smile at each other, then start walking up to ground level, finding a lift to take them above.

Chapter 31

Harriet pulls off the wig and prosthetic in the taxi. She's supposed to use soapy water to loosen the glue, but she's too hot and uncomfortable to wait. Her sweat provides almost enough lubrication to make it come off without too much pain.

She checks the camera app, no sign of the boys there, then regrets checking *Get Level*. The hate is as vociferous as ever. There's an anti-bot march planned, a mob more like it judging by the state of some of those who say they'll be there. It'll start on what's left of 2, then make its way up. It'll be peaceful, the Flesh Fraternity says. We're gonna cut up some bots, say some others, the Human Front still spearheading that mentality. This is Harriet's main worry now. She trusts her boy, trusts his abilities and his determination to find her. Harriet can only hope the march fizzles out quickly enough, certainly before it gets to 5.

Why do journeys take forever when frantic? The taxi is slow, the lift down to 5 takes an age, and the short distance between the lift and her house stretches out for miles. When she makes it home, she falls through the front door expecting Oliver to be there already, but she's greeted by Monty wearing paint-covered overalls, taking up most of the width of the hallway fixing up a battered old wardrobe.

'No sign of him?' Harriet says, though there's no hope in her voice.

Monty shakes his head. 'No. Not yet. I've been checking the camera every minute.'

Harriet slumps against the wall. 'Yeah, me too.'

She goes through to the kitchen and Monty follows, putting the kettle on without saying a word. He presents her with a cup of tea as if it'll cure all ails. Harriet doubts there's a tea or pill strong enough to take her current anxieties away. She sips and enjoys the flavour, but it's impossible not to worry. At least Monty is home more at the moment. She couldn't handle Monty getting into trouble right now. One problem at a time.

The front door opens and they both jump to standing, then Harriet groans when Theo and Beatrice walk through.

'Well, that's a nice welcome,' Theo says.

'Sorry. I was hoping for Oliver. Why are you not at school?'

'Workshop is shut for now. Too many sharp things for the children to cause trouble with. And I told Dexter it's not safe for Beatrice. He went on about that not being important, but I brought her home anyway.'

Harriet sits back down. Tea is definitely not strong enough for today. 'It's that bad?'

'Carnage.'

'How's Josie?' Beatrice asks.

Harriet looks at Monty, guilt inching over her for not asking first. She didn't even check on Josie before she left this morning.

'Pretty bad today,' Monty says. 'She's deteriorated a lot from last night. She's not drinking water and can't swallow pills. I've checked on her every half hour or so. It's warm in there, but she's freezing. My sister was the same at this stage.'

Harriet rubs her hands over her face, her back rounding over.

'It's not going to be long,' Monty continues. 'The doctor finally called, though. She really needs some decent pain relief now. The doctor can give her patches, I think, so she doesn't have to swallow. Anyway, the doctor said they'll be here in an hour.'

Harriet rests her forehead in her hands and squeezes her eyes shut. Colours start to shimmer like an early migraine. 'If the boys are coming back for her, she's got to hold on.'

'That's what I said to her,' Monty says. 'But she's really gone downhill. You know how it is with this. Let's see what the doctor says.'

They all know, Josie included, how the final stages accelerate quickly. Harriet can't imagine the fear Josie is likely feeling. Though she's always seemed so strong and brave, not the sort of person to put up with an abusive husband like Harriet did, or abusive parents. If it were any other sickness, Josie would probably cure herself with grit and determination alone. Harriet gets up to go and be with her. Even the hardiest need friends sometimes.

Before she's left the kitchen, Theo's phone rings.

'Mum?' He stands and goes to walk out of the room to take the call.

Harriet smiles. She adores Theo's parents. They were always so kind to her when they were children. Then her heart skips several beats as she listens.

'They're with you?' Harriet gasps as Theo's voice breaks into a squeak. He faces Harriet and smiles the biggest grin and gives her a thumbs up. 'Oh, thank God. Thomas too?' He laughs. 'Nice to know they're behaving. Are they with you now? It would be nice to . . . Oh, okay. Thanks so much, Mum. We'll be around as soon as we can. We can't leave for an hour, just waiting for the doctor for a friend, but we'll see you soon. Thanks again.'

Harriet's eyes light up as Theo nods, then she squeals and hugs him. 'They're there? They're really there!'

'Yep. The clever lads. They walked all the way there from London. Mum was at the Health Centre since there's no electricity at their place. The boys are dad-sitting. But they're there, at their house.'

Harriet could cry happy tears. She hugs Theo again, then sits, checks the time and bounces her knees up and down.

'You go,' Theo says. 'I can wait for the doctor.'

'No. The boys can wait one more hour. I need to be here for Josie and I want to hear what the doctor says.'

One more hour. Her lungs inflate, and she's walking on air. Her clever little boy. One more hour and she can be on her way to see her son.

Harriet goes through to Josie's room. It's stifling, the wall of heat hitting her straight away, causing her to take a step back. The smell too. It smells like there's already a dead body in there. Then, when she enters the room, her breath catches as she looks around the place. What is normally a dusty workroom for Monty and Theo now looks beautiful. Coloured twinkling lights and decorations hang from the walls. Scented candles burning take the worst of the smell away when Harriet's inside, and a lamp makes sea patterns on the ceiling.

Monty is standing behind her and whispers, 'I did my best to add some colour. I don't think she can see much but I figured, the more colour the better.'

Harriet smiles and gives his hand a squeeze, and then mouths, *Thank you*. Beatrice is tending to Josie, tucking in her blankets and replacing her cold tea with a hot fresh one. Not that she'll drink it, but Harriet smiles at the gesture.

Harriet sits next to Josie, who stirs. Her eyes are hazy, deep in their sockets, her face yellowing.

'Hey,' Harriet says.

Josie squints and moans. 'Don't look at me like that.'

'Like what?'

'With pity.'

'It's not pity.'

'All right, disgust. You're all blurry, but I can tell. And I know I look awful.'

'You don't look awful,' Harriet says, her acting skills failing as Josie chokes a laugh in response.

Monty perches on the end of the bed. He reaches over and lifts some of Josie's hair. It's thin and patchy and mostly matted at the back from her time lying down. Even the twinkling lights fail to give the illusion of shine. 'Well, why don't we fix you up a bit? I can do something with this,' he says as he twists the ends. 'A stylish up-do, some colour, and glitter?'

Josie's cough turns into a laugh. 'Dying in glitter. Sounds perfect.'

***

The doctor arrives a few minutes late, and Harriet shows her through to Josie's room. Josie is lying in bed, but as promised, Monty styled her hair. Her coppery blonde hair is always brittle, but he's made it have a bit more shine with sprays and gels, added some twists and plaits and piled it on top of her head with a generous coating of glitter spray. He's also applied some makeup, most notably some bright pink lipstick, and some glitter varnish to her nails.

'Well,' the doctor says as her eyebrows shoot up, 'looks like you've made an effort.'

'If I'm going to die, might as well die with a bit of glamour,' Josie says. It's the brightest she's seemed all morning.

Harriet finds it hard to laugh with the rest of them. How Josie can be so light-hearted when she's in so much pain is beyond what Harriet can fathom. Harriet isn't sick, yet next to Josie she feels weak. Theo is standing with her, propping her up, being the support she needs whereas Josie is taking it all in her stride. Harriet sweats in the humid room, her heart races as she wishes she could run, wishes she didn't have to see this illness take another life. She's afraid enough for the both of them.

The doctor inspects the rash spreading across Josie's back, measures her temperature, then takes a vial of blood that she puts into a box machine. It whirrs and flashes some numbers on the screen. Josie shivers from the touch of the stethoscope as the doctor listens to her heart.

'Tell me, doc,' Josie says with a breathy voice, still with a smile on her face. 'I know I've not got long. How long do you think?'

The doctor makes some notes of her measurements, then looks Josie directly in the eyes. 'I'm sorry. Just a few days most likely. Here—' She takes out some pills and patches from her bag. 'The morphine patches will make these days a bit more bearable.'

'And how much do I have to take if it all gets too much?'

Harriet gasps and Theo grabs her hand.

The doctor looks down a moment, then up again. 'There's one big pill in the packet. That's the legal way, when you're ready.'

Josie reaches to take the packet, her skeletal hand grasping at air and the doctor helps her, putting the packet in her hand. She holds Josie's finger and traces it over the packet, letting her feel where the big pill is. 'You can't have help taking it. If that's what you decide, you must take it yourself. You can dissolve it in a drink to make it easier.'

Josie nods, then sniffs. 'Got it.'

They thank the doctor, and Theo shows her out.

Harriet kneels next to Josie's bed and takes her hands. They're like icicles. 'You've got to hang on till the boys get here.'

'I know. I'm not taking that pill before they get here.' She takes a laboured breath between each word. 'But I'm not letting Thomas watch me die slowly. I should have been honest with him when I said goodbye. I just couldn't do it. So I'll hang on now, as long as I can. I'll see my boy, then that's me done.'

Harriet releases Josie's hands to wipe her eye.

'Don't you get all sad now. I can hear you snivelling. There's no point trying to fight this.'

Harriet nods and rubs Josie's arm. 'I know. I know.'

From the hall, Theo's phone rings again. The tone of his voice makes Harriet sit upright. 'Mum? What! When?'

Harriet dashes to the door, her wide eyes staring at Theo. He locks eyes with her, and his face tells her everything she doesn't want to hear.

'Okay. Shit. Okay,' he continues, shaking his head. 'No, we've not left yet. We were just about to. That's a shame.' He closes his eyes and rubs his temple. 'Don't worry, Mum, it's not your fault. Give Dad a hug from me. Love you. I'll come visit soon.'

Harriet can't draw breath, her body in limbo as she waits for Theo to confirm what she fears.

'They've gone,' he says. 'When she got back home, they'd left a note. Said they were coming straight to see you and couldn't wait.'

Harriet whimpers, her hands go to her chest. 'Why would they leave? They knew we were coming.'

'The amount Mum was going on about electricity rations because of the "damned new tech above" might have had something to do with it,' he says, making air quotes.

Josie groans and fidgets.

Harriet walks to her and adjusts her pillow. 'Sorry, Josie. You're going to have to avoid that big pill for a while yet.'

She nods and Harriet opens a packet of morphine patches for her.

'He's being sensible,' Theo says. 'This proves he knows there are some who don't like bots. He's avoiding trouble, and he's going to places he knows. He'll find his way to our old place. It's just a couple of minutes away from here. And it's not like we've got anything else to do today. We go there and wait.'

Wait. Harriet is expected to sit still while her boy is alone in the world, a world he hasn't stepped foot in for years. She helps Josie stick the patch to her torso and tries not to gasp when she sees her ribs jutting out of her ghostlike flesh. The boys need to get here soon or they'll miss their chance.

'I see that look in your eye,' Theo says. 'You heard what Beatrice says. She remembers every place she visited when she was a kid. These bots, they have homing instincts like no other. They found my parents' place, walked all the way there! They know where you are. You just have to sit and wait.'

'There's this march, though.' Harriet loads up her phone and shows him an article. 'You've heard about that? It's starting on

2 then moving up. They're marching against the electricity use. It's all those bloody Devil fanatics and unions. The boys are going to have to come through that.'

Josie sniggers, and Harriet assumes she's high. 'Don't you worry about the boys,' she says, still chuckling. 'Your boy Oliver, he can handle himself. And he'll be looking after my Thomas. Those boys are the best there is.'

Oliver, being able to handle himself? Harriet shakes her head and leaves Josie to rest. She must be high on morphine already.

'It's not on 5 yet,' Theo says in a hushed voice behind Josie's door. 'It probably won't be for a while. They've only got to get a lift. Let's go wait at the café by our old place. Monty and Beatrice can wait here with Josie. The boys will get the lift straight to five and be here before you know it.'

Harriet wishes she shares Theo's optimism, yet still she joins him, dashing to the café as if she's drunk three coffees already, telling herself again and again, her boy will be there soon.

Chapter 32

'What level?' Thomas asks Oliver when they're at the lift, his fingers hovering over the control panel.

'4.'

'You think your mum is still at the refuge? Isn't that just for women with children?'

Oliver shrugs. 'That's where she lived when I last saw her. And Sylvia never said she lived anywhere else.'

'We should have asked. Or at least asked where Theo's new place is.'

'How bad would that look?'

They agree on 4, and the lift arrives in seconds. They step out onto a street that feels so overwhelmingly familiar, Oliver could run straight to the park and heave himself up the climbing frame. He remembers the one for bigger kids, the one he was never able to go on, though he has little desire to now. He remembers Delilah, helping her up each rung. She wasn't very brave with such things but keen to learn. He was meant to look after her. An ache spreads across his chest and his muscles tighten every time he thinks of her. He failed to keep her safe. He can't fail anyone else.

He knows the way to the refuge, as does Thomas. They walk there in silence, almost on autopilot. Bounty hunter posters adorn every notice board and Oliver worries TRI will put out posters for them. None of the posters have their picture on . . . at the moment.

They get a few stares from other pedestrians and, looking at each other, they realise why. They're a mess. What fits in below ground does not up here. They don't need to look smart like people do on top levels, but less grubby would be best. People give them a wide berth, probably assuming they're covered in the below-ground toxins. There's nothing they can do about their appearance, so they ignore all the stares and keep walking.

It's less than twenty minutes to the refuge and they reach the big metal gates and buzz the intercom. Oliver recognises Rosa straight away. The kind lady who originally showed them around. She looks exactly as he remembers. A wizened face and kind eyes.

'Rosa!' Oliver shouts and waves.

Rosa's brow furrows and she approaches the gates, but doesn't open it. 'Can I help you?'

'My mum, do you remember her? Harriet Chapel. Is she here?'

'I can't give out information about residents.'

'But I'm her son, Oliver. Remember me?'

She looks him up and down briefly and Oliver really wishes he looked tidier. Rosa shakes her head. 'I'm sorry, no.'

Oliver appears much more grown up than he did back then. His voice is deeper, he's twice the size he was then, and his messy state doesn't help. 'It was years ago. I lived here with my mum. Please, I'm trying to find her.'

'Or my mum, Josie,' Thomas says. 'I lived here with her for a short time.'

Rosa shakes her head again. She's frowning instead of smiling. 'I'm sorry, young men, but I can't help you. If you hang around the gates, I'll be forced to call the police. Now, on your way.' She walks away.

'No!' Oliver's protest is little more than an exhale as Rosa walks back inside.

Oliver and Thomas walk back to the park and sit on swings, not saying anything, just rocking back and forth for a while. The little kids' climbing frame looks so tiny now. Swings aren't as exciting as they used to be.

'Your mum delivered letters to mine,' Oliver said. 'I never asked where she was. She never told me.'

'Hey, don't blame my mum!'

'I'm not. I didn't mean that. I—' He huffs. 'I don't know what to do.'

'She must be at your uncle's.'

'But you heard Sylvia. He's moved to a new place.'

They kick against the floor, setting the swings in motion. Other people are dressed up snuggly in scarfs and hats. Oliver and Thomas only have their usual grubby beige tops and trousers and jackets, with flimsy cloth shoes that do nothing to protect their feet. The crashing rubbish sound is constant. Oliver had forgotten how annoying it is. He supposes he was used to it before and so hardly noticed.

'You know where she used to work?' Thomas asks. 'We could go there.'

'She got chased out of there on her last day. I guess she might be in another one of those bars. I think we should just wait here. Sylvia would have called her. She'll know we're looking for her from our note. So, she'll assume we came here.'

Thomas nods. 'Okay. Agreed.'

They move to a bench to make way for some rowdy kids. Oliver is slightly reassured that at least the world hasn't fallen down. Everything appears much the same as it did before they went to the Institute. No imploding land or carnage, no people being crushed and injured. A little boy falls off the climbing frame and scrapes his knee and as much as Oliver is upset for the child, it's not a disaster on the scale of Oliver's nightmares or that awful film.

They sit for hours on that bench, or for what seems like hours, with nothing to do except wait and watch people go about their day. Oliver listens to people chat, catching snippets of conversation. And the hot news on everyone's lips is to do with bots.

Two men stand just next to their bench. They have coffees in one hand and sandwiches in the other, talking between bites still with their mouths full.

'If I found one, I'd cut it up. Rights for bots? The world has gone mad.'

'Shut it, Pete. It's not human rights. But it's too weird they look just like us. I find it creepy.'

'You know what isn't creepy? The things you can do to them.'

'Gross.'

'Not gross. They're not people. And they're programmed to just do it.'

'Really?'

'That's what I heard. Whatever your wildest sick fantasy you don't ever want to ask your wife to do. You visit a MechaniSlut and they make it happen.'

Oliver keeps his head forward but moves his eyes to the side. The man's Adam's apple bobs up and down.

'Really?' one of the men says. 'Like, anything?'

'Yep. There's this bar down on 3 that has them. Exclusive, apparently. Some early test of those little teen sluts out on work experience. Ravi at work was telling me all about it. Not all about what he did, and I didn't want to know. But I've been thinking about it ever since.'

'Gosh. Yeah, I can imagine.'

'Fancy popping the cherry of a MechaniTeen? A real virgin slut?'

Oliver gasps, disguising it as a cough. The men don't seem to realise. They keep talking.

'Fuck.' One man looks at his watch. 'I guess it's Friday. We can take the rest of the afternoon off.'

'That's what I'm talking about!'

Oliver's hands make tight fists. He doesn't want to imagine what sort of things they're going to be making the teen girls do. He and Thomas lock eyes, a silent conversation passing between them.

Thomas whispers, 'Evie.'

Oliver nods. 'Let's go get her.'

Chapter 33

Harriet can't just sit still and wait. What sort of mother can be that passive while her son is lost? She sits in the café, drinks too much coffee, and picks at the slice of cake Theo put in front of her. She's no appetite for anything but her fingernails as she paces.

They move to the park where her restlessness stands out less. It's freezing, rain spilling over the walkway fences and adding to the constant noise. It smells of damp tarmac, which irritates her more. She should go back and spend time with Josie, but she's in no state for calm company. Josie needs rest.

On every wall, Harriet looks for bounty hunter posters with her son's picture. Would TRI use such methods to track them down? She can't be sure. She checks her phone. That march has moved onto 3. The advertising billboards flash up with news headlines intermittently. Footage shows hundreds, maybe thousands, of people wielding banners, the glint of knives in their hands. Not the sort of march that's going to fizzle out any time soon. She watches a video, and chills cascade up her arms. The chants, impassioned with venom, blare from the speaker. Harriet can feel the atmosphere from the video, the air, thick and brutal, a suffocating tension. 'Bots don't bleed,' is repeated over and over, knives waving in the air.

From the arms, cuts dribble blood to prove they're human, to prove they don't need to be cut more.

Harriet's throat tightens, a constricting pain shooting through her head. She closes her eyes, rubs her temples, and concentrates on simply breathing.

Theo says nothing. No words of reassurance, as there's nothing he can say. The boys need to hurry up. If they get the lift straight to 5 soon, they should miss the trouble.

Harriet gives up pacing and sits on a bench. How many times has she sat on a bench at the edge of the park, watching Oliver play? The flowers in the beds here are artificial and mostly trodden down to stumps. There's barely an insect to be seen. Oliver loves all the bugs and the birds but right now, there's no essence of him here at all. There are children on the climbing frame, swinging from the top rung like he used to. She opts to stand and pace some more.

'Just sit still,' Theo says. 'Or go home. I'll wait here. You go and be with Josie.'

She scowls at him. It's an unkind look, but he'll get the gist that way. 'I have to find him, Theo. I can't just wait.' She sits again, huffs, and then idles some more time away by scrolling *Get Level* again. 'Shit. The march. It's about to start on 4.'

'But we're on 5.'

Harriet groans and palms her forehead. How could she have been so stupid? 'I'm an idiot!' She thumps herself in the temple, which does nothing to help her looming headache but is the punishment she deserves. 'The refuge! The damned refuge! I'll bet that's where they've gone.'

'Oh. You might be right, but there's no way to be sure.' Theo leaps to his feet. 'You wait here and I'll go to the refuge. You might get recognised by the bot-haters. There's no way you can be seen at that march.'

'I can't sit here any longer! Give me your hat. I'll wear that. *You* wait here.'

Theo takes off his hat and Harriet snatches it.

'I know it's pointless trying to argue with you,' Theo says, 'but for the record, I'm saying I should go and you should stay here.'

Harriet gives him a peck on the cheek. 'You're right about one thing. It's pointless to argue.' She smooths her hair back, not that it needs it. It's still pancake flat from the wig. 'You've got battery on your phone? Call me the second you hear anything.'

She's running towards the lift before he replies.

If there's a march on 4, she needs to be there for Oliver; they may even let her in at the refuge if it's riotous, just to wait it out. They'd be safe behind the refuge fence.

When she gets down to 4, the march greets her immediately, the sheer scale of it taking her breath away. The videos on the news and socials didn't capture it entirely. The walkway vibrates with the footsteps of the thousands—and there are definitely thousands now—holding banners and signs, 'Humans first,' is chanted, along with, 'Bots don't bleed!'

In hands are blades, people with wounds up their arms, only a small trickle of blood from each, but together it leaves a coppery smell in the air.

Every face in the march wears a grimace, anger burning in their eyes. The streetlights flicker and dim and every time the electricity reveals itself to be subpar, knuckles glow white from tightening fists. The trash still smashes from beyond the fence, a constant percussion that creates a marching beat. Clenched fists punch hands, chants shout through gritted teeth. The air is the hottest Harriet's known it on 4.

On the advertising billboard, a Divine Flesh Fraternity advert comes on—they're actually using Divine in their title now. Harriet wants to retch at their piety. Images fill the billboard screen of some apocalyptic scene as a speaker shouts their slogans, insisting that bots will cause the end of days and are the Devil. Then, filling the screen is her picture, Harriet's face, calling her a traitor of the people. Harriet swallows, pulls her scarf up and hat down, glances right then left, and lifts her shoulders. Perhaps Theo was right.

No. She shakes that thought away. Oliver is her son. She should be there to greet him. She's not afraid of a few fanatics. Her cowering days are over.

She lifts her sleeve and keeps her scar on show, the one she got when Anthony broke her arm. Such injuries denote her as human now. To suffer is to be human, to know pain. Her blood runs cold at the thought of him. That man is regarded as human when he's the most inhumane person she has met.

He's a voice for this movement of hate. How has the world come to this? Oliver is more deserving of this world than a hundred Anthonys.

The refuge looks bigger than when she was last here. The fence reaches the ceiling from the walkway above, and has been reinforced with thicker posts and barbed wire woven between. When she makes it to the refuge, she's greeted by her old friend, Rosa.

Rosa is at the fence, watching the commotion outside, when Harriet waves.

'Harriet?'

Harriet smiles and stands as close as she can to the fence. Rosa's face is as kind as it was years ago. It's nice to see that she hasn't changed. 'You remember me.'

'As soon as I saw you on TV last week, I remembered you. How are you?'

'I'm fine, but looking for my son, Oliver. Have you seen him?'

'He was here earlier. I'm sorry, I didn't recognise him and I can't divulge information. He went over there—' she points to the park '—with the other boy he was with. Red hair, same age. Sorry, I can't recall his name.'

Harriet's stomach sinks. She tries to keep smiling and to disguise her drooping shoulders. 'Okay. Thanks Rosa. I under-stand.'

'If you both need somewhere to hide out, with all that's going on, you come straight back to me. It's not safe out there for you . . . or him.'

Harriet's eyebrows rise. 'You know?'

'I always knew. A mother is a mother. You're all welcome here if you're in trouble and your children. I'm not here to judge.'

Harriet reaches through the fence bars to shake Rosa's hand. 'Thank you, Rosa. So much.'

Harriet turns around and faces the park, breathing in lungfuls of air. He was there, not that long ago. Beatrice is right about his homing instincts. Her clever boy. Her skin tingles, as if the air around carries his essence. She's so close to him.

Harriet dashes away and towards the park. She shouts Oliver's name but there's no sign of him. The park is empty, the march putting off other families from playing outside. She sits on the bench she always used to when Oliver would play on the climbing frame. He always wanted to be able to climb the bigger one. Perhaps he did just now. She walks up to it and runs her hands over the bars, searching for smudges of his fingerprints, a lost hair. They're cold, as if no one has touched them for hours.

She sniffs and wipes her eye on her cuff. There's no point staying here. The final place he'll try now is their old place. The only option left is for Harriet to make her way back and wait like Theo said, hoping he dodges the march. But Oliver has a head start. He could be there any minute.

It's impossible not to worry. She'll worry about her boy forever, like it's hardwired into her body. But she'll worry a hell of a lot less when he's in her arms again.

She's going to have to get through the protest undetected. She leaves the park, keeping her head down and skirting round the crowds. This crowd seems to have no support for Anthony's business model either, but they're even more extreme. It makes her squirm to think that such reasoning puts Anthony as some sort of moderate. This is a crowd of the Flesh Fraternity's people, claiming bots are the Devil and Oliver has no place in this world. There's pain in so many of the chants, from people blindsided by their own poverty. If Harriet still lived below or even lower than she does now, if she'd never met Oliver, would she think the same? If she worked in a job that suffered without electricity, she probably would. If she'd never lived on the top levels and experienced the opulence, the waste, she might well blame the bots. She always aspired to live so high. She never knew until she got there those levels were only built by reducing the lower levels to caves.

So many below ground idolise the lifestyle of the top levels, aspire to be that way, to have the means to waste so much, but there's nothing glamorous or worthwhile about such a lifestyle. There's no compassion in greed.

As Harriet skirts the crowd, she mentally drafts post after post she can put out on *Get Level* to try to make people see sense, to show who the real criminals are, to show that it's not her son.

She walks, thankfully undetected, trying unsuccessfully to shut her ears to the angry slogans and upset, calling her son a product of the Devil. The Modern Testament is going to be a fun read by the sounds of it. All fabricated horror stories and apocalyptic prophecies. She's read worse novels. She's tired, her movements sluggish, laced with lassitude, a leftover exhaustion from her worries and sleepless nights. She should eat some food if she's going to keep her strength up. There's a café not too far away, and she plans to grab a sandwich there.

She takes another few steps around the edge of the crowd, then stops, holding her breath as the ground shakes.

What the—?

A rumble, distant, joins the shakes, a parting of the crowd as some scramble. Harriet holds her ground, waits for it to calm and for the screams that fill the air to settle.

Then, silence. Everyone is still. Looks are exchanged and people reach for their phones. There's one word on everyone's lips: bomb.

Chapter 34

Oliver and Thomas are in a lift going down to 3. Oliver knows this end of town. His mum used to work around here and it's the route they used to take. She'd wear fancy costumes and deal with lecherous men all night, but she never complained. Oliver could tell on their way back she was tired; she'd walk slower, like her feet hurt. But they'd chat all the way home and sometimes even stop at the park for a few minutes while it was quiet. There are plug-in points near his mum's old work, he remembers, though that's not too urgent right now as his battery is still okay, still about twenty per cent full.

The walkway vibrates with footsteps of so many people. It's not immediately busy around them, but far away there's a dense crowd all walking together. It's like a constant rumble. Carrying in the air are thousands of voices that sound angry and un-friendly, their words making Oliver tense and shiver. 'Humans first,' the voices are saying. And, 'Bots don't bleed.'

Oliver's never been upset about not bleeding, but now it's all he wants to be able to do.

'What's going on?' Thomas asks. 'What do they mean by that?'

'Probably trouble. Come on. Let's keep following.'

As they approach the strip of bars, they lose sight of the men they're following for a moment. Those men blend in with so many here. It's mid-afternoon, he thinks, Friday. Like those men said, people are leaving work early and heading straight for their weekend shenanigans. The lights on the strip glow all sorts of colours, with sculptured lights made into shapes of women and breasts. Oliver and Thomas both blush. Oliver never noticed it before. He was a kid; he didn't understand what these things were. Now he knows and wants even more to rescue Evie.

They stop by a billboard and wait a while. The billboard is as bright as anything. All those people protesting about the electricity Oliver and Thomas use, but there is always enough electricity for advertising and late-night bars. He shakes his head. Questioning such priorities is a waste of time coming from him right now.

They stand close together, feeling too young and too naive to be in such a place. In the Institute, Oliver never felt so small. He's smaller than George and some of the teens, but here, he feels like a kid again, as unworldly as one anyway.

'This place is horrible, Oliver.'

'I know. But it's our best chance of finding Evie. That man said teens are on exclusive trial at a bar. We just need to find it.'

Finding a seedy bar among other seedy bars is tricky. Oliver glances up, then diverts his gaze again when he sees sites of debauchery and images of women in positions that make him blush even more. He looks down, shoves his hands in his pockets, and rolls his shoulders forward. They just need to listen for a while.

'I'm not hearing Evie's name,' Thomas says. 'And nothing about bots. What's a slut?'

Oliver shrugs. 'I don't know. Let's take a slow walk in front of the bars.'

The strip spills out onto the walkway. Here, people don't seem to throw their litter over the fences. They leave it strewn about the street and Oliver and Thomas stumble across it as they walk, splashing in puddles of liquids. From the bars, lights flash, all sorts of colours, and music is loud enough to mostly drown out that crowd of people and their angry voices.

At the doorways, bar workers shout to get attention.

'Private booths for those who want it!'

'Buy one get one free on beer!'

'All your fantasies can come true in this place. You name it, we've got it!'

There's one bar with no one shouting outside. The lights in there don't flash, the music seems a bit calmer. Oliver and Thomas slow their pace when they approach that one and spot those two men going inside. Oliver freezes and grabs Thomas's wrist as they stop to watch them go in. A few people walking about bump into them and Oliver apologises.

'You little sicko,' one man says, but wears a grin. 'Fancy a bit of bot action, do you? Well, I guess below-ground lads need to take what they can get.' He laughs and walks away.

Oliver's eyes widen, and he turns to look at Thomas. The quiet bar. That must be it.

They take a step closer to the doorway. The neon lights on the outside of this one are much softer, and there's the smallest sign in the bottom corner of the door that reads: *MechaniSluts, exclusive here!*

'That must be what a slut is,' Thomas says. 'What's our plan? We haven't got any money and I definitely don't want anything they're charging for.'

'We'll just go in, have a look around, see if we can see Evie, and go. Then, when we find our mums, we can tell them and maybe they can do something.'

'Okay. That sounds sensible.'

That crowd is now much closer. The angry voices are as loud as the pumping music from the other bars. Being inside seems safer than waiting for whatever trouble that crowd is causing. They look over each shoulder before going in.

The air instantly is hazy, pinkish lighting, frilly lampshades and gaudy carpet. The music is soft and over the top of it, Oliver can hear groaning, men and women, then men shouting, banging, curse words and insults. It reminds him of Anthony. Is this what men do to sluts? They beat them up?

'Welcome, gentlemen,' a woman says as she approaches. She's old and wears a ton of makeup that collects in her wrinkles. On her body she wears a gown that shows the top of her breasts. Her hair is so still Oliver wonders if it's glued in place. 'My name is

Candy. What can we do for you? Are you looking for anything in particular?'

Down the hallway, Oliver sees the back of the men walking away with some girls. One of them has the same bright blonde hair as Mia.

'Erm,' Oliver wants to lift his head and appear brave and confident, but he cowers.

'Now, now. Don't be shy. There's nothing we haven't heard in here. You can say whatever you want.' She clasps her hands in front of her. She has the longest fingernails Oliver's ever seen, painted pink with a large ring on each finger.

Oliver chews on the inside of his cheek a moment. He looks to Thomas, whose lips are pressed together so firmly it's like he never plans on speaking again. 'We want a slut,' Oliver eventually says.

Candy smiles. Her teeth are too white for her age, they look fake. 'Well, all we have here is sluts.'

'I want a nice one,' Oliver says, then describes Evie. 'Curly long brown hair. Young. Pretty.'

Candy nods along with his description. 'I have a couple that match your requirements. Wait here. Have a seat, why don't you, and I'll bring some out. You can choose whichever you like.' She walks behind them and takes out a heavy key. 'Gotta lock the door, I'm afraid. There're haters out there. They'll be walking past soon.' She takes the MechaniSlut sign from the window and pulls some curtains across. 'You boys got here just in time.' She smiles at them again and walks out back.

Along the wall there's a pink velvety sofa and they both sit. Just yesterday Oliver thought sitting was nice. Now he's rigid and uncomfortable. He wonders if he's ever felt more awkward.

It's only a few moments later when Candy arrives back, four girls following her. They're wearing almost nothing. Oliver's jaw drops. His eyes bulge so much he can only look at them briefly, then straight at the floor again. Thomas is much the same and they shuffle a bit closer together.

'These are some of our most beautiful sluts,' Candy says. 'They have all been tried and tested, but can perform whatever you want. Just tell them what you want them to do and they will please. Guaranteed.'

Oliver braces, then looks again, and freezes when his eyes land on Evie. She's shaking, as if it's zero degrees in the room, wearing a see-through dress. Oliver can see her nipples. She has some blue-black patches around her neck, the kind of bruises like Oliver's mum used to get from Anthony.

The teen standing next to her is fidgeting and groaning. 'I really want to fuck you right now. I need it. Now. I'll beg,' she says. She's touching herself in that private place, her eyes keep rolling back and she's panting.

'That's Monique,' Candy says. 'One of a kind. A prototype actually. She is absolutely gagging for it twenty-four seven. She won't stop.'

'I need your dick in me now. I need it so bad.'

Oliver shakes his head. 'I don't think that's for me.'

Candy faces Monique. 'Go raid the toy box again.'

Monique runs away, her groans getting louder a moment later. 'Quietly, Monique!' Candy shouts, before facing Oliver and Thomas again. 'She's a live wire, that one. Not everyone's cup of tea, but some adore her. Now, who do we have left?'

'That one,' Oliver points at Evie. He can't tell if Evie is relieved or mortified. Surely, she doesn't think they're here for . . . that.

'Ah, the timid one. You sure? You seem like you could do with a bit of . . . guidance.'

Oliver swallows. 'I like her hair.'

'Fine. Evie, sweetie, take this young man to suite A.' She faces Oliver again and looks him up and down with raised eyebrows. 'It's payment up front. You paying card or cash?'

'Er . . .' Oliver stiffens. His hands go to his pockets to stall; he knows there's no money there. He searches his mind for an excuse. They've found Evie, which is all he was hoping for, but the door is locked. They can't just run away. That crowd is now really close. The whole building vibrates with their footsteps. He doesn't want to go outside.

Candy's eyebrows are still raised, she's pulling her chin in, she's not smiling anymore. Time passes slowly, stretching out in all directions as Candy's face morphs from welcoming to impatience.

The ground shakes. A low noise, a boom, a rush of air. A blast comes from outside, the windows rattling, a tinny noise like wind chimes before they bulge and burst out, shards of glass scattering like dust.

Oliver grabs Thomas and jumps onto Evie, pulling her beneath him. There's screaming coming from everywhere, louder than the smashing glass and brick.

And then it all goes silent.

Chapter 35

Harriet holds her breath as the ground steadies. Billboards all stop their usual trawl of adverts, the screens going blank for a moment and the streetlights flickering. Across the crowds of people there's a stagnation in movement, the air tense, static like before a storm, some collective apprehension in that moment before confirmation. The streetlights return to normal, the billboards flash back on, all now reporting the same news headline: *Explosions on 3.*

Harriet checks her phone for news. With the busier than usual walkways and everyone wanting to know the latest, the signal is dire, the news site taking an age to load but when it does, the headline confirms there were two explosions on 3. Not on Oliver's route home. She releases a breath, invites a little relief as she doesn't know anyone on 3. It's a selfish reaction, but she doesn't need to take on anyone else's heartache in addition to hers. She reads on as she progresses just inches through the dense crowd. The news story merely quenches her curiosity now rather than causing any worry. One bomb went off at a brothel. Poor souls. How cruel can some people be? Death toll unknown.

The headline updates: *Brothel has the exclusive first stock of MechaniTeens. Human Front claims responsibility.*

Harriet stifles her gasp. All around her people are reading the same article and cheer when the update was announced. All around her people are pleased about the possibility of death.

In her mind she sees limbs, blood, blue-black fluid of bots seeping into the walkway. She sees Joshua and Delilah. She mustn't give away her upset. She must continue to blend in, to be at one with this crowd, to act like she's sharing in their joy. The only joy she feels is the brothel wasn't on Oliver's way home. He'll be on his way up to 5.

She's moved through the crowd only a few metres since the announcement. She pushes a little more, taking advantage of a small gap opening up ahead. An incident like this makes the lifts busier, like an explosion is a damned tourist attraction. They all want to know what it looks like when a MechaniTeen burns.

She pauses a moment and thinks again of Delilah. Delilah with the different programming. If she'd lived, she might have been at that very brothel. There are no girls at the Institute at the moment, they're all on work experience. Oliver will know some of those victims. Her son is going to know loss at a young age like she did. She hopes he doesn't see that headline, though if he's on his way anywhere, he will. Billboards are everywhere.

He'll see that some of his classmates could be hurt.

Her palm goes to her chest, her lungs skipping a breath. Oliver, the hero, the protector. In his letter he mentioned a girl. What was her name again? Evie. He'd want to find her; he'd want to make sure she's safe. Harriet's gut knows. He'd save his friends before he'd try to find his mother.

She side steps through the crowd, less polite now, forgetting she's in character. She needs to get to the lift before it's overrun. There's the glint of knives, people bleeding, willingly, their hips on show. She rolls up her sleeve, exposing the scar from when Anthony broke her arm. There's no point yanking her trousers down to show her hip. She's too old; no one will think she's a bot. It's the pretty girls she's worried about, the Beatrices of this world. Exposed, bleeding, fair game according to this crowd. It's okay to attack a pretty girl. She looks like a bot.

And what of the boys? What of her Oliver? Assaulted too or attacked some other way?

Oliver is too sweet for this world.

From somewhere behind, her name is shouted with scorn and contempt. She pulls her collar up, ducks her head low. They're shouting about her TV performance and not that they'd spotted her. There are hundreds of people here. This isn't her stage. Not now.

Oliver has been all alone in the world for so long. He's made it this far. He's just a few levels away from safety. She checks her phone, the camera app, then messages Theo and Monty again to tell them what she suspects. Monty replies, Josie is still hanging in there. She needs to keep going. It's been so many hours since Oliver left the Institute, since he left Theo's parents' . . .

Harriet's breath catches. She freezes a moment.

Hours. She counts on her fingers. Literally hours. No way would he have charged while below ground. He'll be running on empty.

Goosebumps break out across her arms, her bones turning to ice. Her boy, a flat battery, with a riot so close.

He's a clever boy, she reminds herself for the millionth time. He's sensible. Her rational mind kicks in. If she's right and he's on 3, then he'll know the bar where she used to work, and the eBike charging point behind it. That makes her certain he'll be on 3. To find his friend, to charge his battery. She can picture him at the charging point, sleeping soundly as a kid. If he's gone anywhere, it'll be there.

The mob are getting noisier, those chants shouting louder. More people or more impassioned, it's hard to tell. She can't see past it, needs to get free of it. She's on the edge, but they're spreading out and within seconds, she's swallowed up and is in the middle, engulfed by it. She tries to escape, to politely weave her way around the throng, but then there's her name again, and her stomach drops.

'Harriet Chapel! The human hater! Bot sympathiser!'

Now she regrets ever saying anything. Her appearance on TV was meant to help Oliver, not stop her getting to him. She should have put up with the itching and kept her Alyssa disguise on. She grits her teeth and curses. Why get recognised now? What shitty luck.

There's a grab at her arm, fingers digging in and she shakes them free, pushing into one person and another. There's no time to apologise or look back. She barges her way through, keeping her head down, the sound of her name being called following her. She makes it to the front of the crowd, echoes of her name from behind. If she turns around, they'll know it's her. All she can do is ignore them and keep going. She runs up to the lift.

It's shut. *Dammit!*

The notice above the lift plays a message, and Harriet stifles a groan. No lifts going to 3. All are being used to take people away from 3.

Away from 3. Harriet's cold fingers clutch her chest as she curls forwards. Her son is on 3. She's sure of it. Otherwise, he'd be here by now. Her little boy always protects others, worries about everyone. He's so close, yet she can't get to him. And the lifts are delivering everyone back here. If her son gets on the lift, there's no way he'll avoid the trouble. He'll be in the heart of a riot.

Chapter 36

Oliver coughs, as if the dust is in his lungs. He knows he doesn't have lungs, but how can anyone be swimming in dust and not cough? Everything is grey. However much he blinks, the colour doesn't change. He wipes his face, shakes his head to get the worst of the debris off. When his vision clears, he sees nothing but rubble.

'Thomas? Evie?'

He checks himself: arms, legs, fingers, toes. He's all present. As he sits upright, more debris falls off him. It's so quiet now whereas before it was so noisy. His chest constricts, a buzz of panic shooting through him. It looks like the movie. The one of the landslide and buried children.

'Thomas! Evie!' He calls again, louder now.

There's some movement and whimpers, just out of reach. Some of the rubble moves, a flash of dusty red hair underneath. Thomas! Oliver rolls onto his front and crawls on all fours, not trusting his feet just yet. His hand reaches for Thomas and his grip is firm, assertive, alive. It's the best feeling Oliver's had in ages. As good as a hug.

With his other hand he starts to clear broken bricks and pieces of plasterboard, revealing more and more of Thomas. When he can sit up, he inspects himself just the same.

'Are you hurt?' Oliver asks.

'I don't think so. Where's Evie?'

A hand reaches through the debris, grasping at the air, Evie's timid voice calling, 'I'm here.'

Oliver takes her hand. How long has he been missing her hand? He doesn't let go but uses his free one to clear some rubble, Thomas helping. Then, they freeze for a moment.

'You hear that?' Thomas asks.

Oliver puts his finger to his lips, straining to listen.

A whisper on the wind, far away but getting closer. The chanting, like before. Only worse, much worse. *Bomb the bots!*

That crowd did this. And that crowd means to finish the job.

The three of them lock eye contact for a fraction of a second, then start the scramble in the debris and lift Evie clear of the mess.

'Are you okay?' Oliver asks as they pull her free.

'I'm fine. But . . .' Just to her side there's a hand, clad in rings, long pink fingernails. 'Candy,' Evie says.

They clear some debris from her too, but quickly realise how futile it is. Her arm is lifeless, and there's a pool of blood flowing towards them.

The chants outside are getting close, the ground vibrating even more with footsteps.

'We have to go,' Thomas says.

'There are others,' Oliver says, his eyes scanning the rubble. 'The other girls. Mia. . .' His voice trails off as he says her name and spots her pale blonde hair on top of some rubble a few metres away. There's not much left of her head. He spins Evie around so she can't see, and holds her tight in an embrace. It's the first hug they've had and Oliver wishes it was for a different reason.

They stay like that a moment, Evie's body shuddering. There are so many more beneath the rubble, so many more they should try to save.

Bomb the bots! Bots don't bleed!

The chanting is closer still, the ground pulsing with the march.

'We need to go,' Thomas says. 'It's them or all of us.'

Oliver looks at the faces of his best friends, then over at the rubble again for just a second. Thomas is right. Digging them all out would take ages and then what if they're all like Candy and Mia? He can't risk those he cares for the most.

'Okay,' he says. 'Evie, are you okay to walk?'

She nods.

They scramble over what's left of the building, the boundary indiscriminate from the mess outside. The roof is still collapsing, raining down tiles and wooden beams. The building goes higher to levels above and the explosion has left a gaping hole in the walkway around it. Thick metal rods support the floor above and they seem intact. Looking down, the landfill that engulfs the level below churns up, plastic packaging billowing in the breeze.

People pile out of the surrounding bars, choking, bloodied limbs. It's like that damned movie. Is this what the point of that film was? To prepare them for getting bombed when in the real world?

Poor Evie is almost naked, and Oliver takes off his jacket to give to her. They all have blue-black bruising in patches over their limbs. Oliver remembers his mum's bruises were yellow and purple, totally different from bots. They're exposed as they are, too obviously bots.

They step away and Oliver feels it, a sluggishness, like he's wading through a thick fog. Is he injured? No, he knows it's not that. It's the more obvious problem. He looks at Thomas, who must be thinking the same.

'Our batteries,' Thomas says.

Oliver nods and feels his pocket. He's still got his cable. 'How's yours, Evie?'

'Twenty per cent.'

'You got your cable?' Oliver asks Thomas. He checks his pockets, then nods. 'Okay, I know a place.'

His mum's old work is around here somewhere. It all looks different with the ashy air and rubble everywhere. There was a place they charged on 4 as well, but making it to a lift right now would be difficult. They look across the walkway at people running away and approaching. Back the way they came looks like the safest route, and Oliver thinks his old charging point is that way.

It's dark, the electricity is completely out, which makes Oliver worry if they'll find electricity at all. They catch glimpses of their surroundings in the sporadic light from other people's torches. That extra night vision the Institute promised would be useful right now.

'Stay close together,' Oliver says to the others as they navigate through panicked people. 'I think it's this way.'

They walk with the crowd. There are lots of women not wearing much, so Evie doesn't stand out. There's a mob behind them, pushing, so many desperate to get away from the explosion and also, so many people still headed that way, like they want to see, or they want to do it again. Those awful words are still on the lips of so many.

Human's first! Bomb the bots! Bots don't bleed!

There's a crush, a scuffle just in front of them, someone hitting another. In their hand, a flash of metal, cutting skin, blood pouring out. Oliver remembers his techniques for conserving his battery. Don't pay attention, don't be curious. Humans call it a meditative state and he hopes Thomas is doing the same.

They round a corner and the electric is back on; the walkway lights are dim but good enough. They sidestep out of the worst of the crowd and the strip is familiar. There's the bar where his mum used to work just a short walk away, the eBike chargers behind. The billboard used to be broken, but it's working now.

There's only one plug.

'You first,' Oliver says to Thomas. His eyes are slow blinking, so he's obviously more depleted than Oliver. 'Half an hour, then I'll do half an hour, then we can do longer.'

They've nothing to put them on standby; that rod is long gone. Oliver helps Thomas plug in, then sits back and relaxes.

'I'll keep watch,' Evie says. 'And I'll make sure you both get charge.'

Oliver is useless. He hates leaving such a task to Evie on her own. He can't even speak to agree now. The explosion wore him out. He's down to five per cent.

***

Oliver stirs to find Evie plugging him in. The rush of electric makes his eyes see clearly again. Even in her dusty state, she's so pretty. She could have died back there. As soon as he has enough charge, he's going to hug her again. Life is too short, he's realising.

For hours they hide, agreeing they all need to be above twenty-five per cent to leave. When Evie is plugged in, she shuts her eyes, relaxes, and Oliver watches her. He still hasn't hugged her again, but even that doesn't seem like enough now. He doesn't know what this feeling is. They never explained feelings at the Institute. He just wants to be close to her.

The billboard plays the news on a loop. When they've all had some charge and are getting ready to leave, they watch for a moment. The riot—that's the word the news is using for the crowd—is on 4 as well as 3, yet from where they are, it's quiet now. The ground isn't vibrating. Right here, it feels safe. Would his mum know to find them here? None of them want to leave.

There's a new interview coming up, the news presenter on the billboard says. Her voice is excited and the three of them sit and watch.

'In the studio on Nightly News, we have a guest who will once again explain the need for bots. TRI's business partner and investor of MechaniSluts. Mr Anthony Miller.'

His face fills the screen. Anthony. Oliver's fists clench, his teeth grit. Then there's the footage of the riot, and people saying they're cutting bots, to see who bleeds, and those people are justifying it. They're saying Anthony told them to. 'Like that Anthony guy on TV said. Cut to see who's real. Bots don't bleed.'

Oliver's nostrils flare. *Anthony.*

Anthony has made people hurt the bots. Anthony has made the bots sluts.

Hatred sears through Oliver. The rest of the world disappears and all he sees is Anthony's horrible smug face. He can see the fear in his mum's face when Anthony came home, can hear Anthony's fist punching her, and knows everything bad in the world is Anthony's fault.

Oliver is bigger now. He's not some little kid anymore.

And he is not afraid.

Chapter 37

Harriet hides around the back of the lift station for hours. She still can't get to 3. There are other people milling around as well, so she averts her face, rests her forehead on the wall, scarf pulled up. She stares at nothing except her phone, watching for updates but seeing nothing except the battery drain. After hours—she's lost track of how long—nothing changes. This tells her for sure Oliver must be charging or his battery is flat. In any other scenario, he'd be on 5 by now.

Her stomach cramps, and she sits on the floor, her body folding in on itself as her thoughts spiral into the darkest worries as to why he's still missing.

He's hurt.

Killed.

Lost.

Captured.

No. She shakes such thoughts from her mind. Charging is the most likely reason, down on 3, where he always charged. He's safe, in a spot he knows. He'll be charging for hours yet.

Her mind goes to the gruff man at the Institute, calling an alert. With TRI aware he's escaped, and the other teens harmed in the explosion, maybe they're on 3, rounding up the teens and taking them away. Maybe Oliver has a tracker and they found him hours ago, destroyed him for his actions. Harriet's hand goes to her chest as she rasps a breath, bile burning her throat. The ceiling lowers, the fences closing in. She's in a suffocating box, airless, drowning in worry.

There are too many bad possibilities and only one good one. But it's that good one she needs to concentrate on, as if picturing it will make it manifest. She needs to think positively. She can't afford to panic now.

The mob is being broken up, she reconciles. No more are joining them on 3. Oliver might be vaguely safe there. But with 2 mostly a no-go zone these days, that means so many are arriving on 4, and the riot will soon spread to 5. She tucks herself more into the corner, wishing again she had her Alyssa disguise. No one ever recognises her from her movie days, or they never used to. Now one TV appearance and some badly filmed video and it's like she's dressed in neon lights.

When the rabble on 4 starts getting more rowdy, she decides to head back to the refuge. Rosa might let her wait out the worst of it there.

She stands up and turns around, bracing herself before she rejoins the crowd.

'Hey! That's that woman! The human hater!'
Shit!
A hundred heads turn her way. She squints her eyes, hunches over, uses her hand to ruffle her hair. Being in Alyssa's character

isn't going to help her right now. There's a wall of them, a semi-circle around her, and her eyes dart from side to side to look for an exit. Not every face is stern with scorn. There are some who appear more bemused or confused, like they're here just to get a lift and are not part of the mob. She angles herself towards them, then ducks her head, like a rhino about to charge, and pummels her way through the crowd.

She barges and wades through people, swimming against the tide. She bats off grasping hands, fingernails scouring her flesh as she flails her arms in front of her like she's swatting flies. One arm encircles her neck and she kicks back, lashing out and jabbing whatever is close.

There are more hands, more people, too many, overpowering her, a tsunami of grasping limbs. She's off her feet, her hat falls off, and she's being carried somewhere she can't see. She's no longer in control. Her body is crushed, head rammed into a sweaty armpit, smothered by their vinegary odour. She screams out, kicking some more, though her legs barely move under the weight of those holding her. Horizontal now, all she can see is the underside of the walkway above.

'Bot sympathiser! Human hater! We've got her!'

She twists and contorts, but their hold only tightens. Her shouts are inaudible against the riot.

She's upright, pushed and shoved and forced vertical, wedged between two people on the remnants of a wall. She coughs and wheezes and blinks to clear the spots from her vision.

Either side of her are Flesh Fraternity speakers, a megaphone in their hands, a live audience below. She's centre stage.

Chapter 38

Oliver, Thomas, and Evie look too much like bots, and that's going to be a problem. Leaving their safe charging place and walking into possible riots and people who hate them is risky, and Thomas doesn't hold back in saying so.

'It's a stupid idea, Oliver. It's dangerous.'

'He's the one making all this trouble for us. You don't understand! You can't possibly understand how much I hate that man. I have to shut him up. For us, for my mum.'

'Thomas is right, Oliver,' Evie says. 'It's so risky.'

'You two stay here. Alone I can blend in better anyway. I'll come back for you.'

'No chance,' Thomas says. 'You always look out for me. There's no way I'm leaving you alone now.'

'And you guys came for me.' Evie hugs them both, giving each a peck on the cheek. Did Oliver imagine it, or did she linger with him a little longer? 'You saved me. There's no way I'm leaving your side.'

'But just for the record,' Thomas says, 'I think it's a dumb idea.' He says this with a smile, and Oliver knows that as dumb as the idea is, Thomas has his back.

Oliver has walked past that studio before. Up on 99 when he was a kid, his mum pointed it out. She said that's where TV shows are made. Making it anywhere without being caught up in the riot is going to be impossible. They need clothes, lots, to cover themselves. Oliver's arms are exposed since Evie has his jacket and they need their heads more covered. Hats would be good.

The bar where Oliver's mum worked is still open. She used to change clothes in there. Oliver peers round the side to get a view of the front door. There's a security guy, and inside there's hazy lighting and pumping music.

'Maybe there's a back door,' Oliver says. 'We can sneak in there and grab something to wear.'

'I'll go,' Evie says. 'Here, take your jacket back.' Without it on, she's so exposed. Oliver blushes at the sight of her nipples. 'I look like I work there, right?'

Oliver wants to hug her again, to keep her close and to shield her. 'I don't want you going in there alone.'

'Where I was working was worse. Trust me.' She has a sadness in her voice, but she turns around before Oliver can argue.

Oliver and Thomas go back to hiding around the back. Oliver hopes he's not blushing half as much as Thomas.

They plug back in while they wait a few more minutes each. The damned news bulletin is still covering the bots. What's happened while they've been in the Institute? Oliver remembers poor Delilah being murdered by someone who hated MechaniKids. Now it seems like the whole world hates them.

He's never done anything wrong. They only want to help people, to work and fit in. Oliver is sure Anthony is to blame. Anthony always hated Oliver. This is Anthony's rage, his revenge on his mum. He's making people hate Oliver's kind and forcing them into unspeakable professions like poor Evie.

After what feels like ages, Evie comes running out. Her arms are laden with jackets and hats.

'Hurry! Security guy's on the toilet. I stole these from the coat hooks. Customers will be looking for them.'

They dress, throwing on whatever they can get their hands on. The bottom of Evie's legs are still exposed. She couldn't find anything to cover them and the oversized jacket only hangs so low.

'It's the best we've got,' Evie says. 'Now let's go.'

They run away from the bar and back towards the lift. There's a big group of people still waiting. Oliver hoped they'd be gone by now, but from the sounds of it, lots hung around to try to find bots that weren't blown up. They're still angrily chanting, knives in their hands, many with blood trickling from fresh wounds.

'Let's try another lift,' Oliver says. They've got enough battery now. They can handle the walk.

Crowds have gathered around the other lift as well. Oliver and the others tuck in behind another billboard, mercifully a broken one so they don't have to listen to any more of the awful news, and wait, hoping the dim light there will conceal them enough.

They peer around and, in the torch lights, metal blades still glint. There are a few men, huge and angry, slashing their weapons side to side at everyone.

'Show me that you bleed, bitch,' one man says to a woman.

She fronts up to him, their chests touching, and she lifts her arm to reveal her already bleeding cut. 'How about you?'

He snarls at her, and she whips her blade down and up, quick as a flash, and cuts his shoulder.

He yelps, his free hand going to the wound, and she smiles. He lifts his blood-stained hand to show her.

The teens stop looking and face away, their backs pressed against the wall.

'How are we going to get through them?' Thomas asks.

Oliver squeezes his eyes shut. 'I don't know.'

Maybe they should have stayed where they were. They were safe there. He feels a heavy responsibility for his friends here. But the more he hears those people with their knives, listens to their threats, he knows he has to do something. He has to stop Anthony making people do bad things.

Their stolen clothes aren't enough of a disguise. They need wounds. Proper human bleeding ones, not bluish MechaniTeen marks.

'We just need some blood,' Oliver says. 'If we were bleeding like humans, they wouldn't suspect us.'

Thomas and Evie don't respond, instead looking at the floor with wide eyes. Oliver squares his shoulders. He'll be the one to do this job. He'll find some blood.

Steps behind them crunch on the gravelly ground. Oliver spins around. There's a man, alone, a huge person, even bigger than the biggest staff member at the Institute. Oliver's eyes flit down and spots a knife dangling from his right hand.

'You look like a few bots to me,' he says, his mouth wearing the kind of smile Anthony used to before he lashed out.

The man lunges forwards and grabs Evie by the wrist, lifting the knife up above his head.

'No!' Oliver cries and puts his arm between them.

The man slices the blade down, and it cuts through Oliver's skin easily, clinking on the metal of his arm.

The man's face lights up, his eyes sparkle with joy, and he opens his mouth to shout.

Before he has time to think, and before the man has made a sound, Oliver's balled fists smacks him square in the mouth, the other punches him in the gut. He's seen Anthony punch before. He knows exactly how to do it.

The man's face goes purple as he bends over. There's a sound, like he's trying to breathe but can't, and the knife drops to the floor. The man has one hand over his mouth, deep red blood trickling through his fingers.

Blood. They need it. More of it. And they need this man to be quiet.

Oliver punches him in the mouth again, another across his head, and the man goes limp, falling to the ground.

'Oliver!' Thomas gasps, his hands over his mouth.

'Hurry,' Oliver says. He takes the knife from the ground and looks over the man's body. Where to cut? They need blood. Enough to make them all look injured. The dribble from his mouth is not enough. Oliver stabs the knife into the man's arm. Not much blood comes out at first, so he digs the knife in a little deeper. When he removes the knife, there's plenty. Oliver uses the knife like a spoon and rubs it on Evie's legs, covering her blue-black stains. There's plenty more and he rubs some around Thomas's wrists and his own as well.

'That should do it,' he says. 'Are you okay, Evie? Did he hurt your wrist?'

She shakes her head.

He looks down at the man on the floor. He's not moving, except for his chest rising and falling a bit. His purple face is more grey, blood dribbling from his mouth. Oliver should feel bad; he should feel a bit of remorse. Looking at Thomas and Evie, they're too shocked to feel anything.

'Okay,' Oliver says. 'Let's go. We look like we're one of these arseholes.'

Oliver puts the knife back in the man's hand and they walk, not cowering, displaying their human blood with faces of pride, then take the lift to 99.

Chapter 39

The crowd in front of Harriet hush their heckles when the speaker lifts his arms, like he thinks he's Moses parting the damned sea. Harriet sweats and shakes, trying to control her shuddering breath. Now is not the time to get stage fright, though she's never performed to a crowd with such hostility. Even on her worst performances in the worst plays, the audience were well-mannered. She tries to convince herself this is an opportunity, a chance to plead her case and make people see sense. Then all she can think is that this crowd are going to tear her apart, and she hopes she doesn't die before she sees her son again. Just once more, so she knows he's safe.

'This woman is a Traitor!' Spittle flies from his mouth as the speaker puts such emphasis on the 'T' Harriet imagines it as a capital letter. The crowd jeers and Harriet scans their faces, searching for one friendly face, one seed of doubt in a crowd of people seeing red. 'She is a traitor to her own kind. She values robots over people! Perhaps she is a bot herself. Shall I cut her to see?'

Harriet struggles against the men sandwiching her in, shaking her head at their accusations. She wants to scream at them all to go fuck themselves, to hurl insults and spit at them. But she knows that won't do. She must somehow show composure, take the bloody moral high road, despite the roiling anger in her gut. She's practised these arguments hundreds of times. One more performance, one more show, her grand finale. She can do this.

'Oh, look!' The speaker says. 'It seems the human-hater has something to say!'

Hundreds of eyes land on her, peeling away every layer of clothing and flesh, reducing her to her atoms. She's nothing to them. Some living hysteria, the personification of madness. She will prove them wrong if it's the last thing she does—and it might be. A man next to her holds a megaphone in front of her. She wants to grab it, but her arms are stuck to her sides from them wedging her in. She wriggles but it's futile, so she leans as much as she can towards the megaphone. She hasn't an expression practised for this situation. Any rehearsals she did for her TV appearance have blown from her mind. She thinks back to her doe-eyed acting days, her girl-next-door image. That's who she needs to play now. Miss Innocent. Their neighbour and kin.

Her brows draw in and she downturns her mouth just a touch and tries to drop her shoulders. 'I was born below and have lived on the lower levels most of my adult life.' She uses her native, below-ground accent, hoping her voice would come out mellifluent and naive, but it has a gravelly roughness, cracking of age and stress. She swallows to clear it and continues. 'How often do we have to go without, as the scavengers can't bring up all they need from landfill because it's too dangerous? We all know someone who has died trying to bring up necessities. Wouldn't it be better if the bots did that instead?'

'Stealing our jobs!' someone shouts from the crowd.

She finds that voice in the crowd, lets his fear and anguish into her heart, as if she can consume all his worries and take the burden from him. Her eyes glaze, a pained look softening her features. 'With all the extra things bought up, there will be a ton more jobs in repairing them. Safely, up here.'

'With no electricity because the bots steal it all,' someone yells.

She looks up, wishing she could free her arm to point. Screw the soft voice. Now she needs some authority. Now she needs to be bigger than the girl-next-door. She needs power. 'Up top!' she shouts, a fierceness about her. 'They take it all. They fly to work on Hel-Es, they leave their lights on, they consume so much and chuck all their waste down here to smother us. Since MechaniKids were first released, we've lost almost an entire other level to their rubbish. They conserve nothing. They are the enemy here. The bots are only made to help.' Her eyes, wild and frantic, scan the crowd. A rare breeze flows through. Dust, like tumbleweed, blows across the crowd, smudging out the faces of many. The lights do their usual flickering cycle and stay dim for a moment before brightening and she can search the crowd again. In their faces she sees fear and anger, a seething rage teetering on the brink. But there are some, a break in the wave of hate, who nod along with her.

'You want the bots to be treated as human!' the speaker says. 'These fake people, as if they are people made by God!'

This is when her acting is put to its test and she hopes Oliver isn't in the crowd. She'd hate for him to hear this. 'I only want them looked after so they remain useful. We should not waste such valuable products like the upper levels do. We are better than them.' A few more nods from the crowd. Enough maybe to stop them ripping her apart.

Where is Oliver right now? That's the worry rampaging through her thoughts. Her skin is covered in gashes from fingernails, bruises are swelling across her knees and elbows, but none of that matters. She'd tear one of her limbs off to save her boy. Yet she doesn't know her son's face. He could be in this crowd, hiding, scared, listening to her deny her love for him.

The speaker is talking, but she can't hear him. Her ears are ringing too loudly, a shrill note of panic. She needs to get away. She needs to find her son. The billboard is lit, playing the news. There's a camera in the crowd somewhere; her face is on the billboard. Her appearance shocks her. Dishevelled and blotchy, as grubby as a below grounder. She searches the crowd again before she finds the camera, and she looks straight at the lens. She can play Miss Innocent damsel in distress. It's not a hard role right now.

'My fight is for all children, all girls, to keep them safe,' she says, a wobble of love and sadness in her voice, though without the megaphone, she's relying on the audience's ability to lipread. 'My argument is with those who would mistreat a bot who appears so young. I wish to protect the young, the innocents, for children to not witness violence.'

Behind the camera there's movement different to the stationary crowd. Someone jumping and waving. It takes a while for Harriet to recognise her. Is it . . . Beatrice? Dread tightens across Harriet's throat, her mouth running dry. Beatrice shouldn't be here. It's way too dangerous for her. Harriet stares at her a moment, trying to force her message through her eyes.

Leave, Beatrice. Go away!

Harriet worries about looking at her for too long in case anyone notices. She looks away, anywhere but at her. In the corner of her vision, she's still jumping and waving. Harriet's heart pounds, a jackhammer grinding away at her insides, her body spent and weak. If she wasn't squashed between the men on either side of her, she's sure her legs would buckle.

Beatrice isn't just jumping. She's pointing. Harriet follows the direction and there she spots Theo, a few metres away from Beatrice on the other side of the billboard. All she can see is the back of his head, but she knows that thinning spot, his jacket stained with his latest repair project. He's crouching down, then Harriet twigs. There'll be an electrical box there behind the billboard. He's messing with the electric supply. Saving her blushes on TV is not worth putting Beatrice in such danger. He glances up at Harriet and they lock eye contact for a split second before all the lights go off.

There are some groans, cursing, a rustling sound as everyone rummages in pockets and bags for torches. Without the streetlights at this time of night, it's close to pitch dark on the lower levels. The speakers either side of her move away slightly and she has just about enough room to free her arms. There's a hand grasping her wrist and she yelps and flinches.

But there's a voice she knows; the grip is soft.

'Harriet, come on.'

Theo.

The speakers are too distracted to stop her. She hops down and Theo hands her a hat and she puts it on. More concealed now, she takes Theo's hand and they speed walk from the crowd.

'Where's Beatrice?' she asks. The slivers of torchlight catch the contours of scowls, narrowed eyes glinting in the beams. As they reach a thinner bit of crowd, Harriet shivers. 'It's too dangerous for her here.'

'She's fine,' Theo says. 'She's this way. She saw you on TV and told me, then we just raced here.'

They keep striding forward, Harriet's gut twisting at the thought of any harm coming to Beatrice. She's supposed to be looking after her, not subjecting her to danger. They're far from the crowd now, yet still the angry voices carry, their shrill violence cutting through the air.

It's another minute before they meet Beatrice, waiting for them at the edge of a park. Relief would hit Harriet more if she didn't have a million other worries gnawing at her.

'Are you okay?' Beatrice asks.

Harriet's heart melts a little. Beatrice is so kind for asking when she's in so much danger herself. 'I'm fine,' she says, panting now with the fast pace. 'Are you?'

Beatrice nods. She's wearing what looks like some of Monty's clothes, well covered and nothing that would expose her charging socket.

Theo slows the pace a moment. 'Where are we going?'

'I need to go to where I used to work,' Harriet says as she catches her breath, still looking over her shoulder for signs of the mob catching up. The lights are still out. That'll make it much harder for them to find her. 'On 3. But the lifts are shut. Oliver used to charge there. That's where he'll be.'

'The lifts have reopened,' Theo says. 'Let's hurry. We can be there really quickly.'

They run then, full speed, non-stop, all the way to the lift. Harriet's lungs burn. She stumbles on weak legs over gravel and potholes. She's running on empty. When did she last eat? Theo can't be doing much better. He finds running exhausting with his limp.

Some of the mob catches up with them, racing past, barging into them. The three of them hold hands. Harriet winces with every shove, wishing she could close her ears to their hateful chants. They sidestep and manage to find clear ground, and after a few minutes, they're at an area that still has electricity. Harriet glances around at Beatrice, who has one hand to her chest.

'Beatrice?' Harriet's eyes bulge and she slows. Blue-black seeps through Beatrice's top.

'Someone got me with the knife across my chest. I'm okay. It doesn't hurt. I'm just keeping it together.'

Harriet stops. 'Let me see.'

'No. It's really fine. My skin will stick back down in a day. I just need to hold it there.'

Harriet shakes her head. 'Theo, take Beatrice home. It's dangerous. She's hurt.'

Beatrice walks off, picking up her pace in the direction they were headed.

'Wait up, Beatrice!' Harriet shouts. 'Wait!'

'I'm going with you,' Beatrice shouts back. 'That explosion. They could be my friends.'

Harriet looks over at Theo, who runs beside her. His face pales. Neither of them had even considered Beatrice's friends.

There's a crowd waiting for the lift, but they push through, ignoring the angry curses behind them. Squashed in the lift, Theo uses his slight frame to conceal Harriet and Beatrice from view. Harriet faces the wall, dipping her chin as Beatrice folds some of her top over her hand to hide the blue-black stain. Harriet bites her bottom lip, willing for no one to pay them any regard, for just a little bit of luck today.

They alight on 3, that one bit of luck finally rewarding them with invisibility in the crowd. Down on 3, they keep running until they reach the bomb site. The walkway has caved in around it giving way to a dark drop to the level below. There are body bags zipped up outside a wrecked building. In a heap to the side is a pile of MechaniTeens.

Harriet's hands go to her mouth, her veins turning to ice as her eyes stream. *No no no no!*

'Wait here,' Theo says. 'I'll go look.'

Harriet doesn't argue. Mothers are supposed to be strong and resilient, but she feels like a puddle. The only thing propping her up is the gratitude she has for Theo. She faces the other way, as does Beatrice. Harriet can't look. She can't see it. She can't see her boy dead.

She looks at Beatrice, her shaking body, unblinking eyes. 'Beatrice?'

She doesn't say anything. Harriet holds her hand and Beatrice doesn't shake free. Her grip tightens, her arm trembling.

'It's all girls,' Theo says, but Harriet's relief is counterbalanced by Beatrice's dismay.

'Beatrice?' Theo says. 'I'm so sorry. Do you want to see if you know any?'

'I . . . I don't think I can.'

Harriet doesn't want to rush her but she also can't wait. 'You two stay here. I'll be five minutes. His charging spot is really close.'

She doesn't give them time to answer. She turns on her heel and runs again. She should be there for Beatrice, and she will be, she just needs to find Oliver first. There are hardly any people here now. The novelty of an explosion has worn off already, the commotion of the riot on 4 obviously keeping the worst of the people entertained.

She makes it to the bar where she used to work. It's intact, thank God, and still open. A few punters loiter outside, a security guy looking bored. Neon lights outside flash their seedy signs, and from the doorway, music pumps and the smell of smoke and spirits linger. Harriet makes her way around the back to the eBike charger where Oliver used to charge.

The last of her strength seeps from her. She was so sure he'd be here. At the sight of the empty space, her legs give up and she sits on the cold tarmac, hugging her knees. She got it wrong. She's a useless mother. In the chilly air, she shivers, her eyes burn, dry, no tears left to cry. Her limbs hurt, her bruises of the day coming to fruition. Everything aches.

She takes Theo's hat off and tugs at her frizzy mop of hair, then massages her scalp, as if that'll keep her headache away. Her hair tangles around her fingers and she has an urge to rip it out, to enforce such wounds on herself to distract from the pain that hurts the most. Her vision clouds, a shimmer tugging on the edges of her periphery. She should sleep it off. She could close her eyes right here and sleep where her son used to, curl up on the ground where he rested so many times. Her body screams at her to concede to exhaustion.

But there's no time. If he's not here, he'll be back on 5 soon. She takes out her phone, checking the camera. No sign of them. There's a message from Monty that makes her stomach drop. *You guys need to get home really soon. Josie won't last much longer.*

How can she will Josie to keep going when she is so defeated herself? She can't go to Josie without Thomas. She can't let Josie die without knowing her son is safe.

By the eBike charger, something catches her eye. A black cable. She shuffles closer and picks it up. A charging cable, the same as Oliver's kid cable, discarded here, as if left in haste. Probably left by a bot worried for his life.

Her breath hitches as she looks at the ground. There are dusty footprints. She turns round so she's on her hands and knees and inspects them, hovering her hand over them. Her heart moves to her throat as she traces their outline. They're exactly the same size as the ones in the tunnel.

He was here. She can feel it. A tingle in her hands as she touches the prints and the cable. He was here, exactly where she thought he'd be.

And now he's gone.

There's a gentle hand on her shoulder. 'We should get home,' Theo says. 'He'll be headed that way.' Beatrice is standing to his side, and she offers her hand.

Harriet nods, takes her hand, then stands, brushing off her backside.

'Beatrice, your friends?'

Beatrice's red-rimmed eyes look at the floor, and she shakes her head. 'They obviously didn't matter enough.'

Harriet's heart aches for Beatrice. There's so much anger with loss yet, at the moment, Beatrice appears almost tranquil with her grief, deadpan and accepting. Harriet wants to scream at her that she does matter, to make her see just how much. She promises to herself as soon as she can, she'll find a way to make Beatrice understand she matters, to help her love herself as she should. She'll take her to see her family from when she was a kid and let them shower her with all the love she deserves. Perhaps that will erase some of her pain.

Harriet takes one last look at Oliver's footprints, then walks away. After a few paces she pauses, mid-stride, a chill travelling down her spine when she hears her ex-husband's name. Before she can take a breath, she looks around and his face fills the billboard.

Studio 99 is announcing their lineup for the rest of the day, as they so often do. The presenter has an overly excited voice, as Harriet's ex-husband's ruddy face fills the screen.

'And next up Live on Studio 99, we'll be talking about why bots are best used as MechaniSluts, and the effect of his "Bots don't bleed" mantra. Anthony Miller will soon be live in the studio. . .'

That clip has been playing on a loop. Every few minutes they've reminded viewers of what's to come. They always do that. Oliver would have seen it. He was charging right here.

He knows where Anthony's going to be.

'He's not gone home,' Harriet says, a breathy voice as fear grips her lungs. 'He's going to Studio 99.'

Chapter 40

Oliver, Thomas, and Evie alight on 99. Oliver remembers the way from when he was a kid. Along the walkway and past the parks. Anthony's apartment building is a little way behind them. Perhaps if they don't manage to confront Anthony at the studio, he can get into his apartment somehow and wait for him there. Somewhere, somehow, he's going to feel Anthony's neck in his hands tonight.

'Woah!' Thomas says when he looks up. 'The sky! I had no idea it could look like that.'

It's a clear evening sky, scattered with stars, the Hel-Es gliding across. He wishes it was daylight so he could see birds flying. The moon is just rising ahead of them, a half-moon, suspended in the blackness. Oliver takes a second to look up, but he's seen it before many times.

'It's amazing,' Evie says.

Oliver never realised he was lucky to see the sky when he was a kid. He never appreciated what was so normal for him. A few moths and insects flitter around, visiting the flower beds. There are a lot of types of grasses too, and the screech of crickets. How Oliver had missed this. He can't smell the flowers so the real ones here or fake ones on the lower level seem similar to him, but he knows his mum loved them when they lived up high. They can't linger, yet he lets the others watch for a few seconds before nagging them to keep moving.

They're still without any way to tell the time, so Oliver can only assume Anthony will be in the studio soon. They need to get there as quickly as possible.

'Come on,' he says. 'We have to hurry.'

Thomas looks at Oliver now and Oliver stares back, his features taut with determination and impatience.

'I've never seen you like this,' Thomas says.

'What? In a hurry? Come on.'

'He's right,' Evie says. She tries to take Oliver's hand, and while he normally loves holding her hand, his fists are clenched too tightly. 'You're scaring me.'

Oliver stops walking then. Covered in blood, all his muscles tense, he's ready to hurt Anthony. He looks at his hands. They glow crimson in the moonlight. He puffs his cheeks out, flaps his hands around as if that'll clear them of their stain, rubs them on his grubby trousers before folding his arms and tucking his hands in his armpits. He can't see them anymore and he doesn't need to think about it. He doesn't feel bad about cutting that man on 3. That man was bad. He was going to hurt his friends, so Oliver knows it was self-defence. But shouldn't he still feel bad? There should be some pain in his chest, at least a slight ache, right?

That man was bad, but Oliver knows Anthony is worse.

'We need to hurry,' Oliver says to his friends again. 'Or you can wait here. It's up to you.' He walks off, not waiting for their reply but a second later, their footsteps hurry towards him. Oliver's a little lighter with his friends by his side. He'd hate to leave them alone.

Oliver's hands are still tucked out of sight so he can't see the blood. He doesn't need to think about what's already happened, just about what he's going to do. His brows lower, his narrow eyes see only the walkway ahead. The sides of his vision disappear. He's in a tunnel and at the end of that, all he sees is Anthony.

'Oliver,' Evie says, 'I think you need to calm down. We need to talk about this.'

He ignores her. Anyone trying to dissuade him might as well be white noise. Oliver was so small when he last had to fight off Anthony. He can do more now. He can stop him for good.

'Oliver!' Thomas shouts. 'I don't recognise you right now. You're so angry.'

Oliver doesn't bother responding. He has every right to be angry. Those two should be angry as well. Anthony is making people hate bots, hurt bots, blow up bots. But those two never grew up with Anthony. They've probably never learned rage. Maybe all those years living with Anthony rubbed off on Oliver more than he thought. But Oliver is not like him, he knows that. Anthony harms innocent, wonderful people. Oliver only wants to protect people.

The walkways aren't busy, the bomb and riot warnings likely keeping everyone inside. On the lower levels, dusty and covered in blood, they didn't stand out too much. But up here, they look a mess. Across the nearest park, there's a duck pond. How long since Oliver saw a duck! He can't stop and stare. There's no time for that. The three of them shed any clothing that has the most blood on, then wash their hands and arms and faces. The amount of dust and blood that comes off shows what a state they were in. With their appearance slightly more passable, they walk on.

'What's your plan, Oliver?' Thomas asks. 'Just walk into a TV studio and beat him up?'

They have a few minutes' walk to figure out what to do. Oliver pauses, finally realising he can't go in unprepared.

'I just . . .' He's just so angry, is what he really wants to say, that he wants to give Anthony the same kind of bruises he used to give Oliver's mum. He wants to beat him and humiliate him for sure. He wants the world to see what kind of man Anthony is so they won't listen to him. He'll do whatever it takes so people won't do as he says. He wants the world to exist without Anthony. When Oliver opens his mouth to speak, he can't vocalise the hatred, he can't choose the words needed to explain. 'I just want to talk to him, to the camera, make the world see what type of man he is.'

They approach the building Oliver knows is Studio 99. A simple black door frame in one of the many skyscrapers. He's sure as soon as he sees it despite its nondescript appearance. It's drawing him in. He knows Anthony's in there. He can feel it. Not in that place where love is. Lower, in his waist, the part that churns when he feels sick.

They stop and look at the doorway.

'How are we going to get in?' Thomas asks.

They step a little closer and round a corner. From fifty metres away, Oliver peers towards the doors. There are two people who look like security and one person behind a reception desk. There's no way they can just walk past them. They look tidier than they did earlier, but not anywhere near smart enough to be allowed in there.

They walk a little further around and press their backs against the wall.

Oliver thinks for a moment. 'Perhaps there's a back door? Let's go look.'

Chapter 41

Harriet tells Theo to take Beatrice home again, but they both refuse, neither wanting to leave her alone.

There's no time to hug them, so a rushed thanks as they have to run once again has to suffice. Harriet hopes they know how grateful she is. Facing Anthony alone and finding Oliver all in the same place is ramming her with so many emotions, she might burst.

Theo gives Beatrice his jacket to cover up her blue-black stain across her chest. It's stopped spreading, though she keeps her hand there to press her skin down. They run all the way back to the lift and take a level 10 fast taxi to the studio.

Theo checks his phone. 'Monty says Josie's bad. We need to hurry.' He scrolls some more. 'The mob is coming too. Up to 99. They know Anthony's there. Some anti-bot fanatics want to hate him, some want to shake his hand.'

'Security might be tight. We have to get there first,' Harriet says as she bites her nails, taps her foot, willing the taxi to go even faster. 'We need to get Oliver out of there.'

There's no way Oliver will even understand what a mob is. He won't have any clue about their violence and hatred. They need to get Beatrice away too, though it's pointless stressing that again. Harriet is sure none from the mob will be taking a fast taxi. They've got an advantage.

They arrive by the studio on level 10. At the lower levels it's all office space and storerooms. The entrance is plain, just a lobby and a lift, which they take up to 99.

The lift pings open in the lobby on 99. There's that echoey floor, the obscene desk. It's the same receptionist, the one who signed her in and also gave her a screwy look about her appearance. She looks a hell of a lot worse at the moment, so she braces for the sneer. She needs to own this, needs to show she's meant to be here. She approaches the desk, holding her chin high and using her movie accent. 'Harriet Chapel. I'm here to be interviewed on the evening news.'

The look she gets is exactly as she expects and more. 'I wasn't aware you were scheduled for tonight,' he says and clicks at his computer.

'Well, I am and I'm late. I've no time for you to delay me further.'

He makes a face as if he's smelled something putrid. To be fair, that could be deserved. 'There's not much time to get you ready. Especially looking like that.'

She smiles, an innocent, carefree kind of smile. 'Bit of chaos going on outside, if you're not aware.'

It does the trick. She tries not to show her relief when he doesn't doubt her story. 'Come through,' he says, then addressing Theo and Beatrice. 'You'll have to stay here.'

'No!' Harriet snaps, a little too much panic in her voice. She takes a breath and smiles again. From her acting days, she knows assertiveness counts for so much in showbiz. This guy can brand her a diva or high maintenance, she doesn't care. 'This is my agent and my . . . security. They're coming with me, but they can wait in the wings.'

Another judging look from the receptionist, this time directed at Theo and Beatrice. 'Okay, just sign them in here.' He hands her a tablet.

Harriet can hear Shelly Anderson's voice coming from the studio. She's introducing Anthony already. That's where Oliver will be. Sod hair and makeup. Harriet walks past those doors and goes straight through to the studio. She waits out of sight of the camera, searching across the wings. Oliver must be here somewhere. She scans the faces, but her attention is drawn to the interview, Anthony's voice making her skin crawl.

'Ms Chapel, you're not actually on our schedule,' a runner says.

'Hang on,' she hisses. 'Let me listen.'

'The PleasureBots are in huge demand.' Anthony wears that glib grin he does when talking business. 'As well as bots for more difficult tasks, dealing with crime and low-level issues. TRI originally thought raising bots to have empathy was a good idea. Now, we raise them to be obedient, to serve, not like humans at all. Any that are deemed to be human-like in emotions will be reconditioned or destroyed. There is simply no need for so much empathy.'

Destroyed. Harriet's blood turns to ice. She can't see Oliver. What if Anthony has already hurt him?

'Ms Chapel,' the runner says, impatient now. 'I'm calling security.'

Anthony is making some joke with Shelly. He laughs and his joy fills Harriet with rage. How dare he laugh about what he's doing, bragging about destroying bots! Harriet's nostrils flare, her fists clench, and she steps out from the wings.

'Anthony!' she shouts and approaches the desk. A silence rips through the studio floor, and a camera swings to face her. 'It's rich for someone like you to say empathy isn't needed. Is that what you told yourself when you beat me black and blue? When you broke my arm? When you got jealous and forced me to end my career? You want bots to be less empathetic because kindness only highlights how despicable you are.'

Anthony's mouth clamps shut and he recoils. As much as he's trying to remain stoic, he's seething right now, his face reddening, too much for studio makeup to hide.

To the side, Shelly Anderson smirks. She'll be loving this exposure.

'Harriet, my wife,' he says with a fake smile and clenched jaw.

'*Ex*-wife.'

Camera crew lean in, whispers exchange, but Harriet blocks them all out, narrowing her eyes at Anthony.

'You look a little flushed, dear. Shame a barren body still suffers with hormones.'

Oh, she's going to smack him in a moment. And why not? He hit her enough. It's time he knew some pain.

'I saw your little speech in the riot,' he says. 'Touching. Interesting you refer to those of us up top as throwing too much away when you threw away our marriage.'

'If I hadn't left, you would have killed me. You got pretty close a few times.' Several gasps resonate, another camera now facing her.

'Like you killed our son?'

Harriet's hands go to her waist, to the part of her body that knew Freddie so well, that loved him before his first breath. Her stomach rolls, empty, vacant. There are no words for how much she hates this man. Somehow, she's going to tear his world apart.

There are more threats from the runner of security, footsteps come up behind but she ignores them. The cameras will be loving this. Let the world see this man for what he really is. Let the world see what true evil looks like.

She's standing far enough from Anthony and can see him with both eyes. There's clarity in that; a binocular perspective. Anthony is all the evil in the world, all the pain and the hurt. He is everything she needs to protect Oliver from. But his actions are desperate. His vendetta against the bots is the work of a coward. She is not at this man's mercy.

He is at hers.

Chapter 42

Oliver walks all around the back of the building. There's no back door he can access. He paces from where Thomas and Evie are and back in line with the front door again, one hand balled into a fist, punching his other palm.

Maybe he could just make something up. Say he's there to repair a light, or he has Anthony's medication. He's made it all this way. Anthony is so close he can almost feel his neck in his hands from here. Oliver curls and uncurls his fingers. He's going to brave it. He'll barge through if he has to.

He walks around to face the door again and as he braces himself to go in, all the staff at the desk disappear, scarpering away. Oliver pauses a moment, unable to believe his luck. A few seconds later, the entrance is still deserted.

'Guys!' he calls over to Thomas and Evie. 'It's clear!'

He races for the door, his friends following just behind. From further away, he hears that chanting begin again. *Bots don't bleed. Human's first.* He shakes his head. He must have imagined it. Or maybe it's on the TV in the studio. He can't have heard it from all the way on the lower levels.

Stepping through those doors, they take a quick glance around. Oliver still can't believe his luck. There are no staff anywhere. There's a sign with an arrow adjacent to the reception desk that points to the studio, so they head that way.

Television screens line the walls and on every single one of them is Anthony's face, smiling in that awful way he does when he means to do harm. Oliver smiles back at the image. It's his turn now.

Anthony's voice booms through the speakers and Oliver picks up his pace to make it to the studio. The lights are dark as they approach, only the studio is lit up ahead.

As they reach the end of the corridor, Oliver slows, gasps, as another voice fills the space. A voice he's missed so much. He walks slowly now, just listening to the sound of her voice, that longing in his chest back to a heavy ache.

He's at the end of the corridor and can see her now. She's shouting at Anthony.

' —because of that, you were going to kill me. You pretty much held me captive in—'

'Mum?'

She's there. She pauses her speech, turning towards him. Her face was so fierce and angry but when she looks at Oliver, all that rage dissipates. For the first time in years, he sees her wonderful face, hears her say his name. 'Oliver?'

Chapter 43

Her son. Taller, mature, so grown up, yet unmistakably him. That rip Harriet has felt since they parted slowly threads itself back together, a euphoria engulfing her when she sees him. How could she ever have worried she wouldn't recognise him? He's Oliver, still her little boy.

She folds over, crumpled with lightness as she steps towards him, and he runs to her. Her arms wrap around him, holding her up. All the emptiness in her is filled. He's so much bigger, she can't lift him anymore. He's the bigger boy he always wanted to be. But it's him. Her Oliver.

'Harriet Chapel,' the security guy is looming over her, along with the reception staff. 'We need to escort you off the premises.'

She doesn't release her hug. Security can wait a few seconds.

She breathes him in, her son, feeling his body convulse with happy cries for her. Is there nothing purer in the world than a bond between a mother and son?

There's a loud buzz and crack, the electric dies for a second. Cursing from the floor staff before a whirr.

'The mob has cut the power. The generator is on,' someone says. 'We're still rolling, still live.'

Harriet doesn't let go of Oliver. The cursing and instructions and machinery are all white noise. Nothing else in the world exists at this moment. The building could fall down around her and she wouldn't release her son. She leans away from him, cups his face, her eyes taking him in. With her thumb she traces his cheek dimples, his eyebrows. She musses up his hair.

'Oh, how precious,' Anthony's voice cackles. 'The little bot boy is here to see his mummy.'

Harriet blocks him out. She can feel Oliver's muscles tighten as he tries to step forwards, but she leans in and hugs him again. She can hug the badness away.

There's a crashing sound, someone shouting from down the corridor. 'They're in here! The riot!'

Harriet looks around. The studio floor empties bar a few. The security meant to escort her out have now raced to the entrance. Cameras are still rolling. Harriet's heart drops. The mob. Here for Oliver. She pulls away, looks at her son straight in the eyes. 'Darling, it's not safe. We have to run.'

She glances around, searching for an exit. Anthony's voice is still ranting from the stage. He's standing now, wearing that face he always had when he was about to pin her to the wall, when he was about to beat her.

Oliver steps in front of her, the way she did for him when he was little. Oliver's as tall as Harriet now. Her little boy. Her protector.

'Why didn't you keep your movie accent, my love?' Anthony says, his voice full of spite. 'Was that just for me? To trick me into loving you?'

The exit is just behind Anthony; the mob is coming from the other way. Harriet and Oliver are stuck in the middle. Oliver takes a step towards Anthony and Harriet grasps his arm. 'Don't, darling.'

He turns to look at her, his eyes glinting like they always did, but narrow, his jaw tight. 'He needs to pay for what he's done.'

She pulls him in. He's with her again and she strokes his face. 'Look at me, darling. Don't look at him. He's just a fool.'

Then there's Theo and Beatrice on either side of her. Behind are two more teens. One she recognises as Thomas. Josie's little boy has grown up so much. She needs to get him home, to his mum, before . . . before . . . she can't even think of what's coming.

Theo takes her hand and with them she feels stronger. There's more crashing from behind, shouts and cries as security try to hold back the mob. In front of them, Anthony takes another step forward. He's sweating, his red face now purple, a vein on his temple highlighted under the studio lights. His eyes reduce to slits, and he pulls his balled fists back.

'Low level slut like you wants empathy? You're a joke, a below-ground whore. A fungus. A fucking parasite. You and your darling bot. I'll rip that thing to bits. I'll rip you in half too, you fucking bit—' Anthony's face twists, his lips press together, his red face draining of colour. He stills for a moment, face twisting the other way, a knot of confusion. He spurts a breath, his brows knit as his hand goes to the left side of his chest. There's a groan, a gasp for air.

Harriet takes a tentative step forward, Oliver tugging back on her wrist. 'Anthony?'

Some spittle ejects with a strained breath. He sways on the spot as his face is now stark white, his eyes bulging, bloodshot, panicked. His knees bend, and he falls to the ground face first.

'Anthony!' Harriet runs to him.

'Mum, no!' Oliver shouts from behind.

'Anthony? Anthony!' Harriet heaves to turn him over, Theo and Beatrice helping. Anthony's head lollops to the side, eyes half closed.

'He's having a heart attack!' a voice shouts, someone from the camera crew. 'Call an ambulance! Get the defibrillator!'

From Anthony's mouth there's a loud exhale, and his chest doesn't rise again. Harriet shakes him, calls his name, her trembling hand feeling for a pulse, snapping it back when there's none.

In that moment, as he lies still and on the precipice of life, she sees a hint of the man she married. Not the abuser, but the man she loved once. As if all his bitterness has left him along with the oxygen in his lungs. His stress and anger exhaled in that last breath.

'Anthony?' she calls him again, barely a whisper, for the man she hates, but she once imagined a future with. The man who without him in her life, she never would have found Oliver.

Beatrice is next to her, nudging her out the way. 'I know CPR,' she says, then starts chest compressions.

More crashing from outside, thunderous footsteps, shouts from security. The sound of broken glass and chanting.

'Mum!' Oliver cries. 'Let's go. Now!'

She stands and races to her son, almost losing her balance as the runner from earlier pushes past her, holding up a red box, a dent in the front.

'The defibrillator,' he says. 'The mob smashed it. It's fried.'

They need to leave. Harriet reaches for Theo's hand, but he snatches the red box. Theo who can fix anything.

'Theo, come on,' Harriet shouts to be heard over the mob. 'Beatrice, now!'

Harriet grabs for Beatrice but she's still giving CPR. Theo opens the defibrillator box, picks at what's inside. They really need to leave. The chants are loud, so close now. A cry from security says they can't hold them back.

'The battery is bashed in,' Theo says to the runner. 'Have you got another one?'

'I've got it,' Beatrice says.

Harriet's gaze snaps to her, her stomach knots. 'Beatrice, no!'

Beatrice puts her hand under that blue-black stained top. Harriet can hear someone screaming at her not to, her own voice it sounds like, but it's slow motion, yet she can't move. There's Theo's voice too. It's all in the distance, like she's watching from somewhere else, somewhere far away, on TV. That's it; this is a stage, a play, a movie set. It can't be real.

There's a hint of a smile from Beatrice. 'Human's first,' she says, and she tugs. In Beatrice's hand is a box, black with wires. Her eyes glance at it only for a second before she falls to the side on the floor.

All the air expels from Harriet's lungs as her chest caves in. Her hands go to her stomach. There's a scream, so raw and primal, it doesn't sound like hers. *Human's first* sounds again and again in her head. But it shouldn't be. Not that human. Not him. Not for Beatrice. The trade is too unfair. Harriet's on her knees, crawling towards the young woman Beatrice is . . . was. Her shiny dark hair fanned out across the floor, her face, still and grey.

Harriet reaches across, her hands grab her, shake, yell at her to wake up. God please, just wake up!

There's someone pulling Harriet away. She's kicking, crying for Beatrice.

Through her tear-misted vision, she sees Theo take the thing from Beatrice's hand and hooks up the defibrillator. He fixes it, like he always does.

The arms dragging her hoist her to her feet and spin her around, and she's in his embrace again, the one she's longed for. The hug that is supposed to make everything better.

'I've got you, Mum. It's okay. I've got you.'

The world is muffled. She's drowning. From somewhere she hears a buzz, a shock. The wail of an ambulance. The chants have stopped. The world has fallen silent.

'I've got you, Mum,' he says again. In the silence, there's only his voice. 'You're okay, Mum. I've got you.'

Her boy. Her world.

Chapter 44

The world is a haze, and in that haze, Harriet dreams. She dreams her son is with her, in her arms. Despite the miasma of everything, his face is clear as day. The background disappears, as if in sepia and smoke. But Oliver is there, pinpoint sharp. He's so strong now, not like the little boy he once was. She's imagined this day so many times, imagined his voice. He can't really be here now, can he?

'Mum?' his voice again as Harriet's stomach churns. Nausea grips her, a twisted sense of loss. If she really was with her son, she wouldn't feel such loss. She would be complete.

'Mum?' His voice again. She's being called mum. It must be a play, a shoot for a movie, someone is playing let's pretend.

'I've got you, Mum.'

She looks to her left, and he's there—a dream but not a dream; she doesn't think so anyway. She reaches and cups his chin, stroking his skin. There's a hint of stubble. He feels real. Her real boy.

They're in a taxi. Harriet can't recall getting there. But she really is sitting next to her son. He has a look about him, a fierce protector, while she's a heap in his arms. She's meant to be strong. She's his mother. She should be the protector.

She traces the contours of his face with her thumb, running her fingers through his hair. His blue eyes sparkle. He grins and tells her to stop it, like he's embarrassed. Next to him is a girl. She looks straight ahead, a cascade of chocolate curls flowing down her shoulders. Oliver mentioned a girl in his letter, Evie. She's embarrassing him in front of the girl. Harriet smiles. She's a pretty thing, like Beatrice.

Beatrice.

She never had the chance to make Beatrice know she mattered, that she was important, not just a spare part. Harriet's eyes well up again. For every happy moment, a sad one steals it.

'Are you okay, Mum?' Oliver asks.

How can she answer such a question? She's not, she's distraught. But she has her son. Her sweet boy who always asks that. 'I'm so much better now I've found you.'

Sitting opposite is the teenage version of a little boy she knew once. All pink cheeks and red hair.

'We need to hurry,' Theo says, checking his phone. 'We have to get back to Josie.'

Harriet fails to draw breath. *Josie.* Has Theo explained to Thomas? The teenage boy looks at his lap, his face forlorn, as if he knows or at least suspects. Harriet buries her face on her son's shoulder, his hand rubbing her back. She has her son. Finally, she has her boy.

When they get out of the taxi and make it to 5, Theo and Thomas run ahead, Harriet and Oliver trailing behind with the girl. Did Oliver introduce her? Harriet's forgotten her name already. She's running on empty, has been for hours. How long will Oliver be home? She needs to savour this.

The house smells like flowers, the floors gleam with the shine of disinfectant. Monty, dishevelled, still with a mop in his hand, greets them at the door with a pained smile.

'You're in time,' is all he says.

Thomas is sitting at Josie's bedside, her hand stroking his face. She'll be almost totally blind now. The room looks beautiful and, thanks to Monty's efforts, doesn't smell like death. Josie wears makeup, has her hair freshly done. Harriet can imagine the conversation when Theo texted to say they're on their way. *Don't let my boy see me looking this awful. Let me die pretty.*

'Oliver,' Josie rasps when Oliver says hello, and he sits next to Thomas, putting one arm around his friend, then takes hold of Josie's with the other.

Evie says hello, gives a sweet smile, and says she'll leave them to it.

Harriet walks around the other side of Josie's bed, fighting to keep her sadness from her voice. 'Can I get you anything?'

Josie shakes her head. 'You've brought me everything I need.'

Harriet has no more tears left. Her body aches with a pain of indeterminate cause. How can a body ache this much? 'Josie, I just want to say—'

'Well, don't. No tears now. I don't want my last time with you like that. Thank you for your forgiveness. In another life, we would have had a future. But what we did have, I've always cherished.'

'Me too,' Harriet says, then swallows in her parched throat. 'So much.'

Josie turns her head towards Thomas, and Harriet stands, placing her hand on Oliver's shoulder.

'We'll leave you two alone,' Harriet says.

She and Oliver walk to the kitchen and they sit with Theo and Monty, silent, a few cups of tea steaming, yet soothing no one. Any desire for food Harriet had a while ago has gone. She's no appetite even for tea.

'You did so much, Monty. Thank you,' Harriet says.

'It's all I could do. And she insisted, you know,' he says with a smirk.

Josie has always had such no-nonsense determination. Harriet wishes they had more time to enjoy together. Her memories are scant and marred by troubles. Why is it that the happiest prospects have the least time?

'What's wrong with her, Mum?' Oliver asks.

Harriet wonders if he has any concept of death. No real-world experiences, certainly. Death to him is an idea, an abstract. How she wishes she could protect him from it forever. 'She's sick, darling. She's dying. Not long now.'

'And dying—is forever?'

Oh, how his innocence makes her love him more! 'Yes. It's a forever goodbye.'

Oliver looks at his lap, his face drawn. 'What will happen? What will it be like for Josie to die?'

Harriet exhales slowly. 'Well, no one knows for sure, just what we believe. And, I suppose, I believe there's a flash. All the pain and bad things in her life go away, and all that's left is a blissful stillness. In that moment she'll see her family. She'll be in her happiest place, like in the kitchen, hearing the clinking of plates, steaming tea on the table, others laughing. Or she'll be outside, under the sky of 99, feeling the grass beneath her feet, her son's hug in her arms. In that last moment, all she'll know is joy.'

'Is that what it was like for Beatrice?'

Harriet swallows back a lump in her throat, then reaches for his hand. 'I think so.'

Thomas comes into the kitchen sometime later, eyes red-rimmed, his bottom lip wobbling. 'Mum's asked for a glass of water. Something about a pill?'

Harriet's chest hollows, her lungs stall in their breath. Pins and needles travel up her legs. She can't do this alone. She looks at Theo and Monty and they all nod.

'It's her time,' Monty says. 'Her choice now.'

When Harriet tries to stand, the room spins.

Her son once again holds her. 'I've got you, Mum.'

She squeezes his hand a moment and on shaky legs, she fills a glass and takes it through.

'You sure, Josie?' she asks.

Josie's smiling. She has a contentment about her. 'Course I'm sure.' With her spindly fingers she presses the pill from the blister pack and fumbles for it, Harriet putting the glass in her hand.

'You all got a drink?' Josie asks.

Harriet shakes her head. 'No.'

'Well, go get one and let's have a toast.'

Monty comes in with three bottles of beer and hands them out. Condensation drips down the glass. Harriet isn't thirsty, the smell isn't appealing, but if Josie wants a toast, she can have one.

'To friendship,' Josie says, 'and family, in this life and whatever comes next.' And they all clink glasses.

Harriet takes a sip, but can't swallow as she watches Josie drink hers. The beer lingers on her tongue, cold and sharp as Josie gulps hers back. It's Josie's final scene, lying there, with her son. Isn't that the climax every drama needs, the family reforming, an embrace at curtain call?

Harriet swallows, then exhales a tremulous breath.

Thomas still holds Josie's hand. 'I love you, Mum.'

Harriet's heart breaks for him. To have known the love of a mother like Josie is so incredibly special.

Josie smiles, her eyes glaze and her body relaxes, a peacefulness overcoming her. She looks far away, somewhere calmer, somewhere where happy memories can be made.

Oliver's arm is around Harriet as Josie breathes her last breath, her smile remaining until the end, and he whispers, 'Fly free, Josie.'

Chapter 45

Anthony is alive, so the news says. The report portrays this as if it's good news, like a deserved resolution for Anthony. If this were the movies, he'd have snuffed it.

'I wish he'd died,' says Oliver. 'Why does he get to live when Josie doesn't?'

It's a question that's been asked for millennia. Why the best ones go and the worst seem to live on and on. Like there's a rugged determination that comes with brutality. 'It's just luck,' Harriet says. Perhaps that's why those from below ground are so obsessed with luck. It takes any sense of responsibility away.

'He should have died,' Oliver says. 'I was going to make sure of it.'

Under different circumstances, maybe Harriet would agree. The world without Anthony would be a better place. But she's seen too much death for one lifetime.

'Beatrice gave her life to save him,' Harriet says. 'We don't want that to be in vain.'

Oliver huffs and folds his arms across his torso. 'I recognise her from the Institute. She shouldn't have done that. She was better than him.'

He has so much anger in him. Growing up with Anthony that was going to be inevitable. At least his heart is in the right place.

Beatrice's body was collected by scavengers, ones who Theo knows. They had to know for sure if she was salvageable. If she'd waited a minute, Theo could have removed her personality module first and saved her. But how was she to know that? And in any case, if she'd waited, perhaps it would have been too late for Anthony.

And what a shame that would have been, Harriet thinks with a sneer. As much as she's trying to shield Oliver from her resentment, she can still think it. She can still hate Anthony.

Anthony's assistant calls Harriet from his hospital bed. Did she want to visit him? Doesn't she feel bad for him, worried? They all saw her run to him; there must be feelings there. His assistant said all this as if reading from a script, undoubtedly written by Anthony.

She ran to him because she's a good person, she explained, something Anthony will never understand. She relived their history in those few seconds, the part where he made her heart swell. The final years of their relationship played out a minute later.

He will never relinquish his grip on her life. He's lived his entire life unaccustomed to being snubbed, always able to obtain anything he wants. Anthony doesn't deserve another chance at life, yet he has all the luck.

Mr Chambers, that awful TRI CEO, has been on the news round the clock, their share prices hitting the roof. The entire ordeal was broadcast live. The whole world witnessed a bot sacrifice herself for a human.

'This just goes to show how useful bots are in society,' Mr Chambers says, on every news programme broadcast. 'We said it before, we'll say it again, bots literally save lives.'

The anti-bot brigade is quiet now. The Divine Flesh Fraternity can hardly label such a bot as the Devil. No one can argue with what they saw. Harriet hopes they'll see that the real Devil is Anthony, though that's a pipe dream. The sympathy for him has been coming in thick and fast, with plenty of nasty comments about Harriet. Some on *Get Level* agree it's her fault Freddie died, that she gaslighted Anthony. Harriet doesn't care. She has a good mind to delete her social media account. It's done what she wanted it to do. The streets are safe for bots again.

Harriet's phone rings. She frowns when she sees who's calling and has a mind not to answer. But she does, bracing herself for a lecture. 'Dexter?'

'I've been thinking about your role here at the school. With all the support for the bots on TV ... Well ... I think it would be a good idea for you to come back.' He says this as if it's a decision made already without her input. Same old Dexter.

Her eyebrows lift, and for a split second, she considers it. Only for a split second. 'Thanks, but no. I have other career prospects now.'

She smiles, then hangs up, and wonders what sort of gossip is going around the parents now, if the likes of Polly Wilson's dad will admit he was wrong about the bots, if Dexter is being nicer to the MechaniKids. She scoffs. Unlikely.

***

Harriet watches Oliver steal glances at Evie. He spends ages trying to make his hair tidy, checking it in a mirror throughout the day, and undoing all the ruffling Harriet does. He shrugs off Harriet's coddling, getting embarrassed when she shows him affection, usually followed by a moany 'Muuuum!' This is only when Evie is around. When they're alone, he's every bit her little boy. He still asks her if she's okay, and tells her facts about insects and birds.

'Did you know some female spiders eat the male spiders?' he said to her this morning when he found a tiny spider in the corner. 'I think sometimes that's not a bad thing.'

Harriet laughed and mussed his hair he'd just tidied.

Thomas is quiet. Harriet doesn't know how to console him, none of them do. He never learned about grief when he was a kid. Harriet tries to explain her feelings about Beatrice, to describe the pain she's experiencing so he understands what that empty ache is. He listens, but then spends a lot of time watching TV. Theo's fixed up an old games console, and he plays that a lot. When Oliver tries to talk to him, he shrugs.

'He just needs some time, darling,' Harriet says. 'Grief is a horrible thing.'

***

They're tripping over each other a lot in the apartment, but having such a full house, despite the looming sadness, is a joy. There's rarely a minute that goes by without laughter. Harriet thinks she could get used to this.

'I don't want to go back, Mum,' Oliver says. He's said it several other times too. 'I want to stay here with you.'

'I know, Monkey.'

'Don't call me that. That's what you called me when I was little. I'm not a kid anymore.'

He's really not. He's a teenager with all the gripes and insecurities that go along with it. How she wishes she could keep him home with her. She tells herself every teenager says this about going to school, though in her gut she knows this is different. It's not just school, not just boarding school even. Oliver should be with her at home. They should all be with their families.

She's thought about it. Running again, taking Oliver, Thomas and Evie and starting anew somewhere else. Somewhere people won't recognise them. They all hate it at the Institute, all three of them being forced to train for jobs they don't want to do. Evie, especially, is a concern for Harriet. She hasn't asked about her job role, but Harriet can guess. She's one of Anthony's playthings. Her body made to line his pockets.

But who's Harriet kidding? Her face has been everywhere. *Get Level* is rife with memes of her face still, from both the fans and the haters. In any case, her legs ache just thinking about it. She's older than the last time she tried to flee, only a few years, but she's infinitely more tired. And here she has Theo and Monty. Their little support network has got her through some dark days. So much is disposable, easily cast aside and forgotten. Friendships, Harriet has come to realise, should never be discarded.

How long before TRI come knocking? Studio 99 showed Oliver and the others with Harriet as Anthony went on his rant and heart attack. They'll know they're together. They'll take Oliver away again. It's only two more years but Oliver is obviously miserable there, and Thomas without Josie is going to suffer. And Evie, poor young Evie, surviving what her friends did not. She hasn't spoken about the explosion, but when Harriet woke them up after standby, Evie screamed and lashed out, her mind still in her nightmare, her eyes looking beyond Harriet, somewhere darker.

'It's okay. You're safe,' Harriet said to her, over and over as her body shook and her eyes regained their focus.

She hugged Harriet then, holding on and not letting go. How can she send these children away? They may be bigger and more mature, but they're still children.

'I'll speak to TRI,' Harriet says today. 'There's a lot of public support for bots at the moment. What Beatrice did was so brave and may have helped you all. Perhaps there's a way now for us to be together.'

'Not for me and my mum,' Thomas says.

'I know, darling. We all miss her. You're going to get through this. Evie, did you have someone you want to see?'

She's holding Oliver's hand. 'No. My parents weren't that great. I'm fine here.'

When Oliver notices Harriet clocking their affection, he uncurls his hand from Evie's and puts it back on his lap as a blush creeps over his cheeks. He smooths down his hair. They all have fresh clothes on, some old bits of Theo and Monty's and Harriet's, some bits they had to buy. They took forever to choose, Oliver especially.

Harriet knows not to ask about Oliver's romantic life. He's old enough now to want some privacy from his mum, but she wonders and wishes she could know. Have they had a first kiss? She caught them making a joke on the sofa the other evening, giggling, a tickle, their flush-faced embarrassment when they noticed her. Harriet gave them a knowing smile and walked away, her heart full to bursting.

They have each other, she reconciles with herself. Whatever happens with TRI, those three have each other's back. Like Josie said.

Chapter 46

They've barely left the apartment, only a couple of times at night to charge the teens. Harriet is so relieved their batteries last so long now. The entire time on their way and then at the charging port, Harriet's eyes darted around, on high alert, Theo and Monty stationing themselves further down the road to keep watch. What would TRI staff coming to reclaim their property look like? Are there still rioters trying to make bots bleed? Theo and Monty have been going about their days as normal and report all is well. But she always worries. She can't keep them all inside forever, as much as she wishes.

Thomas is flicking through the channels. He's spoken a little more, laughed along with some jokes. Theo is sitting with him. Those two have really clicked, but then, Theo could click with anyone. They settle on some live broadcast from 99. Then, the TV goes blank, an error message filling the screen.

Theo walks over to the TV, then checks the wire, grabbing some tools that display numbers Harriet doesn't understand. 'Weird,' he says. 'Our electric is fine.'

'It's good, actually,' Harriet says. 'Have you noticed the streets? The lights are actually working well. I even closed my curtains last night.'

Monty comes through from the kitchen, chuckling into his teacup.

'Monty,' Theo's accusatory tone makes Monty chuckle more. 'What have you done?'

'It wasn't all me.'

'Monty!'

'Okay.' He puts his cup down. 'So you know the guys from the bar, Eli and Jason and—'

'Yes,' Theo replies with narrowed eyes. 'The guys who have had bounty hunters after them for all sorts of things.'

'Well,' Monty says, dragging out the word. 'I may have borrowed some of your tools and we may have hijacked the electricity a bit.'

Theo tuts. 'They'll just switch it back. How many times have people tried that before? It's pointless, and they'll cut us off for ages as punishment.'

'Actually,' Monty steps further into the room, taking centre stage. 'We learned that it's not just the wind and solar on top levels that doesn't filter down. The incinerators from the landfill, all that electricity, also goes straight up.'

Harriet and Theo both gasp. 'No!'

'Yep. Electricity is power, we all know that, and up top take the lot. That's meant to be low-level electricity, and it never lasts long, as we're always told it's not that effective. But the truth is, up top takes most of it. So, we redirected that.'

'A couple of rowdy guys from the bar figured that out and rigged the electric?' Theo's tone still smacks of suspicion, though Harriet wonders if he's actually annoyed he didn't think of it himself.

'A couple of resourceful below grounders who happen to go to a bar, yes,' Monty says, beaming a smile. 'With a bit of help from yours truly. It seems I do pay attention to you when you're fixing things.' He gives Theo a quick kiss. 'Anyway, it'll take up top ages to figure it out and even when they do, everyone's going to know now. We've made videos. All the incinerator workers, all the landfill scavengers down there will know how to keep that electricity where it belongs. We've told other towns as well, so it's not just Reading who can redirect their supply. If those up top want the electricity shared, they're going to have to share theirs too.'

'Look at *Get Level!*' Harriet says, wide eyes scrolling. 'He's right. Electricity is out at the top and it's spreading down. Everyone above 80 is in blackout at the moment.'

Theo sits back on the sofa and rubs his forehead. 'They're not just going to accept this.'

'So?' Monty says, crouching before him. 'The reason why we've had to put up with whatever shit the top levels throw at us—literally—is because they have control of all the electricity. Freedom from that is freedom for us. They can't just fill the news with broadcasts biased for the top levels now. They can't ration our electricity as punishment, lie to us about upgrading the supply and expect us to just put up with it. This control for us down here is well overdue.'

'He's right, Theo,' Harriet says. 'We're always told to be efficient, so maybe this way *they* will have to be.'

Theo nods, gazes at Monty, then smiles. 'Well done.' He pulls him in for a hug.

Harriet looks at the three teens. They've been paying attention, Evie squeezing Oliver's hand and he's not even stopping her. Thomas is leaning in, enthralled wide eyes and listening to every word. Electricity has always been Harriet's main worry about them and has been the reason so many hated them. Maybe, this way, they could stay with her.

Chapter 47

Harriet walks the streets with her head high, her son and his friends close, not fearing for their safety.

Monty's little intervention has worked, with the lower levels having enough electricity, any residual animosity has gone. There are still speakers about, saying the bots are the Devil, but they're such baseless claims now. The real Devil has been exposed. The real electricity thieves are known.

She constantly checks bounty hunter posters for pictures of the three teens, assuming that's one method TRI might use. It's a stupid idea. TRI are far more resourceful than that. They'll know where she lives. It's a matter of time.

She's posted pictures of the children on her socials, *Shamed Parents* now not remotely ashamed. Oliver has admirers, so many comment on how handsome he is. He has an affinity for the camera. He could be in the movies.

Where before Harriet denied her love for him, now she shouts about it. With the fight won for bots being allowed to exist, her campaign has stepped up a level. She still needs to ensure their safety in the workplace. She's trying to tell everyone that these bots can feel. They have empathy. They can love.

Harriet had a call yesterday from a woman called Eileen who lives on 6. Beatrice's mother. Harriet had plans to take Beatrice to see her one day soon. Now that'll never happen. The pride and sadness from Eileen was heartbreaking.

'At least she made the world a better place,' Eileen said through her tears.

Harriet agreed because she did. She really did. Her innate need to care and protect never broke, even when so much else of her did.

Harriet sits on a bench now, like she used to do so many times when Oliver was a kid, and watches as Oliver and his friends kick a football. He doesn't need parental supervision; he's not a little boy anymore. She just wants to drink in these moments. For every second to be filled with her son as she knows it won't last. He's still TRI property. They'll be coming for him soon.

Sometimes Harriet wonders what the three of them get up to when she's asleep. She hasn't set any rules or boundaries. Those first ventures into adulthood are so exciting and nerve-racking for teenagers. Let them have their freedom while they can. Who knows how long before they'll lose it.

Thomas is coming out of his malaise bit by bit. Oliver takes him for walks, they kick a ball around the park, play frisbee and basketball. Oliver has a competitive streak but keeps it under wraps for Thomas. Though when Evie is around, like now, he shows off. There's a cheer from Evie as Oliver kicks the ball into the goal. Thomas doesn't sulk. They high-five. Like Josie said, those boys have each other's backs. Oliver waves at Harriet, flashing her a smile.

Oh, how she loves this boy.

***

They've not been home long. Monty is cooking, delicious smells of curry coming from the kitchen, when there's a knock at the door. Theo opens it and he comes into the living room a moment later, flanked by two suited men Harriet doesn't recognise.

'Harriet, guys. It's some people from TRI.'

Harriet closes her eyes for a second, then stands.

'Harriet Chapel,' one says, 'or should I say, Alyssa Wade.'

'Well, that didn't take you too long.' Harriet hasn't been back to work at the Institute since finding Oliver. She didn't want to miss a second. 'Cup of tea?'

'No. We won't be long. Just here to collect the teens.'

Oliver is still sitting and she puts a hand on his shoulder, gives it a little squeeze, and feels how tense he is. 'They don't want to go back.'

The second man steps forward. He's a tad less cold. 'We have discussed your actions at TRI and have, as a gesture of goodwill, decided you can maintain your employment. So you will still have access at standby time. You can leave the wig at home.'

The teens all look at Harriet, confusion etched across their brows. She hadn't told them about her disguise.

'It's not enough,' Harriet says. 'You can see what's being said. The bots raised with families are suffering. You can't simply turn them into mindless robots.'

The first man tuts. 'They are mindless robots.'

Harriet bristles. 'No. They're not. You told us to teach them empathy. There are lots of jobs that require that. It's not fair on them to simply try to undo that. We want guarantees.'

'We?'

'Yes. Me. The public. The other parents. We want guarantees they will not be killed simply because they are not suitable for a backorder of job roles. We want guarantees they will be treated with kindness and respect. And we want access. Not just me, all the parents who bonded with their kids.'

The two men both fold their arms and pull their chins in, like the Tweedledee and Tweedledum of TRI. 'Or what?' the first one asks.

Harriet stands as tall as she can, Theo and Monty either side, the teens joining them. 'I have witness statements, from Josie, from the teens, not to mention this interview. Your mistreatment so far will be public knowledge. These bots can save lives, as everyone knows. They can do so much good. They deserve respect.'

The first man huffs and unfolds his arms. 'I'll put it to the boss. Now, you three, this way.'

'No.' Oliver says.

Monty and Theo both hold up their phones, recording, as the men push their jackets to one side, their hands hovering over tasers on their belts.

'When we have it in writing those guarantees will be met, we'll return them to the Institute,' Harriet says.

The first man raises his eyebrows before his lips curl into a sneer. 'Then, Harriet Chapel, you will be arrested for theft. For concealment of stolen goods.'

'I didn't steal them. As you well know. These teens turned up. I am merely caring for them. Our reunion was caught on camera at Studio 99, which I'm sure you've seen.'

The second man sighs. 'Fine. We'll be back with a warrant in due course.'

They turn and leave, Monty walking them to the front door and slamming it behind them.

Oliver is still tense when they've gone, stroppy and sulking. 'Why did you have to say that?' he says to Harriet.

'What?'

'That we'd go back if they give those guarantees. Why not just say we'll stay here?'

She looks at her boy as he sits on the sofa and folds his arms. He's achieved so much in getting away and finding her. He must think the world will bend to however he wants it now, and after all he's done, he deserves his hard-earned freedom. As mature as he is now, he has a lot of growing up to do, a lot of learning about the hardships of the real world. He's lived in a bubble all his life and it's her job to teach him how cruel the world can be.

She sits next to him and gives his arm a squeeze. 'While I would love that, it just wouldn't happen. TRI are too big and too powerful. I had to pitch an argument I can actually win.'

He looks down before meeting her gaze, his brows drawn in, his lips pressed in a thin line. 'The fight's not over yet, is it Mum?'

'No, darling. I'm not sure it ever will be.'

Chapter 48

Oliver holds Evie's hand all the way to TRI, and doesn't even care if his mum sees. His mum is taking them all the way back, only a better way than Thomas and Oliver went before. They haven't had to walk below ground at all.

Two weeks they've been away, and it's been the best two weeks of Oliver's life. He's been able to hang out with his friends without the horrible staff making them do boring and awful things. And he's had his mum.

Thomas even seems a bit better now. He's talking like his old self and they can mention Josie without him clamming up. Oliver wonders how he'll be when they're back at the Institute, if he'll struggle there more, but he knows he'll look out for him. That's what friends do.

They walk to a lift quite far away and even though they're way down on level 5, it's still nice to be outside. He thought about suggesting they walk up on 99, but he didn't want to be any trouble. 5 is still better than the Institute. He can kind of tell what time of day it is, and there are a few gulls and pigeons.

When they're back at the Institute, Oliver wonders if he'll be able to hold Evie's hand or anything else. He thinks about Evie a lot and there are things he wants to say to her he doesn't know how to explain. He doesn't have the words for these feelings. Holding hands isn't enough. Even a hug isn't. He wants to be so much closer to her than that. He saw some TV shows of people doing some things that made his eyes bulge and his face heat. He'd really like to try those things with Evie one day.

Maybe Evie will say something eventually, and she'll know the right words and what to do. She always seems to be able to say what's on her mind.

Oliver's mum says things will be different at TRI now that all of her guarantees were met and she'll be able to visit every day. She showed Oliver the outcry on social media, about how many people support the Mechani-Rights movement. She says Oliver is a pioneer, that he's helped change the world for the better. Oliver doesn't know about that. All he knows is he never wants to have to cover himself in human blood again.

He still doesn't feel bad for stabbing that guy and doesn't know if he should. He never told his mum. The others said not to. Maybe she'll love him less if she knew.

Perhaps someday, Oliver can ask his mum what this thing is he feels for Evie. When he thinks about asking his mum, he can't. His face gets hot on the inside, like his inner workings are in overdrive, and he knows that makes his skin turn pink. He wants to hide, or at least be in another room. He has two secrets from her then. That seems like a lot. He hopes she doesn't keep secrets from him.

Two more years at the Institute. Two more years where he can't protect his mum and he won't know for sure that she's staying away from Anthony. What if Anthony finds her and hurts her? Oliver is so angry he lived. He shouldn't have. It's not right that he's alive and Josie and Beatrice are dead.

He tries to rid his mind of such thoughts, to look to the future, to remind himself that two years isn't that long. At least they got to see the night sky. He'd like to take Evie back to see the night sky again one day, to read about the stars and tell her about them. He thinks she'd like that.

When they walk through the front door of the Institute, Oliver notes the added security features on the door. They're not going to be able to leave again. They've no access to TV here, no radio or newspapers, and only occasional access to computers. None of the other teens will know anything about what's happened in the real world. That's probably a good thing, Oliver thinks. He doesn't want them to know how much some people didn't like them.

Their usual charging area is empty, the rest of the teens milling about in their regular spots. Evie isn't staying. It'll be just boys again for a while yet. Oliver wonders if any of these boys were friends with Beatrice or the girls from Evie's work. He's not going to tell them anything, but he wonders what the staff will say. Perhaps Evie will tell them when she gets back.

'Well, well,' George says. 'Look what's been dragged back.'

Oliver isn't scared of him at all. George has never even been alone in the world without a parent. He's never survived an explosion or a riot. Sod George.

Oliver turns his back on George and kisses Evie on the lips. Not like a mum kiss. He's seen this kind of kiss on TV and thought he'd try it. He's been worried she wouldn't kiss him back, but she does, and Oliver's entire body turns to jelly.

'I'll see you soon,' she says when they pull away. 'A month more of work experience and I'll be back.'

The world is in soft focus. Oliver can barely move his mouth to speak. 'Can't wait,' he manages to say.

His mum says goodbye with that kind of knowing smile mums seem to always have. He gives her a quick hug, not the long hug he'd like to, since there are so many people around. But she'll be visiting every day. He'll look forward to that and when he asks, she tells him she's going to be just fine. Oliver watches as they walk away, and he leans against the wall for support, sure he's going to faint in a moment.

George makes a tutting sound and turns around and Oliver can't stop smiling. He can still feel Evie's lips on his. He bets George has never kissed a girl like that.

Thomas, next to him, giggles and rolls his eyes. 'It's about time,' he says.

A month till Evie's back and then, maybe, another two years at the Institute won't be so bad after all.

Epilogue

Drama school is finishing early today, only half an hour to go. Lexi is doing well. She's really gained some confidence. Ashleigh never puts her hand up but this isn't school. It's a weekend and after-school club, and Harriet says such rules don't apply.

The class was instantly popular and Harriet was pleased to have her assistant. Evie is a natural with the children and Theo's tests confirmed she was programmed to be empathetic, like Oliver. Harriet sees so much of Beatrice in her. Her joy in work, nothing is ever too much trouble. She adores all the children.

The public hall on level 5 where Harriet hosts the club is a little tired, but some decorations have gone a long way. Monty has built a stage and curtains, Theo has rigged up some spotlights, and they're preparing for their first big play. *The Legends of Dragonsville* is a month away from its premiere. Harriet's hoping to convince TRI to let Evie out of the Institute to watch. It's a long shot, but with the support for bots still peaking, there's a little hope.

Harriet says goodbye to the class, their parents meeting the children at the doorway, and some tell Harriet how much they appreciate the class. There's no animosity from these parents.

Some even tell her well done for all she did for the MechaniKids and teens, not even in a whisper. Loudly. With no shame.

Evie makes her way home, back to Harriet's apartment, but Harriet has a visit to make first. There's static in the air, a brooding storm. Perhaps it's Harriet's motivation causing a spark. She used to watch storms from Anthony's penthouse window, the bright cracks across the sky, counting the seconds. Now, she can only listen as the rain adds to the racket. A bolt of lightning might be bright enough to flash down here. What a treat that would be, if only from a meteorological perspective. The light isn't needed. Monty's actions have so far kept the wattage decent down here.

When Harriet arrives on 2, she's delighted that even here the lights are on, though that doesn't seem like such a good thing. The landfill is spilling onto the walkways everywhere. It won't be long before 2 is totally inaccessible.

The underside of the level above is so close Harriet has the urge to duck her head. She trips over some loose gravel and a pothole as she doesn't keep her eyes on the walkway. It's better to look up or straight ahead. No way does she want to know what she just stepped in.

The prison is little more than a cave since the landfill rose up and took over. There's only one entrance to it on level 2 that doesn't involve a deep swim through trash that smells like it's as bad for the lungs and skin as it probably is. As Harriet walks towards the prison, she covers her mouth with a scarf and winces against the eye-burning fumes until she gets to the door.

She uses a gloved hand to press the intercom button. It buzzes so loudly she jumps back.

'Hello?' the crackling voice down the line shouts.

'I'm here to visit Amber Delaware. An inmate.'

There's some rustling followed by silence, long enough that Harriet considers buzzing again. She's visited the prison frequently over the last few years and the intercom gets worse and worse and the waits get longer and longer every time.

Eventually, the door buzzes, and she enters.

The security is minimal, only a pat down before she is allowed through to the visitor's room. Amber is already sitting there, unhandcuffed, though sporting a black eye. She's thinner than Harriet's ever seen her.

'How are you?' Harriet asks, then regrets asking such a stupid question.

Amber responds with a shrug.

'Not much longer now.'

'Another three months,' Amber says with a sigh. 'Maybe less.'

'That's great news.' As upbeat as Harriet tries to make this sound, Amber doesn't respond with any hint of happiness. Her forlorn face is fixed.

The place smells like sweaty socks, though that's a pleasant change from outside. The hum of air purifiers makes quiet conversation impossible and Harriet wonders if that's on purpose, so the guard can hear everything discussed, yet the guard looks more interested in playing a game on her phone than paying attention to them.

'Though I've no idea what I'm going to do when I get out. Without Delilah—' Amber's voice trails off, and with the guard not paying any attention, Harriet reaches for her hands.

Her decline since she's been inside has been severe. Locked away with her grief has left her too much time to dwell. Too much time to spiral. Harriet had already decided not to tell her about Josie. She's not here to make Amber even more upset.

Tears come easily when Harriet remembers Delilah, the sight of her battered body after the MechaniKid hater decided Delilah wasn't worthy of life. Amber was sentenced to three and a half years for trying to defend her daughter, for injuring the attacker. Shay received no punishment at all. According to the police, all she did was damage a device.

'You have so much to live for still,' Harriet says. 'Here.' From her pocket she takes a ribbon, one from Delilah's hair. She hands it to Amber.

Amber gasps, fresh tears rolling down her cheeks. 'Is this. . .?'

'Yes. Some scavengers found her. They found Oliver's kid body too.'

Amber holds the ribbon to her face and cries into it. When her sobs mellow, she wipes her eye on her sleeve. 'I saw you, on TV and *Get Level*. You've really made the world a better place for them.'

'I hope so. TRI have agreed to the Institute doing better, but when they're released, they'll still have no rights at all. None.'

'That Shay getting no punishment for what she did makes me feel sick every day.'

'The world needs to hear our stories. It's not right that they've no protections at all. When you get out, you can help me, if you like? It would be great if the world knew Delilah's story.'

Amber's eyes are on her lap where she holds Delilah's ribbon, running it through her fingers.

'I read about those Divine Flesh weirdos,' Amber says. 'They're still shouting some crap.'

'Not like they were. They're quiet now. And the Human Front have totally disbanded. There are no more bomb threats.'

'After what that girl Beatrice did, I'm not surprised. She was so brave. It was such a waste on that man.'

'I know.' Harriet's muscles tighten a bit. Every time she thinks of Anthony living instead of Beatrice, she gets tense. He's still rich and powerful. Even after calling below grounders fungus, he still resonates with so many. It baffles her as to why people don't see him for what he is.

'You don't need to say anything now, okay?' Harriet says, forcing her thoughts away from Anthony. 'You'll be out soon and then you can do great things. Delilah's law, I'm going to call it, if you like? To make her story known, so no MechaniBot, however old and however raised, is treated as nothing more than a device again.'

Amber leaps forward and wraps her arms around Harriet. Her sobs are so loud the guard lifts her head, though doesn't move any closer. Harriet's hug and back rubs and soothing sounds do nothing to stop Amber's crying, and Harriet cries with her.

Their hug lingers, Harriet's shoulder wet with Amber's tears before she pulls away. Her thin face is red and blotchy but has more determination in it now. A set jaw and steely gaze, rather than the vacant stare she has worn for so long.

'In Delilah's name,' Amber eventually says, 'this needs to be put right.'

Harriet swallows, smiles, then nods. The curtains haven't closed on her performance yet. She will make this world safe for their children.

It's what any mother would do.

A note from Emma

Oliver and Harriet continue their story in the final book of the trilogy, Daybreak.

Thank you so much for reading Spotlight. I really hope you enjoyed this book. The QR link above will take you to the Amazon page to leave a review. Reviews are so vital for authors such as myself, and helps other readers find books they'll enjoy. Knowing you enjoyed my work makes all the hard work worthwhile.

Check out my website and Facebook page for updates and news about upcoming releases and sales. Subscribers to my website receive a few free stories, and there will be many more in the near future.

Litter has always been my bugbear. My old dog, Toby, was the sweetest boy. A real gentle giant. I've adopted several senior dogs over the years, but he was the only dog I've raised since puppyhood. My partner and I rescued him when he was about four or five months old, and he grew into a fifty kilo loveable lump. He was never much one for toys, never learned the joy of a ball or a stick. But whenever we were out on walkies, my partner and I always picked up litter. We still do.

Toby, bless him, figured rubbish collecting was the thing to do. He'd pick up a discarded cigarette packet or can of Stella, and carry it in his mouth until we got to the bin, then hand it over. We never trained him to do this. He wasn't a particularly clever dog, but this task was something he took upon himself. The sight of a large dog with a beer can in his mouth often raised eyebrows, as I'm sure you can imagine.

Toby went over the rainbow bridge a few years ago, but I still miss him so much. In the world of this book, he'd be a low level dog for sure. Level 2 would be right up his street. Piles of rubbish to chase and sort would give him endless joy. It's funny how something like litter—which still annoys me—can bring happy memories too.

Toby, my darling boy, this book is for you.

Emma's other works

The Eyes Forward Series. This best-selling series is set in a world where the population has escalated, and governments employ ever more sinister ways to reduce it. Three stories set in a world where fertile women are branded a nuisance, every child is deemed a burden, and every citizen is a spy.

If you are in the mood for some more twisted dystopian, my first series, The Raft Series, is also available. In this world, the entire country has been sterilised and all non-human life made extinct. But poison comes in many forms and Savannah Selbourne must discover the truth.

For thriller vibes, gore, twists, and some rather unhinged characters, check out the Be Her duology!

Acknowledgements

Spotlight would not be in print without the help of my wonderful betas and critique partners. Thank you to Danica, Emily, Allison, Katie, Jaime, and Barry. Their time and honest feedback made this book what it is today. Thank you also to my editor Shannon, for being so incredibly thorough, and Lawrence for his proofreading skills.

Thanks especially to my partner, John, for giving me the space and time I need to write, for his support, patience, and encouragement.

And thank you for reading it.